CAVANAUGH JUSTICE: THE BABY TRAIL

Marie Ferrarella

HARLEQUIN

ROMANTIC SUSPENSE

If you purchased this book without a cover you should be aware
that this book is stolen property. It was reported as "unsold and
destroyed" to the publisher, and neither the author nor the
publisher has received any payment for this "stripped book."

Recycling programs
for this product may
not exist in your area.

ISBN-13: 978-1-335-75962-7

Cavanaugh Justice: The Baby Trail

Copyright © 2022 by Marie Rydzynski-Ferrarella

All rights reserved. No part of this book may be used or reproduced in
any manner whatsoever without written permission except in the case of
brief quotations embodied in critical articles and reviews.

This is a work of fiction. Names, characters, places and incidents
are either the product of the author's imagination or are used fictitiously.
Any resemblance to actual persons, living or dead, businesses,
companies, events or locales is entirely coincidental.

This edition published by arrangement with Harlequin Books S.A.

For questions and comments about the quality of this book,
please contact us at CustomerService@Harlequin.com.

Harlequin Enterprises ULC
22 Adelaide St. West, 41st Floor
Toronto, Ontario M5H 4E3, Canada
www.Harlequin.com

Printed in U.S.A.

Was he actually pushing for her to go home?

"I don't need a keeper, Cavanaugh."

"Oh. I don't know. Maybe you do."

Kori felt her temper flaring but managed to bank it down. No, he couldn't have said what she thought he'd said. The man would have known better.

"Excuse me?" she challenged.

He shrugged, then told her why he had said what he had. "I've got a lot of people in my family who push themselves too hard and they don't even realize it."

Kori realized that she was clenching her hands into fists and forced herself to relax—she was only marginally successful.

"I'm sure that they all appreciate you taking an interest in their lives." Her eyes narrowed as she concluded more sharply, "But I don't need that."

He knew that she expected him to back off—but he couldn't. "Oh, I think everyone needs that once in a while."

Maybe he didn't realize how dangerously close he was getting to having her explode, Kori thought.

* * *

Be sure to check out all the books in this exciting miniseries:

Cavanaugh Justice—Where Aurora's finest are always in action

* * *

If you're on Twitter, tell us what you think of Harlequin Romantic Suspense! #harlequinromsuspense

Dear Reader,

A couple years ago, my son and sweetheart of a daughter-in-law gave me the most wonderful belated Christmas gift ever. They gave me something I've been wanting for a very long time—a short person in my life, otherwise known as Logan. (I had to promise not to spoil him, but you can't be held accountable to a promise made in the throes of ecstatic delirium.)

My brain works in mysterious ways (just ask my husband), and it was while coming to the hospital to visit with Logan and his mom and dad that the plot of the book you are holding in your hands came to me. What if, in the middle of all this happiness and swirling emotions, someone made off with the baby?

At first it seemed rather impossible, especially after I discovered that the old-fashioned nursery with its cute little residents on display had become a thing of the past. Infants were kept in their mother's rooms, giving said mama a peek into what was in store for her for the next twelve to eighteen months. Like I said, babies were kept with their moms—but not all the time. With enough ingenuity and planning, there were still possibilities where someone could actually steal a baby—and that's where my story started.

This is also a slightly different Cavanaugh series book with a bit of a twist. I hope that it entertains you and keeps you coming back for more.

As always, I thank you for taking the time to read one of my books, and from the bottom of my heart, I wish you someone to love who loves you back!

All the best,

Marie Ferrarella

USA TODAY bestselling and RITA® Award–winning author **Marie Ferrarella** has written over three hundred books for Harlequin, some under the name Marie Nicole. Her romances are beloved by fans worldwide. Visit her website, marieferrarella.com.

Books by Marie Ferrarella

Harlequin Romantic Suspense

Cavanaugh Justice

Cavanaugh Rules
Cavanaugh's Bodyguard
Cavanaugh Fortune
How to Seduce a Cavanaugh
Cavanaugh or Death
Cavanaugh Cold Case
Cavanaugh in the Rough
Cavanaugh on Call
Cavanaugh Encounter
Cavanaugh Vanguard
Cavanaugh Cowboy
Cavanaugh's Missing Person
Cavanaugh Stakeout
Cavanaugh in Plain Sight
Cavanaugh Justice: The Baby Trail

The Coltons of Colorado

Colton's Pursuit of Justice

Visit the Author Profile page at Harlequin.com for more titles.

To

Logan Asher Ferrarella

Welcome to the world, little man

You are very loved

G-Mama

Prologue

The heart-wrenching, terrified scream tore through the darkening fall night air. It would have instantly grabbed his attention, even if he wasn't part of the Aurora Police Department. He ran toward the sound even before he could completely identify it or pinpoint the source.

The next second, he knew. It was a child.

As the father of four, Captain Brian Cavanaugh was more than familiar with the sounds made by a screaming child. He was also able to differentiate between the kind of scream uttered in play and the kind that was uttered in pure, unadulterated terror.

This scream was the latter, reverberating with genuine grief-stricken distress.

As a newly promoted police captain, Brian Cavanaugh was keenly aware of sounds that were out of sync with the streets of Aurora. Streets he had sworn to serve and protect from the first moment the badge had been pinned on his chest.

Half a second after his brain registered the terrified scream, he made out the form of the sobbing little girl on the pavement. Eight, maybe nine years old, the distraught child was on her knees, her body rocking to and fro as she clutched the bleeding body of a man Brian presumed had to be her father, or perhaps her uncle.

The image immediately tore at his heart.

Coming off what had wound up being a very long double shift, Brian had just pulled up and gotten out of his vehicle at one of the few convenience stores in the recently incorporated city of Aurora. All he'd wanted to do was buy the half-gallon container of milk that his wife had asked him to get and go home.

They were out of milk again. His four kids went through the white liquid as if it were destined to quickly evaporate.

He had just finished parking his car when he'd heard the three shots ring out in quick succession. The pitiful scream and gut-wrenching cry echoed in the wake of the gunfire.

Brian was running toward the sound, his gun drawn, before he was even aware of doing it. When he saw the little girl, his first thought was that she was wounded. There certainly was enough blood for that.

The small blonde looked up at him. Tears streamed down her thin face.

"Help him," she begged. "Please help my daddy. He's all I've got."

A quick scan of the area told Brian that the person responsible for this dreadful scene was nowhere in the vicinity.

Brian dropped down to his knees, swiftly checking the

bleeding man for vitals. After a moment, he located the faintest hint of a pulse.

Relieved, Brian pulled out his phone and called for an ambulance. All the while, he was keenly aware that the little girl on the ground was watching him with huge eyes, eyes that silently said she was praying for him to perform a miracle.

"This is Captain Brian Cavanaugh," he told the responding dispatcher who answered his call. Brian rattled off his shield number, identified the type of crime that had just transpired, gave the address and requested an ambulance be sent out immediately.

By then he saw the convenience store clerk stumbling to the front door. Looking as if he was in his late fifties, the clerk appeared barely able to push the door open. He was bleeding from a head wound and seemed on the verge of passing out.

"You might want to make that two ambulances," Brian quickly amended.

He felt small hands on his arm, holding on to him tightly and clutching him as if contact with this man who had driven up out of the darkness was the only thing that was keeping her father alive.

"ASAP," Brian stressed emphatically in a deep voice that brooked no argument as he slipped a comforting arm around the trembling, sobbing little girl. "It's going to be all right, honey. Your daddy's going to be all right," he assured her.

The future chief of detectives didn't know it then, but that was the night he became Korinna Kennedy's larger-than-life hero.

Chapter 1

Looking back at that night, she had no idea where she would be if Brian Cavanaugh hadn't been there to call for an ambulance, one that had arrived just in time to save her father's life. If she were to take a guess, most likely she would have been lost somewhere within the deep recesses of the social services program. Probably bundled off into the foster care system.

Or worse.

To Korinna Kennedy, the larger-than-life Brian Cavanaugh was her guardian angel, hero and patron saint all rolled up into one.

Even at that young age, Kori had known that this police captain who'd come to her and her father's rescue hadn't had to do any of it. His job had ended with calling the crime in. Instead, he had remained with her throughout that whole terrifying night. He had rescued her, but more importantly, she was convinced that he was the reason her father hadn't died that night.

Sometimes, in her dreams, she could still see the whirling, flashing-red ambulance lights, still hear that wonderful, piercing siren sound that told her help was on its way.

For the first year, Korinna had relived the whole traumatic scene in her dreams every night, watching her father being loaded into the back of the ambulance. And rather than being moved aside by paramedics focused on just doing their job and saving a shooting victim's life, she'd been allowed to ride beside her father in the vehicle.

Again because of the man who had showed up out of the blue.

Brian had convinced the paramedics to allow her to go in the ambulance. He'd told them that she'd needed to go with her father. When one of the paramedics began to protest, Brian had told him that it was all right. He was taking full responsibility for the child's presence and planned to also accompany her.

At the time, she'd just thought of him as being the kindest man she had ever met, as well as her hero. She hadn't realized that the tall, extraordinary police officer was also the son of the chief of police, which was what gave him such an air of authority. To her, it was the man's deep, booming voice that made people obey him without question.

In her eyes, because of Brian, her father had gotten the care he'd needed quickly and she'd been there to see it all taking place.

Despite his waiting family and his police duties, the then police captain remained waiting with her in the hospital for what seemed like forever. He'd spent part of the time coaxing her to eat a sandwich he'd gotten from the cafeteria even though she'd politely refused at first, telling him she wasn't hungry. She'd finally eaten the sandwich because he'd said it would make him happy.

To partially distract her, Brian had told her about his daughter and three sons, as well as his many nephews and nieces.

And whenever there was any news about her father's condition, he'd kept her abreast of that, too. He'd treated her, she felt, like an adult, not like a child. Years later, she'd found out that he'd kept certain facts from her in an effort to keep her from worrying.

And in the end, mercifully, everything with her father had turned out well. He'd survived that terrible night as well as the surgery that followed.

No one could ever tell Kori that it wasn't all due to the efforts of her newly found patron saint.

When she could no longer stay in her father's hospital room, the remarkable police captain had come to her rescue again. Leaving the hospital, there'd been no social worker, kindly or otherwise, to collect her and ferry her over to a group home. Instead, Kori had discovered, Brian had pulled some strings and rather than being taken to a bed in a shelter, she'd found herself going home with the man who had saved her father.

That one simple event wound up shaping her life to the present day.

Brian's diligence and kindness were the main reason she'd become a police officer and eventually a police detective. It was also why she was always so determined to go the extra mile, to go out of her way to help people, especially children.

Even after all these years, she could relate to those distraught children. She could see the haunted looks in their eyes and remember what it had been like to feel that way herself.

In her opinion, being cut off from all hope was just the worse thing possible.

It was also why she tried to be so upbeat even when everything seemed to take on such a hopeless bent. In her heart, Kori knew that, despite everything, hope could always be found. She knew that because, when she had been so beside herself, thinking that all was lost—her mother had died the year before and then her father had been shot before her eyes as he went to buy her something to eat with their last twenty dollars—someone had come from out of the blue to save them both. To make everything right when it seemed to her as if there was no more "right" to be had left in the world.

She remembered how afraid she had felt when Brian had brought her into his home. Afraid of being rejected and sneered at by his wife and children.

But that hadn't happened.

Brian Cavanaugh and his family had showed her nothing but kindness. Showed her that there was "right" in the world. And that it was not an anomaly, but the norm.

Every single member of his family, in their own way, had demonstrated it to her right from the very beginning. That sort of thing, in turn, had gone into building her foundation.

Brian's kindness to her had not been just some fleeting thing. It continued.

She was invited to stay with Brian and his family while her father was in the hospital, recovering from his surgery. And she'd remained there while he was in the convalescent home, undergoing physical therapy and, very slowly, growing stronger. Somehow, Brian had managed to find a program that wound up covering the expenses for that as well.

When her father was finally able to retake the reins of his life and unsteadily get back to his feet, it was Brian who'd found him a job within the police station in a civilian capacity.

She loved her father dearly, but Korinna was convinced that she loved Brian Cavanaugh as well. Not only that, she knew that the undying loyalty he had earned would have her following the man through the gates of hell.

After all, the man had given her back her father and her life. There was no way she could ever return the favor, but that did not stop Kori from continually trying.

"Going out to keep our streets safe, Kori?" William Kennedy asked his daughter just as she walked into the living room.

Both father and daughter had always been early risers. Technically, this was actually late for Kori. It was seven thirty on a Monday morning.

"You might not have noticed, but they pretty much keep themselves safe, Dad," Kori replied.

Aurora was known not just as the safest city of its size in California, but was currently inching its way into that position in the country as well.

"Oh, I've noticed," her father assured her. "Which is the reason I know I don't have to worry about you out there—although I still do," Bill confessed without any embarrassment.

They had had this conversation before. More than once. "Dad, you know I can't live in a bubble," she reminded him, then added with a shrug, "Stuff happens."

Bill Kennedy sighed, nodding his head. "I know, I know," he said, making his way into the kitchen. "But you're my little girl…" he began.

Kori turned as she leveled a look at the still handsome older man.

"Dad, I'm not a little girl," she reminded him patiently. "I'm twenty-five years old."

Bill waved his hand at the statement. "Kori, you could be eighty-five years old. If I'm still around at that point, you'd still be my little girl," her father told her without any shame.

"Uh-huh." There was no point in arguing. Kori knew she wasn't going to win. Instead, she nodded her head and changed the subject. "You don't look as if you're ready to ride into work. Shouldn't you be dressed by now?" Korinna asked her father.

"And that's why you're such a good detective," Bill quipped. "And to answer your question, I'm not dressed yet because I'm going in later."

That stopped her in her tracks. Her father prided himself on never missing work, even when he wasn't feeling a hundred percent. It was just the way he was. Once close to being homeless at the lowest point in his life, he was grateful to be able to pay his own way. He never took that for granted. It was a point of pride for him.

"Something wrong, Dad?" Kori asked, concerned.

"Nothing is wrong, honey," he assured her in a patient voice. Having her worry about him was nothing new. "Just time for my annual exam, that's all. Nothing to worry about." And then he smiled at her. "Certainly beats the alternative."

"The alternative?" she questioned, not entirely sure what he meant by that.

"Yes. There was a time when it looked as if there wouldn't be any exams, annual or otherwise," he reminded her matter-of-factly.

Smiling at him, Kori bent over and kissed the top of her father's head, a head that still sported a very thick, healthy mane of dark brown hair, although it was now streaked with gray.

"Good point, Dad. Okay, I'll leave you to get to your exam. Give me a call when it's over, okay?" Kori requested.

He arched a brow. "Who's the parent here?" Bill deadpanned.

"We all know the answer to that one, Dad. I am," she told him, sporting a very straight face that told him she was only half kidding. "See you tonight," she said by way of parting.

Getting into the four-door vehicle she had left parked in the driveway, Kori buckled up. But rather than start the car, she sighed and glanced back toward the house.

It had taken hard work on her part to stop constantly worrying about her father, to stand back and allow him to reclaim his independence. It had taken a real effort to stop hovering over him, prepared to instantly jump right in to help whenever she thought he needed her.

That, too, was thanks to Brian's laidback manner and counseling.

Might as well get going, she mused.

Kori turned the key in the ignition and started up her car. With one last glance at the house, she pulled out of the driveway.

Not a day went by when she didn't think of the tall, distinguished, handsome Brian Cavanaugh as her own personal godsend.

The police chief helped her in so many countless ways. Different ways. There was no way she could possibly *ever* find to thank him.

The only way she knew how to even begin to express her gratitude was to do her job to the very best of her ability—and to never complain, no matter what the circumstances were or how frustrated she temporarily might feel.

That wasn't always easy.

Deciding to put her father's annual medical exam out of her mind—it did no good to worry—Kori drove to the police precinct.

First, though, she stopped at the nearby local coffee shop that had recently opened on the adjacent corner.

The precinct coffee wasn't all that bad as far as that went and, in a pinch, it did the trick. But the coffee offered at the coffee shop was so much better.

Kori stopped there to get what had quickly become her customary, exceptionally strong, container of black coffee. Actually, she ordered two containers. One for herself and one for her partner.

It wasn't until Kori was back in her car and buckled up, the newly purchased containers planted securely in the cup holders, and driving toward the police station, that she remembered she no longer *had* a partner to give the coffee container to.

Or at least, not the partner she usually supplied with coffee.

Detective Weldon Wills had decided to go into the private sector to work. Or rather, his wife had decided that he should enter the private sector. Consequently, her now former partner had handed in his gun and shield and given his notice.

Without the slightest warning, Friday had suddenly turned out to be his last day.

Kori was still reeling.

That also meant, she thought sadly, that sometime during this week, she was going to be meeting her new partner.

New partner.

The words echoed hauntingly in Kori's brain, taunting her.

She supposed she was in sincere denial. That was why the fact that Wills would no longer be sitting at the desk facing hers had just conveniently slipped her mind, sinking to the bottom of the pool like a large lead brick.

If she were being honest, she would have to admit she didn't like change and had always had difficulty adjusting to it. It had been that way ever since her mother had died. Kori freely admitted that was why she had always liked hanging on to the status quo rather than embracing moving on, the way her father—and Brian—had always advised her to do.

Maybe she was being shortsighted, but in her eyes, there was absolutely nothing great about moving on. Nothing.

It was painful.

Before she realized it, Kori found herself pulling into her usual space in the parking lot at the rear of the police station. She had next to no recollection of the trip.

Turning off the ignition, Kori sat there for a moment, looking at the two containers of coffee. Jumbo-sized, one was more than enough to sustain her for the day, but for a number of reasons, she couldn't very well leave the other one in the car.

It had always been beyond her to waste anything, even something as nominal as a container of coffee, she thought as she got out of the car. She supposed the reason for that was rooted in the fact that she could vividly remember, in the days just before her father had been shot outside the convenience store, when he had lost his job and they'd been inches away from living out on the street.

Kori walked into the station. There certainly hadn't

been any money to waste or to spend on things that weren't totally and absolutely necessary.

She supposed that she could easily find someone to give the other container of coffee to. The hard part, she decided, pressing for the elevator, was deciding just who that someone would be.

Since joining the force, she had made it a point to get to know as many of the officers as possible, especially the Cavanaughs. They were Brian's family and so, by proxy, she felt that they were hers.

But there were just so many of them and she didn't want to just single one out arbitrarily. Not that any of them would care—other than to possibly tease her about it—but she would care.

She would definitely care.

Kori really wished that Wills was still there, just for another five minutes or so. Just so that she could hand him the coffee and talk to him one last time.

Maybe he'd stop by, she thought hopefully. Just one last time, to say final goodbyes, or pick up something he'd forgotten to take with him when he'd left the precinct on Friday.

Kori's mouth curved. Now she was really just grasping at straws.

What did it matter who she gave the large coffee to? The Cavanaughs, every single one of them, were not the kind of people to feel slighted by something so minor as being given a container of coffee—or *not* being given a container of coffee.

She was making a big deal out of nothing.

This was just her nerves getting the better of her, Kori thought with a sigh. Well, she had adjusted to Wills when she had partnered up with the man and, she reminded herself, he hadn't been the easiest man to get along with. If she did it once, she could certainly do it again.

And, in the interim, she could find some appreciative soul to give the extra coffee to.

Heading toward her desk, which was located in the middle of the Missing Persons' squad room, she suddenly slowed her fast pace. There was someone sitting at the desk that faced her own.

The broad-shouldered, dark-haired man looked vaguely familiar—

And yet he didn't, she thought.

Closer scrutiny told her she didn't know the man.

It wasn't unusual for people who were escorted into a squad room, looking to speak to a detective, to take a seat in order not to stand awkwardly out.

"Excuse me," Kori said to the man as she set down the two containers of hot coffee in the center of her desk, "May I help you?"

"No, but I think that, if all goes well, we could wind up helping each other," the stranger answered.

And then he flashed her what she could only term to be a wide, magnetic smile; the kind that totally reeled the recipient—in this case, her—in, and created butterflies in her stomach.

Chapter 2

It was the smile that did it.

The moment it appeared on the stranger's lips, curving the corners of his mouth, the warm smile seemed to instantly light up the entire room. It identified the man sitting at what had become, as of this morning, the "unoccupied" desk.

The man seated there was definitely a Cavanaugh, Kori thought.

He had to be.

While every member of that extensive family could easily lay claim to deep integrity as well a number of the same physical traits, the one attribute they all seemed to have in common, at least the ones she had met so far, was that incredible heart-stopping smile.

Granted, she knew that she hadn't met them all. But as mystifyingly improbable as it might seem, all the Cavanaughs she *had* met possessed the same sort of killer smile. One that not only seemed to light up a room, but instantly generate a warmth within the soul of the recipient.

Conversely, the steely look a Cavanaugh leveled at someone could send a chill down the person's spine. It conveyed the message that this was someone *not* to be taken lightly, discounted or messed with.

However, Kori had learned not to jump to conclusions, even if those conclusions seemed to be all but inevitable. So, for now, Brian Cavanaugh's protégé proceeded with caution.

"Let me guess," she said as she slipped into her seat, facing this new person with the incredible magnetic smile. "You're my new partner."

The man at the desk against hers inclined his head as he nodded to himself. "The chief told me you were sharp as well as quick." With that, he half rose in his seat, extending his hand toward her as he introduced himself. "I'm Brodie Cavanaugh," he said. "But I suspect you already knew that."

She felt her pulse jump. There was that smile again. She could swear she could almost feel it burrowing straight into her chest, spreading out and settling in.

Kori did her best to ignore it or, in lieu of that, to sublimate it. If she didn't somehow manage to dampen its effects, she instinctively knew she wouldn't have a prayer of being able to work through any caseload that came along or to even be able to attempt to think clearly.

His smile was *that* potent.

This one was good-looking enough to have his own squadron of groupies following him around wherever he went. He probably did.

"The last name," she admitted, referring to what he'd just said about feeling that she already knew him. "But not the first. Just where are you within the family dynamics?"

Kori asked, quickly adding, "Not that it actually matters when it comes to our working relationship."

Brodie nodded, a hint of his killer smile surfacing again. "Good to know," he murmured and then told her, "But if you're curious—and to answer your question— Finn's my brother."

"Finn," she repeated, her mind quickly reviewing all the members she had been introduced to at the various times Andrew Cavanaugh had thrown parties under one pretext or another. These days she didn't have time to attend them any more, but she had initially. "That would make you…" Her voice trailed off and then she happily declared, "Donal's son," as she identified Brodie's place within the family.

She noted that the smile was back—and widening. Was it her imagination, or was it growing warmer in here?

"Damn, you are good," Brodie told her. "There are times that I can't keep who's who straight myself. It was hard *before* Uncle Andrew stumbled across our branch of the family. After he brought everyone together for the most mind-boggling meet-and-greet, I feel that absorbing all that information as to who's who is just about impossible."

There was a spark of admiration in his eyes as he looked at her.

Kori could see that happening. Because she had been so very anxious to assimilate *everything* there was to know about her white knight, she had made it a point to learn about Brian Cavanaugh's family as well—and there was more than the usual amount of information.

The way that had come about was because Brian Cavanaugh's great-grandfather and his great-grandmother had divorced back when that sort of occurrence was far from the norm. When a divorce created a dark stain on the family tree.

Even so, the young couple had split up and never looked back. They'd each taken a son and gone their separate ways.

Consequently, Brian's father, Seamus, because of his young age, quickly lost track of his little brother, Murdoch. It wasn't until decades later that Brian's older brother, Andrew, Aurora's former chief of police, had learned about the divorce. He, in turn, had gone hunting for his grandmother. She had hidden her trail well and discovering what had happened to her hadn't been easy.

Refusing to accept defeat, Andrew'd kept at it and finally found out what had happened to his father's younger brother.

Sadly, he'd learned that his grandmother had passed away, as had Murdoch. But not before Murdoch had gotten married and fathered three sons and a daughter. Those offspring, Andrew's cousins, all went on to have children of their own.

And that, Andrew liked to say, was when the story turned unique. Oddly enough, Murdoch's children and grandchildren had all either gone into law enforcement within the city where they lived or into some branch *affiliated* with law enforcement.

Once Andrew had found this heretofore "lost" branch of the family, the members had slowly begun to migrate to Aurora. Drawn by what seemed like some sort of a powerful attraction to either be with this new branch of the family or, at the very least, to meet with them and decide whether or not moving to Aurora seemed like the right thing to do.

Eventually, they'd decided that it was and every one of them settled in Aurora.

The new and old members of the family would often joke that they had enough relatives to populate their own entire police force—and very possibly their own town.

"Not impossible," Kori told Brodie, commenting on his assertion that learning everyone's name was difficult. "Just kind of challenging." Without missing a beat, Kori changed the subject. "You transferred from another department." It wasn't a question.

He was new to the Missing Persons department and she'd just assumed he'd had to have transferred from another section within the police department.

"But nobody told me which one," Kori admitted. Then added, "I barely knew that Wills was leaving."

It occurred to her that Brodie might not know who Wills was. She didn't want to start out on the wrong foot and have him think she was taking things for granted—or worse, that she was rubbing his nose in the fact that she knew things and he didn't.

"Wills was—"

"Your last partner," Brodie interjected. "Yeah, I know." Because he didn't want her thinking he had inside information—that wouldn't be the best way to start their working relationship—he said, "At least, I'm assuming that was who you were talking about. Nobody really told me anything. I just applied for a transfer from Homicide on Friday, thinking it would be a long process and that I should at least start by setting it in motion. I was surprised when I was told that one had just opened up that morning in Missing Persons."

Half a dozen questions filled her head, jockeying for position and searching for answers. "Do you mind if I ask why?" Kori asked then realized that her question might have come across as ambiguous, so she elaborated. "Why you applied for a transfer from Homicide, not why one just opened up in Missing Persons. I already know why that happened."

Brodie flashed a smile at her again. This one was just as lethal as the last one—and the one before that. She would have to learn how to block the effects of that smile. There were just no two ways about it.

"That's easy enough to answer," Brodie told her. "I have to admit that the sight of all those dead people was really beginning to get to me. I want to be able to help people *before* they've gone stone cold." He shrugged philosophically. "Working on a case after the fact might help the victim's family feel as if they're getting some sort of closure, but personally I joined the force to help *save* people, not just bring their killers to justice."

When he saw her smile, he couldn't help wondering if the reason he had just given her came across as being entertaining.

"What?" Brodie asked.

Kori shook her head. "Nothing," she murmured. Then, because she saw he was waiting for some sort of an answer, she told him, "It just sounds like the same reason why I joined the force."

Actually, she had joined the force because she wanted to be like her hero, but the reasons that Brodie cited had been her secondary reasons. That was also why she had opted for the division she was in once she was able to request a division assignment.

Listening to her, Brodie nodded. "Then I'd say that we are going to work well together." Her new partner seemed to take full measure of her, his eyes washing over her. "Mind if I ask you another question?"

Kori braced herself to be on the receiving end of any one of a number of questions from "the new guy," ranging from how strict their lieutenant was to how to most effectively get around protocol. Those were all things that Wills had wanted to know when he had come into the squad.

Instead, Brodie nodded at the two containers she had placed on her desk when she had sat down.

"Are you planning on drinking both of those?" he asked.

That caught her off guard.

"What?"

She looked over to where Brodie had nodded and realized that she had forgotten all about the coffee containers once she had seen Brodie. Kori replayed his question in her mind.

"Oh no." Wrapping her hand around the bottom of the container closest to Brodie, she pushed it in his direction. "This one's for you," she told him, adding, "I hope you like it black. If you don't, there's what passes for sweetener in the break room."

Taking possession of the container, Brodie smiled his thanks. "I take it that the coffee isn't from the break room."

She willed her pulse to settle down as she slowly drew in a deep breath. "Oh lord, no. I wouldn't do that to you on your first day as part of the squad." She nodded at the container between them. "This is from the coffee shop that's across the street," she told him. "It might not be the world's greatest coffee, but it definitely is head and shoulders above anything you'll find in the break room or living in the vending machine."

"'Living in'?" he echoed, arching one eyebrow quizzically.

"Sometimes the vending machine coffee tastes as if it had a life of its own," she warned him.

He decided to leave that alone for now. Instead, he focused on the container in his hand. "And you bought this for me?" he asked, nodding at the coffee.

She was about to say yes, then thought better of it. The truth was always the best way to go. "Full disclosure, it was my turn to buy coffee for my partner and me. I honestly forgot that Friday was his last day here," she confessed.

Brodie removed the lid on the container and set it aside. "Were you and your partner close?" he asked her as the steam from the coffee seeped into his senses for a moment.

She wouldn't have exactly called Wills and her close, so she diplomatically replied, "Well, we worked well together."

Brodie processed the information. "I'll do my best not to disappoint you. So how much do I owe you for the coffee?" he asked, pausing as he took his first sip.

Brodie drew in his breath sharply as he felt a jolt shoot through him as the all but solid dose of caffeine kicked in.

"You don't owe me anything. Call it a Welcome to Missing Persons gift," Kori told her new partner.

She watched as Brodie's smile formed beneath the container as he took in another, somewhat larger, sip of the inky coffee. His green eyes seemed to penetrate right into her as they shone with humor above the rim of the container.

"On behalf of my now fully awake consciousness," he told Kori, "I would like to offer my sincerest thank-you."

It took Kori less than a second to find her tongue, but, lost in the glow of his smile, it was a second she was acutely aware of.

"No need for thanks. You get to buy the coffee next week." Kori did her best to sound matter-of-fact and removed.

"Sounds fair to me." Brodie took another deep swig, waiting for the coffee to wind itself through his system. "Where did you say you bought this?"

"The shop is called Morning Wake-up Call," she told Brodie. "The coffee shop is located on the corner across the street from the precinct. You can't miss it. By eight thirty, there's usually a line of police officers feeding into it. There has been ever since the shop opened up. Most of the officers swear by it. These days the only reason anyone drinks what's in the vending machines around here is if they can't get away or are too busy to spare the time to hotfoot it to the coffee shop."

"Seems to me someone should look into whatever it is that they're using to brew the coffee and put that stuff into the coffee machines around here." He finished off the rest of the coffee in his container. "I guarantee you that productivity would go up."

"Well, you're a Cavanaugh. Why don't you suggest it?" she told Brodie.

But her new partner shook his head. "Technically, I'm a new Cavanaugh," he told her. "I'm not into making changes at the moment. Right now, I'm into being part of the team until I get more entrenched in the family."

She looked at him uncertainly. "Hold it," she told him. "You're serious? You're actually 'new'?" That would explain why she hadn't seen him around earlier.

He laughed softly. "Well, not exactly 'new,'" he clarified. "I should have just said new to the Aurora police force. Before that, I worked on the force in Littleton."

"Let me guess, you worked the Homicide Division there?" she asked him.

He grinned. She *was* paying attention. "Very good, you *were* listening. When I applied to join the Aurora police department here, they put me into the exact department

I was initially working in the last city I lived in. But, like I said, I really wanted a change."

Kori nodded. "Because you were tired of dealing with dead bodies." Thinking about that now, she had to admit that was rather a sensitive reaction on Brodie's part. In her book, that spoke well of him.

"Nothing like a dead body to make me feel helpless," he told her.

"Certainly can't argue with that," Kori responded.

He nodded, taking in the last remaining swig of his coffee. "I've got a feeling we're going to work well together."

Kori studied him for a long moment over her own container, having only taken a few token sips so far. She could only hope that the good-looking man wasn't just blowing smoke. Just because the other Cavanaughs she had met and interacted with were men and women of integrity didn't necessarily mean that they all were.

In her experience, a lot of good-looking men just depended on their looks to get them through any situation.

Still, she gave him the benefit of the doubt. "Might be a while before we find out. We don't have as much crime here in Aurora as they do in other cities—except, I suppose, when it comes in comparison to small towns, of course."

"That might be a pleasant change. But that's okay. I'm good at kicking back," he told her.

Just then, the door to the lieutenant's office at the rear of the squad room opened and Lieutenant Dan Rafferty peered out. He quickly scanned the area for a moment. Recognition set in when he saw who he was looking for.

"Hey, Kennedy, Cavanaugh," he called, beckoning. "Come into my office."

Kori pushed her chair back from her desk and rose. "Guess he wants to say hello."

"That didn't quite sound as if that was part of meet-and-greet," Brodie observed. Rising to his feet, he gestured ahead of him. "After you," he told Kori.

She smiled to herself as she led the way to their lieutenant's office. At least the man was polite.

Chapter 3

There were rumors that once upon a time, in his early twenties, Lieutenant Daniel Rafferty had been a track-and-field star and had even entertained the idea of competing in the US Summer Olympics. But that was twenty-four years ago.

Looking at the man now, it hardly seemed possible. Rather than move with the ease of a gazelle, Rafferty lumbered back into his office. Reclaiming the seat behind his desk seemed to require a lot of effort on his part.

The body that sank into the upholstery all but spilled out on the sides, seeming to cover every available inch of space. These days Rafferty was always either just going on a diet or just coming off one, the latter motivated by his frustration in not being able to achieve the weight goals he had set for himself.

There was more than a little envy in the lieutenant's dark brown eyes as he scrutinized the young man who had just been sent to join his department.

Kori had the very distinct impression that the words Rafferty uttered to the new man who was just joining his squad weighed rather heavily on his tongue. It seemed difficult for the lieutenant to interact with someone whose physical fitness was an acute reminder of just how much he had let himself go over the years.

After gesturing toward one of the empty chairs in front of his desk, the lieutenant told Brodie, "I've heard good things about you from Captain Jeffers, Cavanaugh. He sounded as if he was really sorry to see you go." Rafferty studied Brodie's face closely for a moment. "Are you sure you want to be here?"

"I'm very sure, sir," Brodie sincerely assured the man.

Rafferty nodded. For several seconds, there was nothing but silence in the room, as if the lieutenant was thinking over his next words. And then, as was his habit, the squad leader sucked in his breath before speaking. "All right then, consider yourself temporarily assigned to this department, Cavanaugh."

That didn't sound quite right to Kori. "Temporarily, sir?" she questioned.

The lieutenant appeared annoyed at having to explain himself. "Well, it should go without saying that if, for some reason, Cavanaugh here doesn't work out, he'll have to go back to his original department." Rafferty narrowed his eyes until they were all but dark slits. "Cavanaugh or not, there is no display of undo favoritism in my department," he told Kori and then he shifted his steely gaze to the newly transferred detective. "Is that understood, Cavanaugh?"

"Yes, sir," Brodie answered, his expression totally unreadable.

Brodie was apparently taking this briefing in stride, Kori thought, but she took offense for him. Rafferty was unduly flexing his muscles. In her opinion, his words could have been more welcoming, especially given Brodie's connection to several of the people in high places of authority, both past and present. If she was the one on the receiving end of this so-called "first meeting," she would have taken offense at the less than hidden meaning in the lieutenant's pep talk. In other words, Rafferty was saying that he intended to watch Cavanaugh like a hawk and if he took one misstep, then Cavanaugh or not, the detective would be out of there.

Once again, Rafferty sucked in his breath and then said, "All right, with that out of the way, looks as if you might just get a chance to prove your mettle, Cavanaugh. Five minutes ago, dispatch got a 9-1-1 call from Aurora General Hospital. According to the caller, a newborn was just reported kidnapped from a mother's room in the maternity ward." Rafferty shrugged, as if not sure just what he believed to be true. "It just might all turn out to be some sort of miscommunication, but just to be on the safe side, why don't you two go and check it out?" the lieutenant suggested. He gestured at the two detectives as if they were joined at the hip.

Kori was instantly on her feet. This sort of thing was the reason why she had joined the police department in the first place. To protect the children who couldn't protect themselves. Who was more defenseless than a newborn?

"Yes, sir," she declared.

Rafferty barely acknowledged her. Instead, he was looking at the newest addition to his department. "Let me know what, if anything, you find, Cavanaugh," he ordered the man.

"I will, Lieutenant," Brodie promised. He waited until they left the lieutenant's office and then looked at Kori. "I'm sorry."

The apology seemed to have come out of nowhere. Kori looked at him. "For what?"

"The lieutenant usurped you." Brodie sounded genuinely sorry that had happened. "I don't think he meant to do that. He was probably just focused on testing what I'm made of. You know, wanting to see if I can really measure up and be part of the team I was 'auditioning' for."

She stopped walking for a moment so that Brodie could hear what she had to say more easily. "I didn't take any offense that Lieutenant Rafferty appeared to hand the lead to this case over you if that's what you're worried about—but thanks for the apology," she told him. "However, you didn't have to worry. I don't have any ego issues here. Especially since there's an infant's welfare concerned."

Brodie took in what she said. "Even so, I know that the case should be handled by you. I'm here to learn and to help," he told her. "Not to try to take over."

Well, that would certainly make him different from her last partner, Kori thought. Until just now, Kori had come to the conclusion that there were some men who couldn't help themselves. For those men, there was just this bone in their body, this mindset that made them inclined to just commandeer the reins of any given investigation.

Her eyes met Brodie's.

"I believe you," she told him. "Now, let's get over there. Maybe there's been some strange, simple mix-up at the hospital that can easily be resolved and that no one actually kidnapped a newborn."

Brodie studied her profile. "Do you really think that's the case?"

She felt as if he were looking straight into her soul. She sighed. "No, not really," she told him. "But I can hope."

When they got to the rear of the precinct, she instinctively headed to where her car was parked. It took her less than five steps to realize that Brodie wasn't walking next to her. He had turned toward his own vehicle.

"Hey, Cavanaugh," she called out and then waited for him to turn to her. When he did, he appeared surprised that she wasn't with him. They had each just assumed that the other was following in their wake. "I think it would make more sense if we drove in one car," she told him.

He picked up on her inflection. She meant in *her* car. Obligingly, Brodie pivoted and headed for her.

He flashed a rueful smile. "Looks like there are a few things we still have to work out."

Well, that was nice of him. He didn't get his back up over that. She was liking her new partner more and more.

"Looks like," Kori agreed. "Since you just admitted that you're relatively new to Aurora, and heaven knows I've lived in Aurora all my life, I thought in the interest of getting to the hospital quickly, I should drive."

Brodie nodded, his dark hair falling into his eyes. He was amenable to having her behind the wheel. "Makes sense to me," he agreed.

Kori had to admit that she had been prepared for some semblance of an argument. The only reason she was the one to drive when she'd partnered with Wills was that, occasionally, the latter liked to let his mind wander.

Brodie, however, seemed inclined to go with the flow. Maybe this *would* work out after all. This job was hard enough at times without having to worry about jockeying for position and possibly offending a fragile ego.

"So," he said, picking up the conversation where they had left off as he got into the passenger seat and buckled up, "does this mean that you really think that this *is* a kidnapping?" he asked her as Kori started up her vehicle.

"What makes you think it isn't?" she asked, curious as to his reasoning.

"Well, from what I've heard, hospital procedures have changed drastically from the days that people could just walk into the nursery and walk off with a newborn under some pretext. Security has certainly tightened, mother and newborn ID bracelets are constantly being double-checked and most important of all, nurseries have pretty much gone the way of the dinosaur. Now the baby is in a bassinette in the mother's hospital room. Instant bonding from the first moment," he concluded.

That was pretty astute for a bachelor, she couldn't help thinking.

Kori spared a glance in her partner's direction and saw that Brodie was smiling to himself. "What?" she prodded.

"I was just thinking that arrangement pretty much does away with the new mother's illusion that she's going to get anything resembling a full night's sleep anytime in the foreseeable future," he answered.

She laughed softly. "I think that pretty much is a given when she decides to become a mother," Kori pointed out.

A thought came to him out of left field. "What if she didn't decide?"

She wasn't sure what he was getting at and didn't want to jump to conclusions. "What do you mean?"

"What if becoming a mother was something that happened totally by accident? An unintended consequence of one moment of wild, unplanned passion?"

He certainly had a point, she thought, but she wasn't about to get philosophical about this. That path was too involved.

"We're not here to debate how she became a mother. We're here to find out if her baby was taken, and if so, when, how and by who," she specified. Of course, there were other questions, she thought, but for now just these would do.

"You're the boss," Brodie told her.

She slanted a look in his direction at the next light. He seemed way too complacent. "Are you trying to stroke my ego, Cavanaugh?"

"No, just stating a simple fact," he told her without displaying any sort of revealing emotion on his part. "Like I said," he continued, "I'm here to absorb and learn."

It sounded almost too good to be true. "And you have no problem whatsoever taking directions from a woman," she pressed. "A younger woman," she specified since that might have made a difference in this case.

"I take it you *are* familiar with the Cavanaughs?" he asked.

She didn't know if he was feeding her lines or if he was serious, but she answered him as if he were asking a legitimate question. "Of course I am—and I figure you already know that."

Brodie didn't answer her one way or another. Instead, he made the point he was trying to get across to her. "Then you know that my family, especially my *extended* family, has a lot of strong-willed, not to mention really stubborn, women in it. Actually, to be completely honest, I don't think there *is* such a creature as a mild-mannered Cavanaugh female. In our family, every single one of them is stubborn as hell. I'm also proud to say that they all know what they're doing. So no, I have no problem observing how you work and learning from you. Any other questions?"

"I'll be sure to ask them when they come up," Kori replied.

Making a left turn in the middle of a side street that came up, Kori followed the zigzag path that took her into the hospital parking lot. That, in turn, provided parking in front of the emergency room. Following that was a small parking lot directly in front of the hospital entrance. In the distance, a parking structure afforded additional spaces—five levels of them—for people coming to the hospital for the purpose of visiting patients as well as to avail themselves of the various diagnostic tests the hospital offered.

Kori parked directly in front of the hospital's main front entrance. Pulling up her handbrake, she declared out of habit, "We're here."

Brodie wondered if her last partner was a simpleton. "I kind of gathered that from the sign they had right out front that said Aurora General Hospital."

"Well, I see that nothing gets by you," Kori deadpanned.

"I do my best," he answered in an identical tone. And then, simultaneously, the two new partners grinned at one another. If there was any tension, it was laid to rest.

Brodie waited until she got out of her vehicle, then walked with Kori to the entrance.

The moment they entered the hospital, Kori got the distinct feeling that the reported kidnapping had definitely not been made in error. There was chaos everywhere. The tension in the air was so thick, it seemed to make even breathing difficult.

Her eyes on the front desk, Kori approached the distraught-looking woman sitting there. Taking out her ID, Kori held it up for the woman's benefit.

"Detectives Kori Kennedy and Brodie Cavanaugh." She nodded at Brodie. "We're here about the newborn reportedly kidnapped from her mother's room."

The receptionist, a grandmotherly woman who appeared almost beside herself, sighed with what seemed like palatable relief.

"Oh, thank goodness!" she cried.

Rather than telling them where to go to speak to the

bereft new mother, the receptionist was immediately on her feet and making her way around her desk. Flustered, she walked *into* the desk once before managing to clear the area and finally get out into the aisle.

"Nothing like this has *ever* happened here before. At least, not since I've come to work at Aurora General." She considered her words, then added for clarification sake, "But probably never."

"Miss, you need to take a deep breath," Brodie advised calmly.

The fact that he had addressed her as "Miss" instead of "Ma'am" put the woman in a more receptive, calmer frame of mind. The hospital receptionist did as he said, taking in a deep breath and then slowly releasing it.

Kori noted that the older woman actually seemed grateful, but that obviously didn't diminish the horror she felt regarding what had happened.

"The maternity ward is on the fifth floor," she told the two people she felt were here to rectify a terrible wrong. "I'll take you up there."

"That really isn't necessary. We can certainly get there on our own," Kori said.

However, the look on the woman's pale face told her that she was wrong. "Oh, but it *is* necessary," she declared in a quaking voice.

Brodie's eyes met Kori's and she could see that he was telling her they shouldn't contradict the woman. It was obvious that the receptionist would feel better if, in her mind, she'd somehow contributed to the solution of this heinous problem.

"Then please," Kori encouraged the older woman, "lead the way."

She saw Brodie smile his approval. She had no idea why that would make her feel good.

But it did.

Chapter 4

The hospital receptionist, who introduced herself midway as Amelia Saunders, was still talking nonstop as she walked into the elevator with Kori and Brodie. Rather than abate, her babbling grew more pronounced as they rode up in the elevator.

"Security put the entire hospital on lockdown," she told the detectives. "Belatedly, I know, but better late than never, right?" The question was followed by a high-pitched, nervous laugh.

"Do you know any of the details about how the baby was taken from her mother's room?" Kori asked Amelia. Since she had to listen to the woman go on and on, she felt that she might as well channel her toward hopefully useful information.

Confronted with an actual question, Amelia abruptly stopped talking. Instead, she raised her hands, palms up, toward the elevator ceiling as she shrugged. Her eyes appeared huge as she answered. "All I know was what I heard. One minute the baby was in her bassinette, the next, she wasn't." Amelia shook her head helplessly. If there was a theory as to how the abduction had been pulled off, no one had let her in on it.

"Were all the surveillance cameras checked?" Brodie asked.

"No one tells me anything," the woman lamented as the elevator came to a stop and the doors opened up. They had reached the fifth floor.

It was on the tip of Kori's tongue to ask the receptionist if she had made any inquiries about the cameras and actually *asked* if anything had been caught on video, but she had a feeling that both questions would lead nowhere. The woman was completely caught up in wringing her hands and proclaiming how in the dark she was about the whole situation.

So instead, Kori merely nodded her head, as if sympathizing with the receptionist and how locked out of everything she felt she was. She just sensed that it was simpler that way.

The sooner they got to question the mother, Kori felt, the better. Maybe they would get somewhere there. At least, she could hope so.

As if reading her their minds, Amelia proclaimed, "That poor mother's room is this way."

It was an unnecessary declaration. Anyone would have suspected that something out of the ordinary was happening and it was all centered around room 509.

There were a lot of concerned-looking people coming and going, not to mention the sound of high-pitched, anguished crying that emanated from that room.

Kori glanced at Brodie. "Well, it looks like this is the

right room," she said just before she braced herself and entered.

Brodie made no comment in response, but Kori could all but feel her new partner's smile, resigned but still very much in play, slipping its way under her skin.

The next second, Kori's heart went out to the woman in the hospital bed.

Rose Williams's flushed face was in direct contrast to her white hospital gown. Her eyes were red-rimmed. She had obviously been crying and there were tear tracks on her cheeks. The petite, gaunt young woman definitely looked worn out and right now appeared older than her age, which, according to the information that they had been given, was twenty.

When they entered the single-care unit, the bereft young mother had her arms wrapped around herself and she was rocking to and fro in her bed. The action was obviously intended to somehow comfort herself, but it wasn't working.

Just then, the young woman began talking. At first Kori thought the words were meant for them, but then she realized that the infant's mother was saying the words to no one in particular. Her agitation increased with every single syllable she uttered.

"It's my fault. All my fault. My fault that my baby girl's gone," she cried.

"Ms. Williams…" Kori began in a soft, kind voice, trying to get the young woman's attention. It took her two more attempts before she managed to finally succeed. The bereft mother looked up at her with wide, frightened eyes. "Ms. Williams, I'm Detective Kennedy and this is Detective Cavanaugh," Kori said, introducing herself as she drew closer to the young woman's bed. "We're here to investigate your daughter's abduction." She held up her badge and her identification for the mother's benefit.

The expression on the tear-stained face was blank, as if the distraught new mother was being addressed in a foreign language and none of it was registering.

And then, slowly, the words Kori had said seemed to penetrate. Rose took in a deep, shaky breath, as if that could somehow help her cope with the ramifications of this terrible situation.

"She's gone because of me," the young woman cried again. The look in her eyes was wild, as if she didn't know where to go, what to think. "My baby's gone because of me."

"Why would you say that?" Brodie asked. He had been prepared to let Kori do all the talking, but in the face of all this anguish, he'd been unable to maintain his silence any longer.

"Because I said I didn't want her," Rose answered, her voice breaking at the end of her sentence. "But I do. I do want her," the woman cried. She looked wildly from one detective to the other. "I was just scared," she explained, sobbing.

Any second, the woman was going to start pulling out her hair and ripping her clothes, Kori thought. She tried to redirect the young mother's attention by getting Rose to talk to them. "Scared? Scared of what?"

Rose's breathing was labored. "Scared of dropping her. Of doing everything wrong. Of not being good enough to raise a baby." She searched their faces for some sign that they understood. "But now I'm even more scared that I'll never seen her again," she wailed, her voice cracking again as she tried to suppress the overpowering fear that threatened to literally swallow her whole. She was trembling now, unable to keep her body still.

"Every new mother—and new father—is afraid of messing up. It's only natural, and it goes with the territory," Brodie assured the young woman who seemed to be completely unraveling right before their eyes.

"But I was going to give her up, give her away, as if she was a sweater I didn't want. I thought she would be better off without me." Her voice dropped as she added, "And I'd be better off without her." There was self-loathing in her voice. "Except once I saw her, I realized that I couldn't go through with it. I mean, I knew I wasn't going to be the best mother or even what she needed," Rose protested, "but heaven help me, I fell in love with that tiny face. And now she's gone."

She raised her tear-filled eyes to look at the two detectives, silently pleading for their help to rectify this awful turn of events. "Please find her. Please find my baby."

"We'll do our best." Kori's vague words were immediately swept away by her partner's far more forceful promise.

"We'll find your baby," Brodie told her, drawing closer to the tearful, distraught young woman. He was rewarded with a look from the mother that all but canonized him where he stood.

"I'm counting on you," Rose told him, emotion quaking in her voice.

"When was the last time you saw your daughter?" he asked the young woman, hoping he could get an answer without having her break down on them again.

The question seemed to throw Rose for a moment as she attempted to think. It was obvious that she was having trouble keeping events straight in her mind. Everything appeared to be a jumble right now.

Finally, she was able to formulate an answer.

"At breakfast. I saw her at breakfast," Rose declared,

nodding her head as if agreeing with herself. Her eyes met Kori's then swept back to Brodie. "I was finally able to eat something—I've been too upset to eat these last couple of days," she added. "And then I guess I must have fallen asleep. I shouldn't have."

"And do you remember where your daughter was when you fell asleep?" Kori asked. She was fairly certain she knew the answer to that, but she wanted to hear Rose say it.

As Rose pointed toward the bassinette, her hand was trembling. Looking at the empty, tiny, enclosure was a painful reminder that the baby had been stolen from her by any one of a number of people, all of whom she had felt she could trust.

Until now.

"She was right there." Rose looked at the detectives, stricken. "I can still hear the sound of her breathing. It was such a peaceful sound, I guess it lulled me to sleep," she told them ruefully. "I should have realized that something was wrong when it stopped. The silence should have woken me up," she cried, her voice growing frantic again. "Why didn't I wake up? She was my baby, I should have been in tune to her, to her sounds," she declared as if she felt it was some sort of a given. Rose's eyes moved back and forth between the two detectives, searching for confirmation of her omission. "Right?"

"Not necessarily," Kori answered, doing her best to be tactful. "This was all new to you." Kori tried to move on before Rose had another outburst. Having the baby's mother blame herself wasn't going to help them with the investigation. She looked at the tray with empty dishes. "Was the tray here when you fell asleep?"

Rose stared at Kori, a bewildered expression on her

face, as if the simple question was too much for her to comprehend.

"Think, Rose," Kori coaxed. "Whatever you can piece together will help us find your daughter. Now, was the tray still in the room when you fell asleep?"

Rose's eyes moved from side to side, as if that would somehow help her think and remember. When she finally spoke, the young woman didn't sound very confident. "I guess so."

Brodie turned to the receptionist. Amelia was still hanging around, like someone observing an accident unfolding and just couldn't get herself to turn away. Amelia dropped her eyes, as if suddenly embarrassed at being caught this way.

Brodie made it a point to keep any accusation out of his voice. "Who would have collected the breakfast tray, Amelia?" he asked.

This time there was no hesitation when she answered. "One of the orderlies would have come in. It's their job to collect the tray," she declared.

Brodie nodded, taking in the information. "Is there just one orderly who does that for every floor?" he asked the woman.

Amelia looked pleased at the question, as if relieved that there was another one she could answer. Her smile entered her eyes. "Yes, as far as I know."

Kori assimilated the information. Could be something, could be nothing, she thought. "All right. Where can we find him?"

"Her," Amelia corrected. "The orderly who works this floor is a woman. Edith Woods," the receptionist recalled belatedly. "She specifically requested this floor." Amelia remembered. "She said she likes to work on the maternity floor."

Kori exchanged glances with Brodie. She could see they were both thinking the same thing. Maybe there was a reason why this Edith Woods had initially requested to work the maternity floor.

"And where is this Edith now?" Brodie asked the receptionist.

Amelia looked over her shoulder, as if visualizing the space she was going to tell them about. "Security has everyone in the break room, questioning them until the police got here," the receptionist told them, happy to be able to share that information.

"Well, the police are here," Kori told her, spreading her hands as if to underscore the fact. "Where is the break room?"

Amelia jolted, as if she was suddenly waking up. There was almost a rueful expression on her face. "Oh, it's this way. I can take you to it."

"Please," he requested.

"And you're going to find my baby," Rose said. It wasn't quite a question but a hopeful statement. "I'm counting on you. I didn't mean the part about giving her up for adoption. I really didn't."

This time is was Kori who paused at the woman's bedside. She squeezed Rose's hand. It felt icy to the touch.

"We know you didn't," she told her because she felt that the young mother needed to hear the reassurance.

Rather than look consoled, the distraught new mother surprised them by beginning to sob again.

Kori felt at a total loss.

Brodie saw the helpless look on his partner's face. He leaned in to her and whispered, "C'mon, let's find the orderly. Maybe she saw something."

"Maybe," Kori murmured. Right now, it was all they had to go on—maybe.

* * *

Edith Woods looked like everyone's idea of a grand-mother. Heavyset, with kindly eyes, she appeared more than willing to tell the two detectives everything she knew, which unfortunately didn't really amount to very much.

They could see that there was nothing out of the ordinary happening on the floor. A variety of people were coming and going from the various rooms, visiting the new mothers, and oohing and aahing over the brand-new little people who had come into the world. While it vaguely appeared that there was something unusual going on, no one seemed to realize the hospital was on lockdown because, unless someone attempted to physically leave the building, life went on as usual.

"In other words, nothing unusual?" Kori guessed.

The woman shook her gray head. "Nothing at all out of the ordinary."

"Did you see anyone in Ms. Williams's room, either entering it or leaving it?"

"No." Pity came over the orderly's face. "As far as I saw, the poor dear didn't have any visitors. Oh, some of the nurses lingered in the room to talk to her, you know, try to make her feel good about her decision…" Her voice trailed off.

"You mean her decision to give up her baby?" Brodie asked.

"Yes, that. You could see that she was agonizing over the decision, but some women just aren't cut out to be mothers," Edith said.

"And in your opinion, Ms. Williams looked as if she belonged to that group?" Kori asked, studying the orderly, who nodded her head with authority.

Right before their eyes, Edith seemed to retract her words. "Well, that's just it."

"What's just it?" Brodie asked, not quite following what the woman was telling them.

Edith cleared her throat, then told them, "You could see she was wavering about that, that she couldn't quite make up her mind. If you ask me," the orderly continued, lowering her voice as if this was all a guarded secret, "she thought what she'd decided was for the best, but then she just changed her mind. I've seen enough of this sort of thing to know."

Kori reverted to hard and fast facts. "And you're sure you didn't see anyone in her room?"

"Not when I came in to bring her the tray—and not when I came by later to collect it—except that she wasn't finished yet, so I left it," she added. "I only saw her nurse go in as I was distributing trays to the other mothers."

The two detectives were suddenly alert.

"Which nurse?" Brodie asked.

"Nurse McGuire," Edith recalled. "I think she's been here as long as the hospital has," she added.

"And where can we find her?" Kori asked.

"Security just told her she was free to go," the orderly answered.

Kori and Brodie went back to the room where the remaining personnel on the floor were being questioned to ask about the nurse who had been told she was free to leave.

The hospital security guard appeared to have been sent directly from central casting, representing a studio's idea of what a run-of-the-mill hospital security guard should have looked like. The rumpled, stocky man reminded Kori of someone who was doing this sort of work only after having tried and failed at several other types of occupations along the way.

"Well, it's about time," the man cried with relief the moment he saw Brodie and Kori enter the room and come toward him. Rayburn Smith instantly seemed pleased to be able to pass the buck.

What was up with that? Kori wondered. "I guess we must have 'police' stamped on our foreheads," she murmured to the man walking next to her.

"Maybe it's our official demeanor," Brodie commented, humor curving his mouth. "Mr. Smith," he said after half a beat during which time he read the man's name on the badge pinned to his chest, "we're Detectives Kennedy and Cavanaugh." He indicated Kori and then himself. "If you have the time, we'd like to ask you a few questions."

"Of course, of course," he said agreeably enough. "But unfortunately, I didn't see anything," he told them right off the bat.

That seemed to be everyone's story, Brodie thought. He still held out the hope that *someone* had seen something useful.

"Maybe you don't even realize that you saw something. Sometimes even the smallest detail can help break a case," he told the security guard.

Smith's dark eyes grew wide as he looked from one detective to the other. "You really think so?"

"You never know," was all that Brodie would commit to. The next second, he suggested, "Why don't we go over there where we can talk without anyone interrupting us?" Brodie nodded to a far corner of the room.

The security guard brightened. He appeared to be more than happy to comply. And then his eyes darted toward the rest of the people still waiting to be told they could go home.

"You want me to tell everyone else they can leave?" he asked.

"Not quite yet," Brodie told him.

Smith nodded, more than happy to comply. "You got it, Chief."

Brodie didn't bother to correct him.

Chapter 5

In the end, after speaking to the security guard, as well as all the hospital employees who had been gathered and held in the maternity floor break room, everyone was finally released.

Kori and Brodie found the interviews entirely unsatisfying, not to mention draining.

Brodie blew out a breath as he shook his head. "I never saw so many people who saw nothing even remotely suspicious," he said wearily. "Either whoever took that baby was exceptionally good at making themselves inconspicuous or invisible, or the baby wasn't taken from here."

"She had to be," Kori insisted.

"Then how would you explain 'Now you see her, now you don't'?"

Kori thought for a moment then ventured one explanation. "My guess is that everyone on the floor was too busy doing their job—one of the nurses said that there've been cutbacks recently, so the employees here are trying to do more than their share," she confided.

"What about the people visiting patients?" he asked. They had interviewed a number of visitors as well.

"That's easy," she said. "They were too absorbed in their own little world, oohing and aahing over the newest addition to the population. That could have easily prevented them from noticing anything unusual that might have been going on."

Tunnel vision. That was a simple enough explanation, he thought. "You're probably right. We should hit the surveillance cameras next just in case *they* picked up anything useful," he suggested.

"You mean like someone making off with a baby?" she asked grimly.

"I was thinking more in the way of a wiggling backpack or duffel bag," Brodie said, scanning the immediate area as they walked away from the break room.

Kori shook her head. "If only," she said with a wistful sigh. "That would make things so much easier. Okay, let's see if whoever is manning the monitors turns out to be more helpful than the security guard was and gives us copies of the fifth-floor videos from the last twenty-four hours." She figured that should cover it on the outside chance that the kidnapper had made the mistake of surveying the immediate area *before* finally going through with the abduction.

"You might want to review videos taken from all the ground-floor exits in that time frame as well," Brodie told her. "After all, the kidnapper had to have left the hospital with their 'prize' somehow."

Kori's quizzical look melted into a smile as she nodded at him with approval. "You just might work out after all, Cavanaugh."

"Is that your idea of an 'atta boy'?" he asked Kori.

"It might be," she allowed, rolling the term over in her head. "I don't like being predictable."

Brodie laughed, amused. "Something tells me that's not one of your shortcomings."

She raised her chin, pretending to dismiss his comment. "I don't have shortcomings."

"Of course you don't. What was I thinking?" Brodie quipped.

"Hey," Kori suddenly called out to Brodie as he bypassed the elevators. "You just walked right by the elevators," she said, pointing to the closed silvery doors.

"I know," Brodie answered as he continued walking down the hallway.

A thought suddenly occurred to her. "You're not one of those people who likes to take the stairs every time he gets a chance, are you?" She was all for exercise, but there was a time and a place for it and that time was not now.

He looked at her as if she were spouting nonsense. "Hell no!"

Her brow furrowed. "If you're not taking the stairs down and you're bypassing the elevator, where are you going?" she asked.

"I just wanted to go see the baby's mother before we left," he told her.

She still didn't understand why he was going back. "Did you think of something else that you want to ask her?" she asked as she quickened her step to catch up to Brodie.

"Actually, I did," he answered. "I want to ask her if she has anyone to call who could be here for her. That orderly mentioned that she didn't recall seeing anyone coming by to visit Rose, and I just want to make sure she has someone she could stay with or talk to." He turned down the hall toward the woman's room. "She shouldn't be going through this by herself."

Kori stopped walking and looked at her new partner in surprise.

When Brodie realized that she wasn't keeping up, he turned around to look at her. He couldn't read the expression on her face.

"What?" he asked.

"Nothing," she answered, waving away his question. And then she replied, "You're just being very thoughtful, that's all." Her mouth curved ever so slightly. "I had no idea that my new partner came with feelings."

Brodie laughed at the comment. "I'm a Cavanaugh," he reminded her, then deadpanned, "I'm told that we all come with feelings."

"Well, there's always an exception," Kori pointed out diplomatically.

He pretended to take her comment seriously. "Not to my knowledge," he answered after a moment.

They reached Rose's single-care unit and pushed open the door. The second they walked in, the young mother sat ramrod-straight, instantly alert.

"Did you find her?" she cried eagerly. "Did you find my baby?"

Brodie hated to have to tell her the truth, but he wasn't about to lie. "No, not yet..." Brodie began to answer.

Rose refused to surrender all hope. "But you do have some leads, right?" she asked breathlessly. "Things you can follow up on, right?"

He didn't look in Kori's direction and he certainly didn't have the heart to tell Rose that so far they had come up empty. He saw no reason to crush her.

So he worded his answer as positively as he could. "We're examining every single possibility. In the meantime, we—" he glanced toward Kori, including her in on this "—wanted to ask you if you have anyone you could call to come down to the hospital. Like a friend or a relative," he supplied when she didn't say anything in response to his question.

Rose seemed lost for a moment. Her eyes moved back and forth, seemingly staring at nothing as she tried to think.

"I suppose there's my cousin, Rachel," she finally said. A small, disparaging laugh escaped her lips as she considered her cousin. "I haven't seen her in a few years, though. Not since she went away to college." She raised her eyes to Brodie's face, suddenly dismissing that choice. "But I can't call her. I'm not part of her life anymore. She doesn't even know I had a baby. And her mother—my aunt Gloria—would be horrified if she found out that I had a baby and wasn't married. They wouldn't want to have anything to do with me," she said sadly. The very thought was pure anguish to her.

"Your aunt might surprise you," Brodie told her. "You'll never know if you don't try to get in contact with them," he predicted. "Why don't you give me her number, or at least her name, and I'll see if I can reach her for you?"

Rose looked very doubtful about the suggestion. But in the end, she relented and gave him her aunt's last name and her last known address.

Writing it down, he pocketed the piece of paper. Patting it, he told her to think "good thoughts."

Rose offered him a weak smile. "That didn't help with my grandmother."

Brodie and Kori exchanged looks. "You have a grandmother?"

"Yes. We were pretty close, too. But something changed when I told her that I was giving the baby up for adoption.

She seemed really disappointed and distant. We still talk, but not as much," she lamented.

"Have you tried calling her?" Kori asked.

Rose pressed her lips together and nodded. "But she's not answering."

"Keep trying," Brodie advised. "Tell her what happened. I'm sure she'll come," he told her. He couldn't imagine a relative staying away after hearing that.

Rose nodded, though she seemed unconvinced. "Maybe."

Brodie said a few more encouraging words to Rose, and then he and Kori left the hospital room.

He was well aware of the fact that Kori had kept her silence throughout the entire exchange between the kidnapped baby's mother and him as he was trying to build up her hope.

"Go ahead," he told Kori as he pressed the down button for the elevator.

"Go ahead?" Koru repeated, raising her eyebrow as she looked at him.

"Yes. Tell me what you're thinking. I know you've been dying to give me your opinion about what I just said to Rose," Brodie said. Partnered with her for a few hours, Kori had impressed him as the type who didn't hold things back when they occurred to her.

Her answer surprised him. "I think you're a lot more thoughtful than I'd expected you to be—and a hell of a lot more thoughtful than any of the other detectives I was partnered with."

"'Partnered with,'" Brodie repeated. "As in plural?" he asked. "Just how many partners have you had?"

In response, Kori laughed to herself. It was a dry, almost humorless laugh as she thought about the men who had filled that position.

"Off the top of my head, I'd say too many," she answered.

"Why so many?" Brodie asked, genuinely curious. Was there something about her that he should be aware of? At first meeting, the attractive young woman seemed nice enough, but he could be wrong. If so, he needed to know in order to be prepared.

"Looking for people who have disappeared out of their lives can take a lot out of a person." She half shrugged as they rode down to the first floor. "I suppose that some people can't handle it."

"But you can?" Brodie asked, studying her face.

Her answer was straightforward. "I live for it." Her eyes almost glowed as she said, "There's nothing like being able to reunite people who never thought they would see one another again."

Brodie caught the note in her voice. "You sound like you speak from experience," he noted.

"I do," she said proudly, thinking of the cases that had gone well. And then she asked Brodie, "Did your uncle tell you about the night I met him?" If he already knew, then there was no sense in repeating the story, she thought.

"Which uncle?" he asked as the elevator came to a stop. The doors yawned open and he put his hand out, holding the doors back as she got off. Brodie followed her out. "You forget, I have an entire stable full of uncles."

She smiled at the way he'd put that. She would have loved to have had more of a family than she did. But she was grateful to have her father alive.

"Brian," Kori answered.

"Oh." He nodded. "You mean the chief of detectives. No, he didn't. Probably didn't think it was important to our working together," Brodie guessed.

He was probably right about that, Kori thought as she

began to go over the particulars of that night. "I was going with my father to the convenience store. We were having hot dogs for dinner," she recalled, then added, "He couldn't afford anything else." There was no shame in her voice. It was just a simple fact. "It turns out that the convenience store was being robbed at the time and we walked right in on the robbery. My father grabbed my arm and bolted out of there."

She paused for a moment, a lump forming in her throat. "He used his body to shield me so I wouldn't be hurt." She shivered as she said, "I just remember this awful sound—the robber fired his gun and he shot my father. Twice. My father fell to the ground right before my eyes." She stopped again, trying to catch her breath and keep her tears back. She always cried when she remembered that night.

"I just remember trying to keep my father's blood from spilling out of his body with my hands over the wound. I was nine," she told Brodie, as if that explained her futile, foolish attempts to stop the bleeding with her hands.

Her mouth curved slightly from the memory. She had been so desperate, so hopelessly naive.

"That was the night I met your uncle. He was just coming off a double shift and his wife told him to stop at the convenience store on the way home so he could get some milk. I will forever be grateful that he did.

"He called for an ambulance and then stayed with me until they came. He even insisted that the EMTs let me ride in the ambulance with my father. They weren't happy about it, but they did," she recalled. "That's when your uncle Brian became my hero," she confessed.

"He stayed with me in the hospital waiting room while my father was in surgery. And when it was finally over and it looked as if my father was going to survive, instead of handing me over to a social worker—I had nobody else—" she explained ruefully. "Your uncle took me home with him," she recalled fondly. "His wife didn't look too happy to see me instead of the milk," she recalled. "That was his first wife," she added. "When she died, he married Lila," she explained. Given Brodie had said he was relatively new to the family, she'd thought he might need to have the dynamics reinforced.

Since they had reached the first floor and had gotten off the elevator, they began walking in the general direction of the room where the hospital surveillance cameras were kept.

"Wow," Brodie said to his new partner, impressed. "I'd say you definitely know a great deal more about my family than I do."

"Only certain members." She didn't want him giving undue credit where it didn't belong. "Your uncle Brian was my guardian angel. All I ever wanted to do was be like him and find a way to repay him for what he did for my father," she told him. "Trying to reunite missing people is my small way of paying a little back."

"If I know my uncle—any of my uncles—he would probably just say that he was only doing his job," Brodie told her. His mouth curved. "That's how they all think."

"Well, it might have just been his job, but it was my life," Kori stressed. She stopped walking because they had managed to reach the hospital's security office with its multiple bank of monitors. "Okay, let's hope that the hospital's surveillance cameras didn't suddenly all go down for some reason or wound up malfunctioning in the last few hours."

"Well, if you ask me, that would be one hell of a coincidence if it happened," Brodie told her.

Knocking on the closed door, he didn't wait for an invitation to come in. Instead, he opened the door and then held it for Kori so she could walk in first.

The lone security guard sitting there, watching the various monitors, looked surprised and was on his feet instantly.

"You can't be in here," he informed the duo indignantly.

"On the contrary," Kori said, holding up her badge and ID for the guard to see, "we can." Giving the man both their names and the police department they were with, she told the man exactly what they needed from him. "We would like copies of the surveillance tapes from this morning. Specifically the ones from the maternity floor and the ones monitoring all the hospital ground-floor exits from the last twelve hours."

The guard, a nondescript man in his fifties, didn't appear to be the type who enjoyed deviating from the norm. "You want copies of *all* of them?"

"Unless you want to give us the originals," Brodie specified.

The guard looked horrified by the suggestion. "Oh no, no I don't. The originals tapes have to stay here."

"Good policy," Brodie said cryptically. "But we need to review them and unless you want us sitting here, crowding you for however long it takes to look those videos over, you're going to have to make copies of them for us." Brodie's eyes met the guard's. "Do you have a problem with that?"

The man's eyes darted back and forth between the two detectives as he took in a deep breath. He seemed ready to protest the decision then, looking at Brodie, he seemed to think better of that.

"No, no I don't," he replied. "I don't have a problem at all. I just have to find where Herman kept the empty tapes."

"Herman?" Kori questioned. Was that the man's supervisor?

"Yeah, the security guard who usually runs this area. He called in sick today."

Brodie could feel his partner looking at him and he didn't have to guess what she was probably thinking. Was this Herman's absence merely a coincidence, or was it all just a well-orchestrated plan set in motion to facilitate the newborn's abduction?

Everything was suspect. He would have to work at finding a way to shed these suspicions once he walked out the door. But for now, he made a mental note to go to this Herman's house and talk to the man—on the outside chance that the guard had had something to do with the abduction.

As for shedding these suspicions, this wasn't like other jobs that could be left behind once he walked out the door. It remained on a person's mind, preying on it in order for him to be able to make something of all the puzzle pieces that he wound up picking up. He needed to try to make sense out of all of these pieces and form them into some sort of a coherent whole that would lead to an answer.

"You have this Herman's address and phone number?" Kori asked the security guard before Brodie could.

"Of course I have it. What kind of a security guard do you think I am?" the man asked her indignantly.

"A conscientious one," Kori answered without any hesitation.

The guard seemed to relax a little right in front of her eyes, placated by her response.

"Okay then," he said. "I'll go get what you asked for."

With that, the security guard went to fetch the information for them.

Chapter 6

Valri Cavanaugh belonged to the family members heretofore thought of as the lost branch and, once discovered, had transferred to Aurora. In short order, Fergus Cavanaugh's daughter had become an indispensable member of the computer lab that was a vital part of Crime Scene Investigations.

Brenda, Brian's daughter-in-law and head of that computer division, had been quick to see the young woman's potential and had taken Valri under her wing, where the latter had flourished.

These days, Valri was the one everyone approached when they needed something done "yesterday." Consequently, Valri could usually be found swamped beneath a pile of do-mine-first requests.

It had taken her time, but Valri had finally developed a tough skin and had learned to turn a deaf ear to all those needy pleas.

Or most of them.

Hence, when Kori finally came to the computer lab and approached the "wizard of the lab" with the stack of Aurora General surveillance tapes, Valri said, "I'm afraid you're going to have to wait your turn," as she gestured toward all the other requests currently covering her desk.

"Normally, I would," Kori told the attractive woman, adding, "Really. But this is an emergency."

"Honey," Valri replied wearily, "they're *all* emergencies." She didn't even bother looking up from the project she was immersed in to make her point.

Brodie knew exactly what button to press when it came to his cousin. "A baby was stolen out of her mother's room in the maternity ward at Aurora General Hospital sometime this morning."

Valri was somewhat partial to the Cavanaugh whose first name was the same as her husband's last name: Brody. But more than that, it was the nature of the crime that had snared her attention.

"Why didn't you say so in the first place?" she asked. Valri stopped what she was doing for now and, for the first time since they had entered, really looked at the two detectives standing beside her desk. "Okay, hand them over," she instructed as she put out her hand.

Brodie did as she asked, putting the stack on her desk. The number of different tapes was not lost on Valri but, in the long run, it wasn't anything she couldn't handle. "What is it that you're looking for?"

"Anything that looks suspicious to you." When Valri raised an eyebrow, Kori got a little more specific. "Someone making off with an infant and making their way out of the hospital rather than back to the mother's room. We had security give us copies of everything they had from the fifth floor as well as from all the ground-floor exits, but we haven't had a chance to review anything yet," she confessed.

Valri was quick to cut off what she suspected was going to be a rambling apology. That wasn't going to do anyone any good and would only eat away at the time.

"Leave that to me," she told Kori. She directed her question at both of them. "How long has the baby been missing?"

"Sometime between seven and ten this morning," Brodie answered. Ten was when they had been called in.

"That's rather a large window," Valri commented.

Kori agreed with her. "The mother fell asleep right after she ate breakfast. She had apparently been under a huge emotional strain."

Interest flashed in Valri's eyes. "What sort of a strain?" she asked as she made notes to herself.

Brodie recalled what the mother had tearfully told them in the hospital room. "Apparently, she had decided to give the baby up for adoption and then had second thoughts about it," he told his cousin. "Consequently, because she had wavered, she felt that the baby's abduction was all her fault."

Valri nodded. "It looks like someone decided to take that decision out of her hands."

"You have to admit that, from one angle, it does look that way," Kori agreed.

Valri frowned to herself as she wrote down more notes. "I guess keeping the baby in the mother's room doesn't completely eliminate the problem of hospital abductions," she said under her breath. Nodding, she looked at the stack of tapes she was going to have to review. "Okay, I'll let you know if I see anything 'suspicious,'" the computer expert promised them.

And then she offered Kori what she hoped passed as

an apologetic smile. "I didn't mean to snap at you like that when you came in. It's just if I didn't try to prioritize what's really important and what someone only *thinks* is important because they've been asked to look into it, I would never get out from behind this desk." She quietly laughed to herself, adding, "Not even for a bathroom break."

Kori could easily see that happening. How many times has she stayed at her desk, working into the wee hours of the night? There were even times when she all but slept in the squad room. She could fully sympathize with the other woman.

"Apology more than accepted." Kori flashed a smile at Brodie's cousin. "Thanks."

But the other woman shook her head. "Don't thank me yet," she told Kori. "Wait until after I've come up with something."

In the face of that, Kori amended her initial statement just slightly. "Thanks for trying."

But Valri barely seemed to hear her. The computer tech was back in work mode.

Brodie led the way out of the computer lab.

"Why don't we grab some lunch and then see if Herman Garcia is as sick as he claimed to be when he called in this morning," Brodie said as he made his way to the elevator.

Brodie's suggestion surprised her. Kori hadn't thought about food since they had caught this case. The very idea of the baby being stolen the way it had, under everyone's nose, had completely destroyed her appetite.

"You can eat?" she intoned as the elevator doors opened and they got on.

"I can always eat," Brodie told her, adding, "I work a lot better if my stomach isn't rumbling and distracting me.

"Besides," he pointed out, "you need fuel to work an investigation." He pressed the button for the first floor. "So, drive-thru or takeout?"

Kori had to think for a moment before answering his question. Her mind was definitely not focused on food. She made her decision based on expediency. "The drive-thru," she finally said. "That way you'll waste a minimum of time."

He wasn't sure how she meant that, but he sensed this wasn't the time to get into any sort of a debate not based on the case.

"Works for me," Brodie replied. Then he couldn't resist adding, "I chew fast."

That meant he'd wind up taking in a lot of air, she couldn't help thinking. "Isn't that bad for your rumbling stomach?"

Brodie smiled, amused. "Do you enjoy arguing?"

She had to pause and think for a moment to word her answer properly. "I enjoy solving crimes," Kori told him. "Anything that gets in the way of that is consequently a problem for me."

His grin grew wider. "So then that's a yes," he assumed.

Kori shot him a look, wondering if this was some sort of game for him. Was he trying to test her or just annoy her?

Maybe she'd been too hasty, thinking they'd work well together. There was still a lot about this overly good-looking man that she didn't know.

"We can skip the drive-thru, you know," she told Brodie. Since she was the one driving, that meant she could call the shots.

Brodie raised his hands innocently, surrendering. "I never said a word."

Since she viewed that as more or less of an apology on his part—he didn't press the matter or attempt to flex his muscles to put her in what he thought was her place—Kori felt she could afford to relent.

"I had a feeling that you'd see things my way," she said. "Okay, what's your preference?" she asked, referring to the drive-thru.

He really didn't care as long as he got to eat. His tastes had always been eclectic, which made him easy to satisfy. "You pick."

She wasn't about to make a selection. For one thing, she didn't know if one place was better than another because she didn't frequent any.

"I don't go to fast-food places," she informed him.

Her disclaimer surprised him. Because of the nature of the life cops led at times, he thought that all law enforcement agents frequented fast-food establishments to a lesser or greater degree.

"You're kidding," Brodie said, thinking she was pulling his leg for some reason.

"I kid on occasion, but never about food," Kori replied. She could see that her answer confused him. She was going to leave it that way, then decided to open up to him just a little. "I like to cook, not grab things on the run." He still looked as if he was having trouble processing that, so she added, "Cooking relaxes me."

When she slanted a glance in his direction, she saw that her new partner looked amused by her answer. "I'll keep that in mind," he told her. "But for now, I don't think we have the time for you to demonstrate your culinary abilities for me—although I'd like to revisit that offer later."

"What offer?" Kori asked, baffled. She hadn't made any sort of an offer, she thought. What was he talking about?

"Sampling your cooking," Brodie answered. "You've piqued my curiosity."

Kori shot him a look. Maybe she had really made a mistake. Maybe the man was an egotist after all. "And you've piqued mine," she replied. "Just when did you hear me make an offer to cook for you?"

"I thought it was implied," he told her.

"No," she replied definitively. "In your case, it wasn't implied, it was imagined."

His eyes smiled at her. "Po-tay-toe, po-tat-toe," he countered. "Let's hit the drive-thru and then get to Herman Garcia's apartment."

Kori sighed as she pressed her lips together. "Tell me, did you willingly transfer out of Homicide or did someone strongly suggest you make the change?" Right now she had the uneasy feeling that Brodie Cavanaugh was a problem waiting to explode. She could easily see a superior wanting this to be someone else's problem.

Brodie laughed. "As a matter of fact, they tried to talk me out of it."

"Out of making the transfer or out of remaining with the police department entirely?" she asked pointedly since his statement sounded so ambiguous.

"Since you seem to have your doubts about me, maybe you should investigate that matter for yourself," he suggested.

Cavanaugh was bluffing, she thought. She decided to call it. "Maybe I will," she replied, looking over briefly to see if Brodie's expression gave him away.

It didn't. The man probably made a hell of a poker player. Okay, Cavanaugh wanted to eat, she thought, so they were going to get that out of the way first.

"Any particular fast-food place you want to go to?" she asked.

"Whatever is closest. I'm easy," he replied, his eyes teasing her.

The hell he was, she thought. Cavanaugh was challenging her and that was far from easy in her book. "So you say."

"Are you saying I'm not?" he asked. There was no missing the amusement in his voice. He was enjoying this. Well, she was not about to encourage that.

"I don't know you well enough to say anything one way or another." Scanning the block as they drove by, she saw a sign proclaiming they were about to pass a taco place. She slowed her vehicle. "How's *Arriba* sound?" she asked him.

"Edible," he answered with a smile.

"Is that a yes?" she asked, wanting to be absolutely sure. She didn't want to go through the drive-thru only to have him change his mind at the last minute and say he wanted to go somewhere else.

"That's a yes," he answered, then added with a laugh, "If this was some other time, I'd be thought of as a cheap date."

Oh no, they weren't going to go that route, Kori thought. "Except that this isn't a date. However, what it does mean is that you have no taste buds," she informed him. "You know what you want?" she asked as they approached the order window.

He looked at her for what felt to Kori like a very long moment. "I do," he answered.

A wave of warmth shot through her. Something in Brodie's voice gave Kori the very distinct feeling that he wasn't referring to the menu. But if she said that, she knew he would make some sort of a crack that would totally get them off track, so she bit her tongue and refrained.

Brodie placed his order, telling the disembodied voice

coming from the sign that he wanted a quesadilla. And then he looked at her.

"Do you want anything?" he asked. "It's on me," he added.

She was tempted to say something about his being the last of the big spenders, but then thought better of it. That would have been mean-spirited. It also wasn't like her.

Maybe she *was* hungry, Kori considered. That sort of response was something a cranky, hungry person would have said, not her.

She really did need to get more sleep, she silently upbraided herself.

Kori looked at the sign and decided to go with the item pictured on it.

"Maybe I'll have a taco," she told Brodie.

"What kind?" he asked. When she didn't answer him, he tried to make the choice easier for her. "You want bean? Chicken? Beef? Or a combo that includes all three?"

"Chicken," she said, choosing the lightest thing she could that was on the menu.

Brodie nodded, adding the item to his tab. "And a chicken taco."

The sleepy voice told them to drive up to the next window to pay and collect the items.

When they reached the next window, their order was already there waiting for them. Brodie paid for it then collected the large paper sack with all the items stuffed inside.

Kori drove away from the last window. She had to admit, if just to herself, that the smell filling the air was really tempting.

"You want me to pull over somewhere?" she asked, nodding toward the parking lot located behind the fast-food restaurant.

Brodie read between the lines. "No need, I can eat while the car's in motion," he told her and then realized she might take that as a criticism. "But if you want to pull over somewhere—"

She shook her head, vetoing that idea. "I'll feel better once we get to question Garcia and find out if he's really sick or if this was somehow part of an elaborate plan to steal a baby."

"If Garcia is really sick, I doubt ten minutes is going to make any difference. If he isn't, then my guess is that he's not home anyway." But one look at his new partner's face told him which way he needed to go with this. "Why don't we find out if he is really sick and just didn't come in?"

Since he was being selfless, she could relent, Kori thought. "Aren't you afraid your quesadilla will get cold?"

"That's the good thing about fast food. It tastes the same whether it's cold or warm. Like I said," he repeated, smiling at her. "I'm easy."

This time, she offered no argument. Instead, she just nodded. "Right."

Parking in front of the Wakefield Arms, an apartment complex that had been one of the first built in Aurora, and while none of the apartment complexes in the city look old, it was apparent that the Wakefield Arms had seen better days.

Garcia's apartment was located on the second floor. Because someone was exiting the building at just the right moment, there was no need to ring a bell to enter.

Moving swiftly, Brodie slipped in and then held the door open for Kori.

Once inside the building, they went up to the second floor, taking the stairs.

Apartment 204 was to the right of the stairwell.

Kori pressed the doorbell. When there was no response, she tried again.

Still nothing.

Before she could try a third time, Brodie gently moved her out of the way and banged on the door. He announced their presence by declaring, "Aurora P.D., Mr. Garcia. We need to have a word with you!"

When there was no answer from inside, Kori realized that Brodie was going to break down the door. Putting her hand on what was a surprisingly rock-hard chest, she stopped him.

"Why don't we go get the manager and see if he or she can—?"

At that moment, the door to the apartment opened just a crack. They could see a watery set of eyes looking at them. A hoarse voice that sounded as if it had gotten that way thanks to a night of next-to-nonstop coughing asked, "Why is the police department looking to talk to me?"

The question was punctuated by several sneezes in a row.

Kori stumbled backward to get out of the range of the sneeze and wound up against Brodie's chest.

"Sorry," Brodie murmured only loud enough for her to hear.

Doing her best to ignore the almost rock-solid chest she'd backed up against, Kori directed her attention toward the man they had come to talk to.

"Mr. Garcia, you called in sick today…" Kori began.

The sick man looked surprised. "Boy," he cried, his voice totally nasal, "when they said that the hospital was going to be cracking down, I guess they really meant it."

The security guard punctuated his statement with another sneeze.

Chapter 7

Kori decided to tackle the situation head-on and not waste any time mincing words. "The hospital didn't send us, Mr. Garcia," she told the rather pale-looking, sweaty security guard.

She realized that the somewhat overweight man appeared to be holding on to his front door more for support than to keep them out. He was looking at them blankly, as if trying to unscramble the words they had just said.

"Then why are you here?" Garcia finally asked in a thick, nasal voice.

"Mind if we come in?" Kori asked him.

Garcia stared at the two detectives, apparently weighing whether or not he should invite them inside. And then, taking a labored breath, the man, swaddled in his bathrobe, stepped back. He cleared the threshold for the detectives, although, even now, he was still partially holding on to the door.

Kori came into the tiny apartment first, followed by Brodie.

"We're here because there was a baby stolen from Aurora General Hospital this morning," Kori told Garcia as she turned to face him again.

"Your absence from the surveillance camera monitoring room seemed to strike us as a rather a convenient coincidence," Brodie added. "We wanted to verify that you were really ill."

Watery dark eyes widened as the security guard stared at the two detectives standing in the small hallway in his apartment. He sneezed then, covering his mouth with a bunched-up handkerchief that had apparently seen much better times.

"A baby?" the man repeated, clearly horrified. Belatedly, his brain seemed to kick in as he blinked. "But you got it on the surveillance tapes, right?" he asked anxiously. "The baby-napping."

"The tapes are being reviewed right now," Brodie told the security guard, answering the man's question honestly. "But so far, we haven't come up with anything we're able to use."

Stunned, Garcia shook his head, as if to clear it. And then he sneezed again before he was able to say anything. When he did speak, what came out was a hoarse protest. "That's not possible," he cried.

"That's what we thought," Kori told the guard, watching his face. He sounded sincere enough, but she wasn't a hundred percent convinced. It could have just been an act.

"Unless there are some dead zones in the hospital," Brodie said, referring to areas that either had no cameras set up or where the cameras that were installed couldn't capture any actual images. "Are there any known dead zones on the maternity floor, Mr. Garcia?"

The man clutched his threadbare robe as he grimaced, attempting to think. Apparently, the effort hurt his head. Kori guessed that he might have been dealing with a killer migraine, but this matter superseded something as mundane as a headache. He sat down on his sofa.

"There are a couple on every floor but that's because the hospital doesn't have the most high-power cameras installed. There're plans to put them in, but…" His voice trailed off and then he sneezed again, his eyes watering before he was finally able to conclude, "Yeah, there are dead zones."

Brodie and Kori exchanged glances. "Looks like we're going to have to talk to everyone on those tapes to find out if they saw anything even remotely suspicious going on," Kori said.

"Or question them to find out if they *did* anything suspicious," Brodie deliberately added.

A loud sneeze prefaced the guard's declaration. "I'll go with you."

It was a halfhearted offer as Garcia pushed himself off the sofa and unsteadily back up to his feet.

At this point, Kori believed that the man was actually as sick as he seemed.

"That's okay, Mr. Garcia," Kori said. "The hospital doesn't need you risking getting all those mothers and babies sick. You just need to take care of yourself. We'll see ourselves out."

Garcia offered no argument. Brodie thought the man even looked relieved to an extent.

"I take it you believed him about being too sick to come in today?" Brodie asked her as soon as they closed the door behind them after leaving the second-floor apartment.

"Garcia looked downright miserable and his eyes were

genuinely red-rimmed. The man didn't strike me as being that good of an actor." Because she and Brodie had only been partners for a matter of a few hours and she didn't want him getting the impression that she was steamrolling him, Kori made a point of saying, "Unless I'm missing something here."

Brodie took her question for what it was: a gesture. But he did appreciate it. He'd encountered people, male and female, who came across as if they had chips on their shoulders, or thought of themselves as having the final word in everything. Kori didn't appear to have that problem.

"Not that I can see," he told her. "The guy looked pretty miserable to me. Not only that, but I got the impression he was really upset that this baby kidnapping took place in his hospital when he wasn't there to catch whoever did it in the act."

Well, at least they were in agreement on that, Kori thought.

Leaving the building, they proceeded to Kori's car. Kori's brain was whirling. "All right, next order of business," she told Brodie, "is to get someone from the hospital to identify all the hospital personnel who were captured on the surveillance tapes."

Brodie nodded, but he just wanted to make sure that his partner hadn't lost sight of one very salient point. "You realize that the baby is long gone by now," he told Kori.

"I know," she answered, "but if we can find out with who, we'll be halfway toward getting that baby back," she emphasized. She refused to entertain any other sort of outcome for this situation.

There was no arguing with that, Brodie thought, although, quite honestly, he didn't hold out all that much hope that they'd be able to locate just who had taken this baby—which meant that, in all likelihood, they weren't going to get her back, at least not any time soon.

Brodie roused. He couldn't allow himself to entertain negative thoughts.

"How can someone do that?" Brodie asked after maintaining several minutes of silence once they had gotten into the car and were traveling on the road again.

Lost in her own thoughts, Kori looked at Cavanaugh, startled. "Did you say something?"

Brodie rephrased his question. "How can someone just take a defenseless infant and make off with her like that?"

He had seen all sorts of bad behavior while on the job, but this sort of thing was beyond him.

Kori glanced in her partner's direction. "Oh, there are lots of reasons," she told him.

"Like what?" he asked.

Because he was probably dealing with this for the first time, she could see how this could be a gut-wrenching mystery to him. Sadly, she had more experience with this sort of thing. At this point, very little surprised her, but it could still sicken her.

"Maybe whoever took her wanted a baby of their own and, for one reason or another, they couldn't have one. Or maybe this person knew that Rose would give the baby up for adoption and they thought, 'Hey, no harm, no foul,' they'd just eliminate the middle man and find a couple who wanted this baby and were willing to pay any sum to have her.

"Or maybe," she said grimly, "whoever took the baby intended to sell it on the black market." She squared her shoulders as if that could somehow protect her from letting this thought eat into her soul. "It's barbaric, but you would be surprised how many babies are actually abducted and sold."

Brodie shook his head as he felt a cold chill work its way down his spine.

"It's an ugly, ugly business," he murmured more to himself than to her.

"That it is," she wholeheartedly agreed.

"How can you be part of it?" he asked, wondering how she could immerse herself in this sort of thing.

"I'm not 'part' of it," she informed him tersely. "What I am part of is reuniting the stolen babies and children with the people who love them and are totally out of their minds with frantic worry. Doing my job right is what makes everything else worthwhile."

Brodie nodded, taking her words in. "I guess I have to apologize."

Kori wasn't sure what Cavanaugh was telling her. "For what?"

"For underestimating you," Brodie said. "You've got a tougher skin than I gave you credit for."

Kori's laugh rang hollow. Then just before she pulled into the precinct, she told him, "I don't have tough skin, Cavanaugh. Under this exterior is just one big bowl of mush."

Brodie caught himself thinking that the woman sitting in the driver's seat had to be just about the most tempting-looking "bowl of mush" he had ever encountered—but he felt he couldn't say as much. That might get him into trouble at this point in their association.

And besides, they were working a case that was far more important than the way he felt himself reacting to this new person in his life.

They went back to see Valri.

They could tell the moment they entered the computer

lab that they wouldn't be hearing the news they were hoping for.

Valri raised her eyes. "Just how fast do you think I am?" she asked the duo. There was an edge to her voice, partially brought on by the fact that, so far, she hadn't succeeded in her efforts to locate whoever had made off with the baby and she was taking this abduction personally. "I mean I'm good, but you people are expecting superhuman good."

Kori felt bad about putting this sort of pressure on a woman who was already overworked. But before she could begin to make any apologies, Brodie rescued the moment.

"We were just looking to spare you the trouble of having to make a phone call, one way or another. We're all aware of the fact that time is of the essence in this case and we were hoping against hope that something would pop out at you from the surveillance tapes," he told his cousin. "Whatever tapes you've gone through, we're going to take those back to the hospital and see if someone there can give us the names of any of the hospital personnel who do appear on the tapes so we can question them.

"Maybe, between all that effort, we can find some information to help us find this baby," Brodie said.

Kori mentally applauded her new partner, impressed by his creativity.

Valri stopped and pulled three of the tapes over toward herself. Those were all she had managed to go through during the time that Kori and Brodie had been gone.

"Have at it," she said, gesturing to the tapes. "You think you can get someone to confess to taking the baby?" Valri asked her cousin skeptically.

"No, but we can question them regarding whatever they

might have seen. Sometimes people don't even know that they've seen what they've seen," he told the petite young woman sitting behind the computer.

Valri pressed her lips together, nodding. "I suppose that makes sense," she agreed. Having turned over the reviewed tapes, she sat back in her chair. "Now, if you don't mind, I've got a ton of work waiting for me. Some of it's not even yours."

Valri actually could get back to what she had been doing.

"Thanks for all your help," Kori told the other woman with sincerity, squeezing Valri's arm.

Valri merely murmured something unintelligible in response, then looked up for a moment to smile at them before retreating into her work.

Half a second later, Valri was totally lost in thought.

"You know, she seemed so preoccupied, I don't think she even heard me," Kori told Brodie, talking about his cousin as they made their way to the elevator.

"Oh, make no mistake about it, Valri heard," he assured his partner. "She's exceptionally good at multitasking."

However, Kori wasn't all that sure about what he had just said. She was fairly certain that in Valri's place, she wouldn't have that ability. She usually needed to focus on one thing at a time. "How do you know?"

Brodie laughed as the elevator doors opened and they both stepped in.

"Trust me, the woman has hearing like a bat," he told her. "I don't know how she does it, but somehow, my cousin manages to hear everything, even when there's noise that would normally interfere with her being able to hear clearly."

"'Hearing like a bat,'" Kori repeated. "Lovely description."

"Accurate description," Brodie countered. "And that's all that counts right now."

Armed with the copies of the surveillance video tapes, Brodie and Kori returned to the hospital. This time their destination was the personnel department. They went straight to the head of that department.

When Kori and Brodie walked into Wade Murray's office, the man looked as if he was getting ready to go home for the night.

He didn't seem pleased to see them. "I'm sorry but you're going to have to come back in the morning. I'm afraid that I'm on my way out for the day."

"And I'm afraid you're not," Brodie countered.

The head of personnel looked as if he might drop a few choice words on these strangers invading his office when Brodie took out his badge and ID. The man swallowed whatever words he was about to utter.

His sloping shoulders seemed to slope even more. "This is about the baby that was taken, isn't it?" Murray asked.

"Smart man." Kori flashed the man a humorless smile, showing the head of personnel her own identification and badge.

In response, Murray dropped into his chair like a man who suddenly was unable to stand under his own power. He sighed helplessly.

"I'm not sure what more I can tell you. The police were already here, and I gave them my statement." He gripped the armrests as he looked from one detective to the other. "I'm afraid I didn't see anything."

The regular department would have sent out officers to take down statements, Kori thought, but she and Brodie, as well as other members of their team, were more organized and focused when it came to abductions.

"This isn't about what you might have seen, it's about what someone else might have seen," Kori told the head of personnel.

Murray's eyebrows drew together in a deep frown. "I'm afraid I don't understand."

"We have copies of all the surveillance tapes that were taken of every conceivable hallway and escape route the kidnapper might have taken with the baby he or she abducted," Kori told the director. "As you can imagine, there are a lot of hospital personnel visible in these tapes. Unnamed people," she emphasized.

"That's as should be expected," Murray said, then added, "This is, after all, a working hospital. A very popular working hospital."

"Yes, Mr. Murray, we understand that," Brodie said. "We'd like to have all the people in these tapes identified. Or at least as many who work in the hospital as possible."

Murray nodded his head almost absently. "Of course," the man agreed as he began to push himself up from his chair.

Just as he reached his feet, Brodie delivered the knockout punch.

"Today," Kori's partner stressed.

Murray eyed him, as if he were having trouble processing what was being asked of him. His gaze moved from Kori's face to Brodie's.

"Today?" he repeated, surprised.

"Yes," Brodie confirmed. "This is time sensitive. So yes. Today."

A huge, heartfelt sigh escaped Murray's lips and his eyes stared in helpless resignation at the tapes that Kori was holding.

"Today," he murmured.

Chapter 8

As it turned out, most of the employees the personnel director saw and could actually identify on the various surveillance tapes had ended their shifts and gone home for the day.

Other than a couple of orderlies who had opted for overtime by taking on a second shift, the employees Murray had named were no longer on the premises.

Drained, Murray leaned back in his chair. He mopped his forehead with his handkerchief and rubbed his eyes. "I'm afraid that you're still going to have to wait until tomorrow to question these people. As a matter of fact, in a few cases, you're going to have to wait until the day after tomorrow," Murray said, correcting himself.

Kori didn't understand why the man was being so thick-headed. Didn't he understand what they were up against? "We don't have time to wait," she told the head of personnel.

"I understand your position. I really do," Murray told the two detectives. "But you have to understand mine. I can't release these people's home addresses without a court order. I'm sorry, but my hands are tied."

Brodie nodded, stepping forward. "I understand," he told Murray in a soft, quiet voice. Out of the corner of his eye, he could see the furious look entering his partner's vivid blue eyes, but he pretended not to notice. "Did I happen to mention that my sister is a journalist writing for the *Aurora Gazette*? As a personal favor to me, she's sitting on the story—for now—about the abduction. How fast do you think the story about the uncooperative head of hospital personnel obstructing our search for the kidnapper—or kidnappers—can circulate after it hits the paper as well as its online companion?" Brodie asked innocently as he pinned the man down with a sharp look.

Murray's shallow complexion turned almost a bright scarlet. "But I'm not being uncooperative," he protested. "I sat here, *after hours*, and looked over all the tapes you brought me. I'm not releasing the employees' addresses and phone numbers because I'm just obeying the law."

"I don't think people are going to see it that way when there's a baby's life involved. Can the hospital withstand that sort of bad publicity? Can you?" he pressed. "How long do you think people will continue bringing their children to this hospital?"

Murray raised his hands in blatant surrender, giving up. He'd half agreed with the detective all along. Now it was totally out of his hands if he didn't want this blowing up in his face.

"You've made your point."

Brodie didn't take the opportunity to gloat. It wasn't about that. He merely said, "I hope so." And then he got back to business. "We're going to need a printout of names, home addresses and phone numbers—ASAP," he informed the man.

Murray nodded, beginning to type again. "Way ahead of you." Kori stepped back, away from the director's desk and out of his earshot.

"I didn't know your sister worked for the *Aurora Gazette*," she whispered to Brodie in a barely audible voice. She had been under the impression that practically all of the Cavanaughs were involved in some form of law enforcement.

Watching Murray as he compiled the information he had requested, Brodie hardly spared her a look. He didn't want to distract the head of hospital employment from what he was doing.

"She doesn't." Brodie's voice was so low, it barely registered.

Kori stared at him. Turning her back to the intimidated head of personnel, she had to ask her partner, "You mean you lied?"

"Not exactly." When she looked at him for an explanation, he gave her the best one he could. "Skylar took a couple of journalism courses when she was in college. At the time, she was toying with the idea of becoming a journalist. That lasted for about six months before she torpedoed the idea."

"But you asked him how he'd feel about the *Aurora Gazette* running a story about him not being cooperative," she reminded Brodie. "You made that up?"

"A fair question," Brodie agreed. "I never said that Skylar could get the *Gazette* to run it."

He looked at her to see if she disapproved of his method or had something to say about his deception. Or worse, if Kori's sense of self-righteousness might egg her on to tell Murray the truth and consequently cause him to stop what he was doing right now.

But none of that happened. Instead, Kori appeared to be waiting for the man to finish printing the list of names and addresses he had come up with.

When the computer stopped printing, she took the list from Murray and quickly scanned it, doing a mental tally.

All in all, it looked like there were twenty-seven people they needed to talk to.

"Thank you, Mr. Murray. If we wind up finding Rose Williams's daughter, we'll make sure that you get the credit," Brodie said, taking the list from Kori, folding it and tucking it into his shirt pocket.

Murray shook his head. The bottom line was that he just wanted this to be behind him so that the hospital could move on.

"Just make sure you find her," the personnel director told them.

"We fully intend to, Mr. Murray," Kori replied, shaking the man's hand. "And thank you for all your help."

Murray merely nodded as they left his office. The man still looked very shaken.

As they left the building, Brodie focused on the list in his pocket. There were a lot of names on it. "We're going to have to get a task force together," he told Kori. "There are too many people on that list for the two of us to be able to talk to in any sort of a timely manner. Not if we want to do a thorough job. Any time we spend talking to one person is that much more time the actual kidnapper might utilize to escape with the baby."

Kori decided that there was no point in her taking offense, but this was *not* her first rodeo and he should have realized that. "I've already got people on standby," she told him.

Brodie nodded. "I kind of figured you would," he replied as they walked down the hospital's driveway.

"By the way, what you did back there with Murray…" she began.

Still not quite sure how to read this woman, Brodie braced himself for anything, including a possible lecture. "Well, you know, desperate times…" he said, allowing his voice to trail off.

She smiled at her partner. "I was going to say that I was pretty impressed by how quickly you picked up on being so innovative," she said, referring to his story about his sister.

Brodie slanted a look at her, feeling relieved. "So then you're not mad about my taking a liberty?"

"Why would I be?" she asked. The truth was that she'd been prepared to be a great deal more creative to get the director's cooperation. "There's a baby's life at stake here," she told him. "The only thing that would make me angry is if we were forced to drag our heels. And thanks to you and your 'sister the journalist'—" the corners of Kori's mouth curved in an amused smile "—we weren't."

Her smile widened as they reached her vehicle and got in. "You know, I really think that this partnership definitely has possibilities, Cavanaugh."

Brodie didn't say anything. He merely flashed a smile at her.

Maybe it was because she had had so little to eat today and was basically operating on fumes, but she could feel his smile burrow into her chest and then spread out warm fingers that seemed to touch every single part of her.

Damn, she was definitely tired, Kori thought.

Kori did her best to block out the effects that Brodie's

sizzling, sexy smile managed to generate, but it took concentrated effort on her part.

Walking into the squad room, before she contacted the people she used to make up a task force, Kori decided to take a little time out so that she could call her father. Given the nature of her job, she knew he worried.

Hell, she thought, the man would have worried if she worked in a library. The specter from the night so long ago hovered over both them, casting a dark shadow. She didn't want her father's imagination running away with him, especially since she normally had a habit of contacting him if she was planning on being late.

It took her five rings to get her father to answer the phone.

"Hi, Dad. Sorry I didn't check in with you earlier," Kori said. It wasn't until just now, when she heard her father's voice, that she remembered he had gone to see his doctor for a checkup. "So what did the doctor say? Is everything all right?" she asked him, mentally crossing her fingers. Since that night when she had almost lost him, she took nothing for granted.

"Yes," Bill's booming voice reassured her. "The doctor gave me a clean bill of health. According to him, I'm going to be around for a really long time." Deftly, her father changed the subject. "So, are you going to be late?" he asked. She was ordinarily home by now unless something was going on at the station.

"I'm afraid I am." She glanced toward the squad room doorway. One member of her team had walked in. "It looks like I might be pulling an all-nighter, Dad."

She and her father had always been on the same wavelength. Now was no different. "Is it bad?"

She wasn't about to insult her father's intelligence by attempting to pretend the situation was better than it was.

"I'm afraid it is, Dad," Kori confessed. "Someone kidnapped a baby girl from her mother's hospital room today."

"And no one saw anything?" her father questioned. His tone told her that he already knew the answer to that, but was hoping to be told differently.

"No one saw anything," Kori confirmed, frustrated.

Her father was quiet for a moment before he said in a confident voice, "You'll find her."

Kori sighed. "I wish I had as much faith in me as you do."

"That's okay, honey. I have enough faith in you for both of us," he assured her with a soft laugh. "After all, you're the reason I'm still alive," he added in all sincerity.

Kori smiled to herself as she turned away from the others to ensure her conversation remained private. "Dad, Brian Cavanaugh is the reason you're still alive," she tactfully reminded him.

"That's not how I remember it, honey. It wasn't Brian Cavanaugh's arms that were around me in those crucial moments, anchoring me to this life and refusing to let me die and slip away," her father said.

This was familiar territory and while Kori appreciated what her father was saying, right now, she didn't have time for it. The rest of her task force had just showed up. She didn't expect them to do much at this hour, but at least they could get started.

"Dad, I've got to go. I've got a task force to put together," she told him.

Kori heard him chuckle. "That's my little girl. You go do what you have to. I'll leave the porch light on for you."

"Oh good," she quipped. "I hate to come stumbling home in the dark."

She heard her father laugh again. "You know, honey, someday that smart mouth of yours is going to get you in a whole lot of trouble."

"It hasn't so far," she returned.

"It's just a matter of time," her father assured her. "Your luck can't last forever."

"Huh. Who says?" were Kori's parting words to her father. "I've really gotta go, Dad. I'll see you later." She terminated the call.

As she tucked away her cell phone, Kori turned around and saw that Brodie had been standing close enough to be able to listen to most of her end of the conversation without any trouble.

"You always eavesdrop?" she asked Brodie in surprise as she crossed the last few steps to him.

He wasn't about to deny that he had overheard. "In my defense, I wasn't intentionally eavesdropping."

Her eyes swept over him. "I don't see any handcuffs holding you in place."

"Not any real ones, anyway," he told her. When she lifted an eyebrow, he clarified. "After all, you said you were going to brief your task force, so I didn't want to go wandering off so that you wouldn't be able to find me when you got started."

She gave him a very cryptic look, not believing a word of his excuse. "How very thoughtful of you."

Brodie pretended to take her words at face value. "I always try to be," he answered. Then he asked her, "Everything okay?"

Rather than automatically say yes, Kori felt her back going up. "Why?"

Brodie shrugged. "It's your tone. You sounded worried

when you were talking to your father. I thought maybe something was wrong."

She felt her irritation growing, then managed to talk herself out of it. The man was a Cavanaugh. Cavanaughs took an interest in everything and everyone around them. He was just being nice, she silently insisted. He wasn't trying to be invasive, or nosy.

"Everything's fine," she told him. "Or it will be once we find this baby and hang whoever took her by their thumbs from the nearest yardarm."

Brodie looked at her, cocking his head. "The nearest what?"

"Yardarm," she repeated. Then, because Kori realized that Brodie probably hadn't read the same books as a child as she had, she elaborated on the term. "It's a mast on a ship."

He looked a little dubious. "Okay, I'll take your word for it."

"You didn't read much as a kid, did you?" Kori asked with a laugh.

"Obviously not the same books that you did," he replied.

"Actually, there wasn't much money when I was growing up. To entertain myself I would read everything I could get my hands on," she confessed.

The smile that curved his mouth was self-depreciating. "I spent most of my time playing video games," he replied.

"That must have made your father very proud," she quipped.

"I don't know about that," he told her. "But it did help build up my reflexes."

She nodded her head. "Which will come in handy if we ever have to battle it out with the undead."

As she said that, she eyed some of the officers in her

task force, They didn't look overly happy about having to be here at this hour.

The oldest member, as well as the shortest member of the team, Roy Valente, was immediately alert as he picked up on the last thing that was said.

"We're going to be up against the undead?" He looked both uneasy and intrigued. "Since when did the undead invade Aurora?" he asked, looking at Kori as if he were seriously asking the question.

"No forces of the undead," she said. "What we've got is a baby stolen from her mother's room in the hospital. If you ask me, that's definitely enough of a 'bad guy' in any book," Kori told the four other members of her task force, looking at Alex and Roy.

"You're right." Mark Baxter agreed with Kori. He looked at the other men gathered around Kori's desk. He zeroed in on Brodie. Raising a shaggy eyebrow, he asked, "And you are?"

Kori realized that she had definitely dropped the ball. She really was tired, she thought. "Everyone," she announced, "this is Brodie Cavanaugh, the newest member of our team. He'll be replacing Wills, who left us on Friday."

Fresh-faced and eternally eager, Richard Spenser was the first to extend his hand to Brodie. This was obviously Cavanaugh's first case with Missing Persons as well as his first day. "I guess you get to hit the ground running," Spenser speculated.

"Best way to learn," Brodie replied.

Spenser grinned at Kori, his recently straightened teeth spilling into a whiter-than-white smile.

"He's a Cavanaugh, all right," the detective declared, then grew serious as he asked the leader of their group, "So what are we doing here in the middle of the night?"

Mark Baxter, another member of the team, rolled his eyes. "This is *not* the middle of the night. You're more of an old man than I am," he pronounced. "This is what we normal people think of as the shank of the evening. But his question is valid…" Baxter continued, looking expectantly at Kori. "What *are* we doing here? I had to break a date with this gorgeous creature that took me *forever* to finally arrange."

"What we're doing here is that we have twenty-seven people to talk to about what they might have seen in the hospital," Kori told her task force. "They showed up on the surveillance tapes in the same time frame that the baby was taken. They were on the maternity floor at the time. We're hoping that at least *one* of them gives us some kind of a lead."

"We're talking to them at this hour?" Valente questioned.

"Yes," Kori answered. She wasn't happy about the hour either, but she had to work with what she had. "You have a problem with that?"

"Not me." Valente spread his hands. "I was just thinking how popular this is going to make us, knocking on doors at this hour," he pointed out.

"I don't care about being popular," she told her team. "All I care about is finding that baby as soon as possible," she told the others.

As she spoke, she divided the list of the twenty-seven people who had been on the maternity floor at the time of the abduction into three separate piles, then handed the pages out. "Spenser, you're with Baxter. Simon, you're with Valente. And Cavanaugh," she said, turning toward her new partner, "you're coming with me."

He bowed his head in compliance. "I hear and obey," Brodie said.

She shot him a look that had been known to melt lesser men, then just continued walking.

"This should be interesting," Baxter murmured, only saying what the other members of the task force were thinking.

Chapter 9

"Well, that was an immensely frustrating couple of hours that led nowhere," Kori said to her partner as they walked away from the last of their share of people to question.

In the interest of fairness, she had given each set of detectives nine hospital employees to interview. However, of the nine that they had drawn, only six were actually at home and none of those six had had anything productive to offer when they'd been questioned. Nobody had seen anything out of the ordinary.

"I sure hope that the others had better luck than we did," Brodie told her as they walked down the street to where Kori had parked her vehicle.

Kori frowned, frustrated. Things could have gone a lot better. She was beyond tired. "The only way they could have had worse luck would be if none of the people were at home," she said.

Brodie didn't quite see it that way. "Actually, not finding these people at home leaves the possibility open that when they *are* questioned, they might have something viable to offer by way of an observation." He glanced at Kori, who wasn't saying anything. "In other words, they might have actually seen something."

Kori sank back in the driver's seat. Her car key was in her hand but she hadn't put it into the ignition yet.

Brodie leaned forward, looking at her profile. "You know, I think I can actually *see* the wheels turning in your head," he told her. "What are you thinking?" In his opinion, Kori was being almost unnaturally quiet.

She shifted in her seat, then glanced at Brodie. He was right. Something *had* occurred to her. "That the people we did get to talk to, for one reason or another, might not have been all that forthcoming."

"Okay," Brodie said gamely. "So how do you propose we find out if they were or not?"

The fastest way she knew of was to look into bank statements. Most criminals weren't nearly as smart as they thought they were and were very prone to making amateur mistakes.

"The best way I know of is to take a look at their bank records or examining their lifestyles. If someone is suddenly spending money like water, there's usually a reason for that and it's not because a long-lost relative died and left them money," she told Brodie. Kori warmed to her subject. "Think about it. This might not be our kidnapper's first time stealing a baby. There might have been other infants taken from other local hospitals."

"Maybe," Brodie agreed thoughtfully. "Or maybe this is just a one-time deal and the kidnapper was prompted by something else—like they want to have a baby but can't—and then they saw Rose's infant daughter and decided to take their shot."

It sounded way too plausible. He could very well be right, she thought darkly.

She frowned at him. "Do you always rain on people's parades?" she asked.

"No," he answered. "I just wanted to point out what we're up against."

"Trust me, I am *very* aware of what we're up against," she returned. Stretching, she rotated her head. She ached in places she didn't know she even had. Kori sighed. "Lord, I feel like someone mopped the floor with my whole body," she complained.

He grinned at her. "Well, for a mop, you look really great."

Kori laughed. "If that's supposed to be a compliment, I think you need to work on it," she told him. Taking a deep breath, she finally put her key into the ignition and started up her car. "Okay, let's see if the others had a more productive evening than we did."

"I'm guessing that they didn't," Brodie said to Kori in a low voice as they walked into the squad room less than half an hour later.

He looked around the all-but-barren room. None of the four other task force members was giving off any sort of a breakthrough vibe and he was guessing they would be if they'd had any sort of success tonight.

The next moment he heard Kori making it certain. "Did anybody find out anything tonight after questioning their list of hospital employees?" she asked, looking from one task force member to another.

"Yeah," Valente said, speaking up. "That I can't pull

an all-nighter the way I used to." The recently divorced detective looked far from happy about the revelation.

"Well, I don't know about anyone else, but in our case, not everyone answered the door," Baxter told the others.

"Yeah, I don't know if they weren't home," Simon chimed in, "or if they just weren't willing to answer their doors at that hour."

"Well, either way, you're right. It's late," Kori said, clearly not happy about today's outcome. If it were up to her, she would go on knocking on doors and asking questions, but she knew she had to pull back. There had to be a happy balance between doing her job and pushing her people beyond endurance. "We're going to have to stop and get a fresh start questioning the hospital employees in the morning."

"Tomorrow," Baxter repeated as he scrubbed his hand over his face, then looked at his partner. "That's the day after today, right?"

Spenser didn't answer immediately. He had to stop to think for a moment before he could actually answer with any sort of conviction, "Yeah," he finally said, "last time I checked."

Simon stared at the detective and laughed. "Just how tired are you?" he asked.

"Apparently very," Spenser answered. He looked at Kori, not sure if she had actually said they were free to go home or if that had been wishful thinking on his part. "If it's okay with you, Kennedy, I'm going to call it a day and go home."

"You wait any longer, and it'll be tomorrow," Brodie quipped.

Because of the nature of the crime, she had been pushing them hard, Kori thought. Too hard. She wasn't asking anything of them that she hadn't asked of herself, but that wasn't really a good excuse. The others had lives to get back to. They weren't like her. This *was* her life.

So she nodded toward Brodie. "Yeah, what he said. Right now, looking at all your bright, shiny faces, I'd say that we're all too tired to be productive. Like I already said, we'll pick this up in the morning," Kori told the rest of the task force.

"You'll get no argument from me," Valente said as he gathered up his things.

He was immediately joined by three other, barely audible voices, all expressing their agreement.

The task force quickly filed out, leaving the squad room and heading for their separate vehicles in the precinct parking lot.

Because he was technically "the new guy," at least in this department, Brodie took his time getting ready to leave. He was well aware that it was never a good idea, as "the new guy," to gain a reputation of being the first one out the door.

About to leave, Brodie noticed that Kori was still at her desk. Taking a closer look, he saw that she was reviewing something as she made notations on her computer. He didn't have the impression that she was just finishing something up so she could leave as well.

He debated just walking away, then decided to say something to her. "You're not going home?" he questioned.

"I will," Kori answered absently. Her attention was on something that she was rereading and she really wasn't paying attention to what he was saying.

"But not now," Brodie surmised.

His voice finally penetrating, Kori raised her eyes to his. Was he actually pushing for her to go home? "I don't need a keeper, Cavanaugh," she told him.

He made up his mind and crossed back to her desk. "Oh. I don't know. Maybe you do."

Kori felt her temper flaring but managed to bank it. No, he couldn't have said what she thought he'd said. The man would have known better.

"Excuse me?" she challenged.

He shrugged, then told her simply why he had said what he had. "I've got a lot of people in my family who push themselves too hard and they don't even realize it."

Kori realized she was clenching her hands into fists and forced herself to relax—she was only marginally successful.

"I'm sure they all appreciate you taking an interest in their lives—" her eyes narrowed as she concluded more sharply "—but I don't need that."

He knew she expected him to back off—but in good conscience, he couldn't. "Oh. I don't know. I think everyone needs that once in a while," he said.

Maybe he didn't realize how dangerously close he was getting to having her explode, Kori thought.

"No offense, Cavanaugh, but I don't really care what you think." Her eyes pinned his. "Is that understood?"

She expected him to back off, but he didn't. Instead, Brodie told her, "I thought that was the whole reason I'm part of the team."

"Are you *trying* to get on my nerves?" Kori asked, doing her best to get back to the notes she was making to herself.

"Not particularly," Brodie answered with an innocent expression. "But then, Pinocchio didn't appreciate having Jiminy Cricket right away, either."

Okay, enough was enough. She was through trying to be nice about this. Kori stopped making notes and put down her pen. "If you were Jiminy Cricket, I could at least squash you like a bug," she informed him, hoping that would get her message across and get him to back off so she could finish what she was attempting to do.

But Brodie ignored what she was saying. Instead, he decided to level with her. "Look, I know the chief of D's is going to ask me how you're doing—I don't really need to tell you that he takes an interest in all his people and that you, because of the nature of the way your relationship began, have a special place in his heart. If I tell him that I stood by and watched you work yourself into a total frenzy, he's not going to be very happy with me—or you, for that matter. I don't want to have to give him a negative report—so help me out here," Brodie requested.

Was he actually missing the point? she wondered. "The negative report, Cavanaugh, is that we haven't gotten anywhere."

"And we're not going to," Brodie stressed, "if you wear yourself completely out. C'mon, Kennedy, do me a favor. Call it a day and go home. Even a superhero like you needs to sleep once in a while." He saw her open her mouth and put up his hand like a traffic cop in an effort to stop her. "Tell you what, since my car is still in the lot, let me drive you home. That way," he told her with emphasis, "neither one of us has to worry about you falling asleep at the wheel."

"I have *never* fallen asleep at the wheel," she informed him indignantly.

Brodie was unmoved. "Doesn't mean that this won't be the first time."

The laugh that escaped her lips was a very dry one. "You really like to argue, don't you?" she charged,

He didn't even try to deny her accusation. "I've got two sisters and a whole bunch of girl cousins. Kennedy, I was *born* arguing," he replied. "So you might as well just retreat," he told her. "Because you're not going to win this."

"You realize that I could just order you to go home," she said.

The look he gave her in response told Kori that she was free to try, but it might not quite go the way she anticipated that it would. "You could waste time like that, sure."

Leaning back in her chair, Kori stared at him, then she sighed and pushed herself away from her desk. "I'm too tired for this."

"Finally," he declared, taking that as a sign of victory. But he made no effort to leave the squad room until she gathered her things together and began to make her way out.

"You know, maybe I should have you meet my father," Kori said as she walked through the door that Brodie was holding open for her. This time, when she smiled, she wasn't forcing it. "I've got a feeling he'd really like you."

He took her assessment in stride. "Why shouldn't he?" Brodie asked. "I'm a really likable kind of guy."

Kori gave him a look as they went toward the elevator. "I'd say that is up for debate."

He was unfazed by her tone. "That's okay. We'll let your father cast the deciding vote."

Did he actually think she was about to bring him home to meet her father? That was not about to happen. She'd only said that in a moment of weakness.

Wow, she really *was* tired.

"In your dreams," she responded to his suggestion that her father cast the deciding vote.

Brodie glanced at her as Kori pressed for the elevator. He noted that her expression had turned rather sad. Something else was up, he thought. Something that didn't fit in with the banter.

"What's the matter?" he asked.

She shrugged, looking away. "I'm just thinking about how Rose must feel."

"Rose?" he questioned. For a moment, he didn't make the connection.

"Rose Williams," Kori elaborated. Then because there was no recognition in his eyes, she said, "The baby's mother."

For a moment, because of the bantering between them, the baby's mother's name had eluded him. But not anymore.

"Don't dwell on that," he told Kori. "Focus on how Rose is going to feel when we bring her little girl back to her."

He was taking things for granted. "*If* we bring her little girl back to her."

"We will," Brodie told her with unmistakable confidence.

"You can't know that," Kori insisted.

"The first step in making something happen is believing that it can—and will," he told her. "The next step is good police work. And your team," he reminded her, "is the best."

She frowned at him as she stepped into the elevator. The doors closed with a resounding whoosh.

"Don't patronize me."

"I'm not," he replied. "What I'm doing is just repeating what my uncle told me when he brought up my being your partner."

"Your uncle really said that my team is the best?" she questioned.

The corners of his mouth curved slightly as they got off the elevator. "He did."

Was he deliberately setting her up? she wondered. After all, she didn't really know this man yet, outside of the fact that he was a Cavanaugh.

"In those words?" she questioned uncertainly.

Brodie didn't hesitate for a second. "In those words."

Kori still wasn't a hundred percent sure if she believed him, but she made a decision. "I think I should quit while I'm ahead."

Brodie's smile began in his eyes and radiated outward. "Good idea. So…" he said as they went outside "…should I drive you home or should I just follow you?"

She didn't understand. "Why would you follow me home?" Kori asked. Was he talking about stalking her?

He looked at her as if the answer to that was self-evident. "To make sure you got there."

Okay, now he was really pushing it. "I don't need you watching over me, Cavanaugh."

"Probably not," he agreed, "but humor me. Just in case the chief of D's is going to ask me, I need to be able to honestly tell him that, one way or another, I saw you home."

"Cavanaugh." Kori's voice went up, a warning note practically vibrating within it. She was very close to telling him what he could do with his insulting effort to keep tabs on her.

But Brodie talked over her. "The chief of D's cares about you, Kennedy. The way he cares about all of us."

"All of us, huh? So does that mean he's going to ask me if *you* got home safely?" she challenged.

"Probably somewhere down the line," Brodie answered without so much as blinking an eye. "The sooner you stop fighting me on this, the sooner you can get home and go to bed." He saw suspicion flare in her eyes, so he felt obligated to add, "Alone," just in case she thought he meant something by that.

Kori lifted her chin defiantly. "There was never any question about that," she informed him icily.

Brodie smiled at her. *Really* smiled. Even though she

was exceedingly exhausted, she could still feel the effects of his smile as it seemed to burrow into her stomach, throwing it into complete chaos.

Brodie was right. She *was* too tired to work, at least productively, Kori told herself.

She needed a good night's sleep so that she wasn't subject to these sorts of thoughts tomorrow and could turn her attention to her work full-time.

"Okay, you can drive me home," she told him almost grudgingly as she got into his police-issued vehicle.

She struggled to keep her eyes open so that she could direct him to the small house she shared with her father. Damn, she was more tired than she had originally thought.

Brodie pulled up at her curb, then turned toward her. "Do you need me to walk you to your door?" he asked her gamely. "No charge," he added.

She didn't know if he was being serious, but she was taking no chances. "I think I can find my way home," Kori informed him.

Rather than make a comment one way or another, Brodie decided to tactfully retreat. He felt it was better that way for both of them.

"All right, Kennedy. I'll swing by in the morning to pick you up," he told her as she opened the door on her side to get out.

She looked at him blankly. "You don't have to do that."

"Yes, I do. Your car is still in the rear of the police station," he reminded her.

Kori rolled her eyes. She'd forgotten about that. "I guess I really am tired," she admitted.

He shrugged as if that were no big deal. "We all get that way sometimes," he told her. "Well, good night, Kennedy. I'll see you in the morning."

"Yes," she said with resignation, "I know." Kori mumbled something else in response as she let herself out and walked up her driveway.

She felt his eyes on her as she closed the door behind her. The man obviously took his promises seriously, she thought.

Chapter 10

Kori was halfway up the stairs, making her way to her bedroom, when she realized that her father was sitting in the living room, sound asleep on the recliner she had bought him for Father's Day several years ago.

Turning around on the stairs, she felt a pang of guilt.

It was obvious that her father had fallen asleep waiting for her to come home. Kori shook her head. He hadn't done that in years. But then, she thought as she made her way back downstairs, she was usually home at a decent hour. This was way beyond a decent hour.

Crossing over to the living room sofa, she picked up the blanket that had been thrown over the back of that piece of furniture for as long as she could remember. Bringing it with her, Kori very carefully covered her father with it. Lately, the nights had been unusually chilly, and she didn't want him getting cold.

"Oh, Dad," she whispered as she spread the blanket

over him, "you should know by now that I can take care of myself. You didn't have to wait up."

Finished, Kori pressed her lips together as she stepped back to make sure that she had covered all of him. For the umpteenth time, she thought how grateful she was that Brian Cavanaugh had been there that night to save her father—and, consequently, her. If he hadn't been there, there was no doubt in her mind that she would have missed all this.

Satisfied that she had done what she could, she moved away very quietly. Retracing her steps, she went to the stairs.

"You haven't found the baby yet, have you?"

Kori stiffened. Her father's sleepy voice, suddenly coming out of the blue like that, caught her off guard.

For a second, she thought she had imagined it. But one look at the man's face told her that she hadn't.

She might have known. He must have heard her come in no matter how quiet she tried to be. The man had hearing like a bat.

Turning on the stairs to face him, she confirmed his suspicions. "No, we didn't."

"You will, Kori," he told her with a certainty that sadly eluded her. "You will."

"Go to bed, Dad," she replied. She wasn't feeling very optimistic right now and she was much too tired to debate over whether or not she and her team would be successful in recovering the kidnapped infant.

Her father drew back the blanket she had thrown over him and left it on the side of the recliner. Holding on to the chair's arms, he pushed himself into a standing position and got up.

"I can now that I know you're back safe and sound," he told Kori as he made his way to his first-floor bedroom.

"Uh-huh. G'night, Dad," she said as she continued on her way up the stairs.

Exhausted though she was, it took Kori a while to unwind and finally fall asleep. Miscellaneous details of the case kept popping up in her head. Not only that but, in the middle of it all, she would suddenly and completely unexpectedly, experience this warming, all-encompassing feeling slipping throughout her entire body. The same one that she felt when she reacted to Brodie's smile.

She did what she could to block it.

Kori finally fell asleep, almost in self-defense.

In the morning, she felt as if she was fighting her way to the surface through an unusually thick serving of oatmeal. Struggling to open her eyes, she was about as rested as someone who had slept on a bed of hot, lumpy coals.

If anything, Kori felt more tired than when she had fallen asleep. She made her way into the kitchen from memory.

Hearing her coming in, Bill, busy preparing breakfast, turned around to greet her. The greeting died on his lips, unspoken as his eyes grew huge. "Wow, honey, maybe you shouldn't go in today," her father commented as his eyes slid over her. "You look as if you're coming down with something."

"I'm fine, Dad," she insisted, taking her usual seat. "Or at least I will be once I find the miserable lowlife who stole that defenseless baby girl and bring her back to her mother."

"Very noble plan," her father replied as he brought over the black coffee he'd just made and filled the empty cup he'd placed in front of Kori. "But right now, I'm thinking of my own little girl."

"Dad," Kori said patiently after she took a long sip of

the coffee and let it wind throughout her body, warming it and bringing it back online, "we've talked about this. I'm not a little girl anymore. I haven't been one in a very long time."

They had a difference of opinion on that score, Bill thought, saying, "You will *always* be my little girl. Case closed," with finality. "So, how's the new partner working out?" he asked as he buttered two slices of very lightly toasted white bread for her.

Kori shrugged. "Not great," she replied noncommittally.

"Why? What's wrong?" he asked. In his experience, the Cavanaughs were all good, decent people dedicated to their professions as well as their commitment to keep the citizens of Aurora safe.

She blew out an irritated breath. "Brodie Cavanaugh was the one who strong-armed me into calling it a night and coming home. I was all for staying at work, but he insisted I go home. He even drove me here so I wouldn't fall asleep behind the wheel." Kori frowned.

She didn't like being told what to do and her father knew it. Even if he didn't, the touch of disgust in her voice would have given it away.

Still, Bill couldn't help grinning. "I like him already." Just then there was a knock on their door. Her father looked at her. "Are you expecting someone?"

"Well, my guess is that it's either a very polite home invader, or my new partner." She scowled at her plate. Now she wasn't going to be able to finish her breakfast. She should have come down earlier, she thought. "Since he drove me home, he's here to pick me up so I can get to my vehicle. It's parked at the police station."

Bill went toward the front door to open it. "Well, at least you know it'll be safe there," he said. "Nobody's going to steal a vehicle from the police station." With that, he opened the door. "Hello," he said to the tall young man in his doorway. "I'm Bill Kennedy. You must be Korinna's new partner."

"I must be," Brodie agreed. "And you're her dad."

Bill nodded as he drew open the door further for Brodie. "Guilty as charged," he said with a smile.

"You know, I think we met once at one of Uncle Andrew's parties." Brodie walked into the house. "As I recall, you came alone," he told Kori's father, glancing in her direction.

Bill nodded. "I think you're right. C'mon into the kitchen," he urged his daughter's new partner as he closed the front door. And then, as they walked into the kitchen, Bill nodded at the stove. "Have you had breakfast yet, Brodie?"

"I grabbed some coffee on the way over here," Brodie admitted.

"That's not answering my question," Bill said and then rethought his statement. "Or maybe it does. Grab a seat." He gestured to one of the remaining empty chairs. "How does scrambled eggs sound to you?"

Brodie saw the plate of eggs her father pointed out. "Great, but I don't want to eat your breakfast."

Bill waved away the other man's protest. "Go ahead, eat. There's more where that came from," he assured Brodie.

"Dad," Kori pretended to complain, "if you feed him, we'll never be able to get rid of him."

Brodie smiled at Kori, as if this was the first time he'd noticed her sitting there. They both knew that wasn't the case. "Maybe if you feed me, you'll bring out my better qualities."

"That's assuming that you *have* better qualities to bring out," Kori countered.

Bill looked from his daughter to the detective who had already gone out of his way for Kori. The older man thought he detected things in her voice that he wasn't aware of ever hearing before.

Bill smiled to himself as he pushed his plate over in front of Brodie. "Anything else I can get you?" he asked.

"Oh no, this is more than enough," Brodie assured him with feeling. "Really. I just came to pick up your daughter." Belatedly, the young detective realized that he hadn't told her father his name. Half rising in his seat, Brodie extended his hand to Kori's father. "I'm Brodie Cavanaugh, sir."

"Cavanaugh," Bill repeated. "I take it that you're also related to Brian Cavanaugh."

It was a given that all the Cavanaughs were related to one another in some fashion, but since Kori rarely talked about her work other than in general terms, Bill was rather curious as to exactly how the man who had saved his life was related to this young man who had been partnered with his daughter.

"Dad, we have to get going," Kori told her father. She was already on her feet and taking her empty plate to the sink.

She wanted to stop her father from asking more questions. He meant well, but that didn't mean he wouldn't ask embarrassing questions.

Bill raised his hands, symbolically indicating that he was backing off.

"Sorry, despite attending some of your uncle's parties, I don't usually get a chance to meet any of the people that Kori works with. I just wanted to make sure that she had someone to have her back."

Heaven only knew what her father was going to ask Cavanaugh next, but she wasn't about to hang around to find out.

"Time to go," Kori announced loudly.

On his feet, Brodie picked up the remaining piece of toast, nodding toward it.

"Thanks for the breakfast, Mr. Kennedy. It was great," he said with genuine enthusiasm.

Her father was preparing a fresh serving for himself. "It was my pleasure, Brodie," Bill said.

"See you tonight, Dad," Kori declared. She paused to brush a quick kiss across his cheek. She was impatient to get going and was out the door in seconds.

Brodie was right behind her, the last piece of toast disappearing behind his lips.

"My car's parked at the curb," he told her.

"I see it," she told him, adding impatiently, "I've got eyes."

He pretended to glance at them. "Pretty ones, too," Brodie acknowledged, then, in case she had some choice words about the compliment he had just paid her, he added, "I like your dad," just as they reached his car.

She slanted a look at her partner. "He seems to like you, too."

Brodie caught the less than thrilled note in her voice. Rather than just ignore it, he asked, "Is that a problem?" When she didn't answer, he pushed it a little further. "Did I miss something here?"

She had the nagging suspicion that her father was attempting to play matchmaker.

Kori sighed, getting into Brodie's car. She was probably just being edgy, but once the thought had entered her head, she couldn't get rid of it. Now that she thought about it, lately her father had been talking about how maybe she should start thinking about starting her own family, and while that seemed like a good idea somewhere down the line, she really wasn't ready to entertain that thought now—or maybe not even for a long while.

"No," she denied. "That's not a problem."

Brodie laughed, shaking his head. "Wow, that wasn't convincing at all."

She was not about to justify herself to him. He might be a Cavanaugh, but as far as she was concerned, he was the "new guy."

"Can we get back on point, please?" she said, buckling up.

"Actually, if you want to know the truth," he told her, starting his vehicle. "I was trying to distract you."

"Distract me?" she echoed, her eyebrows drawing together as she stared at him, perplexed. Why?" she asked, confused. And then her expression transformed to one of concern. "Why?" she repeated. "Did anything happen with the case that you're not telling me? And why would you be the one who was notified anyway? I should be the one in charge of this investigation."

"No one is disputing that," he told her. "I just thought if you were able to be a little more clear-headed, it might be a lot easier for you to think and investigate this awful kidnapping."

"Clear-headed?" she questioned.

"Yes." Looking to his left, he pulled away from the curb and headed straight for the precinct. "From what everyone told me about you when I asked them, they all agreed that you have this laser-like focus. And if anything else got in your way, you could just eliminate it and zero in on what you felt were the important details of the case."

"You *asked* about me?"

He hit her with another lethal smile. "Hey, I'm a Cavanaugh. Cavanaughs like to know what they're getting into."

She didn't care for being dissected this way—or the way he had put it—but there was no sense in reading him the riot act. That wouldn't help any of them find the baby any faster—or get along any better. He was right about one thing, though. She needed to focus.

"Well, the first thing we're 'getting into' is getting the rest of the team together for a strategy session. We're going to rattle some cages until someone says something that we can use to find out just who took this baby and what happened to her. Babies do *not* just disappear into thin air."

"This one apparently did," Baxter muttered, frustrated when Kori said the same thing to the four other members of her task force in the conference room half an hour later.

"Well, I am not about to accept that," Kori informed Baxter passionately. She turned toward another member of the team. "Spenser, find out just how much this baby weighed when she was born and how many inches she measured."

"On it," Spenser replied. The detective started to leave the conference room to head for his own desk in the squad room.

"She was six pounds, two ounces and a total of nineteen inches long." Brodie spoke up before Spenser was able to leave and log onto his computer in order to get that information.

Pleased, as well as surprised, Kori nodded at Brodie. "Good work," she told her partner.

"How is knowing how much she weighed at birth supposed to help us?" Simon asked.

"Simple," Kori answered. "Since according to all the

surveillance tapes we reviewed, the baby didn't appear to be carried out in plain sight, I have to assume that she was smuggled out in something." She glanced around the room at the men working the case with her. "This gives us a starting point. We're going to go over all the tapes again—" her words were met with groans, but she continued talking "—to see if we can see something that the kidnapper might have used to smuggle the baby out of the hospital.

"For instance, a laundry hamper, or those food delivery wagons the orderlies use to bring trays to the patients. A drugged baby could just as easily be smuggled out in one of those."

"You want us to check the whole hospital?" Baxter asked.

"Only as a last resort," Kori answered. "For now we concentrate on just that morning and just on the maternity floor—as well as the exits during that time period." Getting warmed up, the volume of Kori's voice increased. "We'll be looking for large handbags, backpacks, or the aforementioned laundry hampers, wagons and anything that could have been used to transport an infant without arousing any suspicions."

"Valri already reviewed the tapes," Brodie reminded her.

Kori nodded. "Yes, but she was looking for someone who was transporting a baby outright, not attempting to smuggle her out inside something. C'mon people, we've got six sets of trained eyes," she said to her task force. "One of us should be able to see something that looks out of place."

"Don't forget you wanted us to look into bank records and credit card statements," Simon reminded her.

"I'll get the list of names and get started on that," Brodie volunteered, adding, "I know some people who can get us those records pretty quickly."

Ordinarily, she might have challenged him. But she wasn't about to ask questions, not when there was possibly a baby's life at stake.

"Then do it," she told him. "The clock's ticking, people, and we're running out of time."

The declaration was greeted by the sound of chair legs scraping along the floor as everyone went to do their part.

Chapter 11

Because she thought there was something they might have overlooked or missed when their second day of investigations turned up nothing useful, on the third day, Kori decided to try another approach. In order to implement it, she didn't go to her lieutenant. Instead, she went straight to the chief of detectives.

Ultimately, he was the one who would have to approve this anyway.

Since Detective Jennings, the woman in charge of the chief of D's schedule, wasn't at her desk, Kori knocked on Brian Cavanaugh's door. When she heard his resonant voice respond, "Yes?" she peered into his office.

"Got a minute, sir?" she asked him, remaining just outside his door.

Brian was just finishing a report he wanted to issue. Looking up, he nodded at Kori. She didn't usually take it upon herself to just pop up in his office this way. This had to be important.

"For you? Always. Come on in, take a seat," he invited, half rising in his chair. "So, what can I do for you?"

Although they shared a special relationship whose roots went all the way back to that night in front of the convenience store, Kori had never just presumed that she could barge in on the man at will. But this situation was different.

"Well, you know about that case we caught, the one involving the baby who just seemed to disappear from the hospital." Replaying what she had just said in her head, Kori laughed at herself. "Of course you know. You're the chief of D's, you know everything."

"Well, not everything," Brian replied. "But I am aware of most things," he allowed, then urged, "All right, go ahead."

"We keep coming up against dead ends," she told him, distressed at the way the investigation was going. "I think we need someone to go to the public and make an appeal. See if someone saw anything that we could use."

Kori was well aware of the downside of making such an appeal. "I know we'll wind up getting a lot of blind leads that go absolutely nowhere." She slid to the edge of her seat, enthusiasm getting the better of her. "But all we need is that one lead that turns out to be real—and it'll all be worth it."

She was all set to try to talk him into it, but it didn't turn out to be necessary.

"That's a good idea," Brian told her. "I'll have Jennings set it up. She'll let you know the specifics as soon as she has them."

To Kori that just represented an extra step that wasn't really necessary. "I don't need to be informed, sir," she told the chief. "I just wanted to get the situation going."

"Of course you need to be informed," Brian contradicted. "After all, you'll be the one who's going to be making the appeal to the public."

The chief's words caught her completely off guard. She replayed them in her head. It didn't help.

"Wait. What?" The import of what Brian was saying finally hit her. "Oh no, sir, I didn't mean to imply that I was the one who was going to make the appeal," she protested.

"Why not?" he asked, then challenged, "Who better than you? You're familiar with all the details of the case, which means that you can answer any questions the reporters might ask," Brian pointed out.

What he was proposing terrified her. "I don't do well in front of an audience outside my own task force. The public…" Her voice trailed off as she shook her head, negating the very thought of having to stand up behind a podium and brief the general public.

Brian didn't accept her excuse. "Don't sell yourself short, Kori. You care," he emphasized. "That's the important thing here. The public can sense that you're being genuine." His tone indicated that, as far as he was concerned, this was a done deal. "I'll tell Jennings to set it up."

Suddenly feeling desperate, Kori said, "Your nephew would be better."

Intrigued, Brian felt compelled to ask. "Why would you say that?"

She shrugged haplessly. "I get the impression that your nephew's used to getting people to listen to him. I guess what I'm trying to say it that he can charm people into seeing things his way."

"I see," Brian replied, rolling the situation over in his mind. "Here's a thought. Why don't you bring Brodie to the press conference for moral support?"

Kori looked at the man she would have willingly followed through the gates of hell if he had asked her to. She had a bad feeling about this. "I'm not going to get out of this, sir, am I?" she asked him.

Brian's smile unfurled very slowly, working its way up to his eyes. In that, she suddenly realized, the chief of detectives reminded her a great deal of his young nephew.

Kori sighed and nodded, resigned to what she was going to have to do, even though the idea really did unsettle her.

"All right, sir. Have Jennings call me when the news conference has been set up."

The chief beamed at her. "Atta girl," Brian readily pronounced.

There was no mistaking the pride in his voice. He had made no secret of the fact that he felt as if he had a personal stake in Kori and in everything that she did and accomplished.

Not leaving anything to chance, Brian was on his landline, calling Brodie the moment that Kori walked out of his office.

He told his nephew exactly what had gone down and what he needed from the younger man. "Your new partner doesn't like the spotlight. All things considered, she would prefer to avoid it."

Brodie tried to read between the lines. "So you want me to be the one to make the appeal to the public?"

"No," Brian said. "I think she needs to learn how to do that. This job requires a lot out of its people." And he envisioned a great future for this young woman he had taken under his wing. "I just want you to back her up, offer her moral support," Brian told his nephew. "I'm counting on her earnestness getting the public on board."

Brodie neither craved nor shunned the spotlight. It was

just another tool to be used if the occasion called for it. "You got it, Uncle Brian."

Brian had expected nothing less from him. "I knew I could count on you to help properly represent the department. Jennings is putting the press conference together right now. My guess is that it'll take place within the hour."

"Don't worry. I'll hold her hand," Brodie assured the chief. As a thought hit him, he suddenly added, "But only if she wants me to."

Brian laughed softly in approval. "Good man, Brodie," he told his nephew.

Kori was positive that the swarm of butterflies was going to overwhelm and get the better of her. Standing there, clutching the sides of the podium and staring into the cameras that were all pointed at her, recording every nuance, every word she was uttering, Kori thought her throat was going to close off, making her strangle on the words she was attempting to utter, all before a live audience.

Doing her best to pull herself together, she didn't even realize that Brodie had left her side as well as the podium. Belatedly, she saw that he had made his way down to the front row of newscasters, all of whom had gathered before her, ready to listen to whatever it was that she had to tell them before firing their questions at her.

Catching a glimpse of him now, Kori saw that Brodie had the most encouraging look on his face, aimed at her. It was as if he was mesmerized by every word she had to utter.

That was some bit of playacting on his part, she thought, considering that the man was already briefed on everything she had to tell this gathering of reporters and newscasters.

And then an incredible thing happened.

Kori found herself talking to only Brodie—just the way one of her teachers had once counseled her to do when she had to give a speech and it all but paralyzed her.

She didn't attempt to dissect it, she just went with it because, for whatever reason, delivering this briefing to Brodie seemed to help her not just manage to get through this ordeal, it also helped her get her message across to the reporters.

By the time Kori finished her briefing, she could feel her head spinning wildly. But at the same time she felt fairly certain that she had managed to drum up the necessary response from her audience to motivate them to get out there and search for some viable trace of this baby, who had somehow managed to disappear from her mother's room and vanish into thin air.

The inside of her mouth was as dry as a desert when she finished and turned away from the reporters. Only then did she blow out a shaky breath. Behind her, she heard the sound of people—reporters—gathering up their things and moving away. She surmised that they were preparing to carry the message she had imparted to them and take it to their various audiences.

The first person at her side was Brodie.

"How did I do?" Kori heard herself asking her partner. The next moment she was bracing herself for an answer she felt would most likely be critical.

"You were every bit as good as the chief of D's thought you'd be," Brodie told her. "Now let's get back to the precinct because the second this hits the airwaves we're going to be inundated with calls." As soon as he said that, another thought hit him. "We're going to need more people manning the phones."

Coming out of a self-imposed trance, Kori nodded as his words penetrated. While giving her briefing to the cameras, she hadn't been able to think past the moment. But now that this uncomfortable ordeal was behind her, her mind began whirling a mile a minute.

The very next moment she was striding toward her car, barely aware that she was leaving Brodie behind her until he called out to her.

"Hey, slow down, Speedy," he cautioned. "Unless, of course, you're planning on running all the way back to the station."

There was an unbelievable amount of energy surging through her veins. So much so that the idea of getting back to the police precinct on foot actually had some merit—for a moment.

"All right—for your sake, I'll slow down," Kori told him.

An amused expression playing on his face, Brodie told her, "I appreciate that, Kennedy."

Many hours later, Kori felt as if, any minute, her head was going to just come right off.

It seemed as if she, Brodie and the rest of her six-person task force, not to mention the score of people commandeered to answer the phones, had been at this forever.

And not really having that much to show for it, she thought ruefully.

Leaning back, she ran her hand across her throbbing forehead, acutely aware of the pounding headache that had moved in and taken up residency there.

In a daze, it took her a moment to realize that someone was saying something to her.

Hanging up, Simon looked around the room. "You know how people are always saying that all babies look alike?" he asked wearily, aiming his question at no one in particular.

"Yeah, people who have never had a child of their own say that," Valente responded. "As the father of two, I can definitely tell you that all babies do *not* look alike," he said. "Even when they're tiny little people, there's a personality there. Ask my wife," he added, picking up a receiver as yet another call had been put through.

Simon refused to surrender the point he had just made. "Well, I've just taken at least ten phone calls from ten different people who all swear they've seen our missing baby being taken from the premises by one person or another. What do you want to bet they didn't see anything?"

It was tempting to believe that, but that wasn't why they were here. "We can't assume that until we've sent someone to check out these different so-called sightings," Brodie told the man sitting to his left. And then, realizing he might have treaded on Kori's toes, he glanced in her direction. "I'm sorry. Did you want to say that to Simon?"

She didn't know if he was being serious or sarcastic, but because he had been there for her earlier at the press conference, silently supporting her, she decided to take his statement in a positive light.

"No, I think you took care of that nicely," she told him. And then she turned to look around at the rest of her team. "Cavanaugh is right," she told them. "We're going to need to check out every so-called sighting just in case it turns out to be the one we're looking for."

"All right," Valente said with a resigned sigh. "Who's going to go?"

There was only one fair way to do this. "We'll take

turns," Kori answered, then scanned the room. "Is that okay with everybody?"

Baxter was the first one to answer her. "Sure."

Valente nodded. "Yeah. Because of you, I get to skip a PTA meeting my wife was dragging me to."

Simon gave Kori a three-finger salute. "You got it, boss."

"I'm not your boss," Kori insisted. "All I am is the temporary leader."

Spenser merely laughed under his breath and said, "Yeah, right."

"Admit it, Kennedy," Brodie said, joining Kori as they left the room to check out a possible lead ten minutes later.

"Admit what?" she asked. She was relieved to take a break from the phones as she led the way to the elevator.

"That you like being the leader, temporary or not," he clarified.

"And if I do?" she challenged, pushing the down button a little too hard.

"That makes you human," he told her with an enigmatic smile.

"I am human," she readily admitted. "No arguing with that."

His eyes were warm as he looked at her. "Good to know."

The call they were responding to had come from a Cyndy Kellerman who had said she had been in the vicinity of the Aurora hospital approximately at the time of the abduction. Working, she couldn't come to them, so they came to her.

Cyndy worked in a fast-food restaurant that prided itself on the number of different kinds of tacos offered on its menu.

"You hungry?" Brodie asked his partner.

Agitated, she wasn't even mildly tempted. "I'll eat later," she told him.

They walked into the small sitting area, which appeared as if it could seat about twelve. At the present time, there were only three people in the restaurant, all seated at different tables.

Brodie led the way to the counter, but he let Kori do the talking.

Showing the tall, gangly teenager behind the counter her identification, Kori asked him, "Is there a Cyndy Kellerman here?"

The teenager looked at the badge in front of him as if he were examining it for authenticity, and then raised his eyes to the woman's face.

"Did she do something bad?" he asked, his voice cracking. Kori decided the teen had to be a late bloomer.

Brodie had a feeling he was shooting the teen down when he said, "No, we just need to talk to her."

"You got one of those, too?" he asked, nodding at the identification Kori was just putting away.

"Yes, I do," Brodie answered, although he didn't bother taking it out. "Now, is she here?"

The teen nodded. "But she's taking a break, man."

Of course she was, Kori thought. "And where does she go when she's taking her break?" Kori asked.

The teen nodded in the general direction of the front door. "Outside."

Kori felt her patience ebbing away. "*Where* outside?" she asked, allowing the edge back into her voice. It had been another exceptionally long day and she was coming dangerously close to the end of her patience for today.

Nervous now, the teenager pointed to the back of the lot behind the building. "She likes to smoke. The boss wants her as far away from here as possible. I guess he hopes the walk back will be enough to get the smoke off her clothes. It's not," he confided, lowering his voice. "I can still smell it on her when she comes back."

"Sounds positively delightful," Kori murmured under her breath as she made her way out the door to talk to the young woman.

Kori and Brodie quickly scanned the area.

Cyndy wasn't hard to spot. The woman, who looked as if she was out of place working at the fast-food restaurant, was standing at the extreme left of the building, an absent expression on her face as she stared off into space.

"Lord, I sure hope she's sharper than she looks," Kori murmured.

"My guess is that she'd have to be," Brodie responded. "But don't judge a book by its cover. She might surprise us."

Kori laughed as she held up her crossed fingers in the air. "Well, here's hoping that you're right about that."

Chapter 12

Brodie and Kori had their wallets open to display their IDs and badges as they approached the woman they assumed had called the precinct, saying she was certain she had spotted the baby that had been talked about on the news.

"Cyndy Kellerman?" Brodie asked as he and Kori crossed to where the young woman was standing, smoking her cigarette. She stared sleepily at the approaching duo.

"Who's asking?" Cyndy asked.

"I'm Detective Cavanaugh and this is Detective Kennedy," Brodie said, indicating his identification and then Kori's.

The woman looked at them blankly, as if unable to fathom why the two detectives were there.

"You called the station, saying that you were certain you had seen the baby everyone was looking for on the day she was abducted," Kori prodded.

The light seemed to dawn on the young server's face. And then her eyes shifted from one detective's face to the other's.

"I did," the server told them defensively. She raised her chin.

"Tell us exactly what you saw," Kori urged, doing her best not to sound as impatient as she felt.

"To the best of your recollection," Brodie added. He deliberately ignored the look that Kori shot him.

"I saw this old lady with this baby in her arms, on the side of Aurora General." She looked from Kori to Brodie then appeared to consciously decide to give the details to Brodie. "She was in a hurry," Cyndy added. "The old lady, not the baby."

"How big was the baby you saw?" Brodie asked. Anything larger than a newborn meant she hadn't actually seen the baby in question.

Cyndy paused to think, then told him, "Not big. Like the one they keep showing on the news bulletins that they keep broadcasting." She became defensive again. "I wouldn't have wasted my time calling in to you guys if what I saw was a big baby."

"Okay, fair enough," Brodie said when he saw that Kori was about to say something he thought might wind up being off-putting. "Can you describe the woman who was holding this infant?"

"I said she was an old lady," Cyndy insisted and then emphasized the key word again. "*Old.*"

"How old?" Kori asked.

"Well, she was older than you," the server said flippantly. Then looking at Kori more closely, Cyndy added, "Yeah, I guess a lot older."

"Nice to know there are people older than me," Kori

murmured under her breath as she turned away from Cyndy.

But Brodie heard her and he struggled to mask his amusement.

"Can you give us an estimate? How old do you think this woman was?" he asked Cyndy. "Was she forty? Fifty? Sixty?" Each time he gave her a number, he looked at their potential eyewitness's face to see if he had guessed a number that came close enough.

But there was nothing to indicate that there had been a breakthrough.

The girl shrugged. "Look, I don't know," Cyndy stressed. "She was just old. Like grandmother old," she told Brodie.

That wasn't good enough in Kori's book. "All right, let's try this," she proposed. "What was this old woman wearing?"

"I dunno. Frumpy stuff," Cyndy said.

"Like a nurse's uniform?" Kori asked.

There was no recognition on the server's face. "I don't know. Maybe. I wasn't looking at her clothes. All I know is I wouldn't have been caught dead in those shoes she was wearing."

"Her shoes," Brodie repeated. He doubted this would lead them anywhere, but maybe it was better than nothing. At least it was worth a shot. "What kind of shoes was she wearing?"

"They were all crepey, rubbery-soled." The fast-food server shivered as she described the shoes. "I'd say they were probably good for a burglar. Nobody could hear you coming if you wore those," Cyndy surmised. There was a bit of vague admiration in her voice.

"Which way was she going?" Kori asked.

The server looked annoyed that the female detective

kept breaking into her conversation with the tall, good-looking detective.

"Away from the hospital…" she said, her voice trailing off. "Or maybe she was going to it. Anyway, she was in a big hurry. At least for an old lady."

This wasn't getting them anywhere, Kori thought. From the looks of it, this Cyndy person was just trying to flirt with Cavanaugh. It was time to wrap things up.

"Well, thank you very much," she said with finality. "If you think of anything else—" Kori took her business card out of her pocket and presented it to the girl "—give me a call."

Cyndy glanced down at the card in Kori's hand but made no effort to take it. "Can I give him a call instead?" she asked, nodding toward Brodie, a wide, inviting smile on her face.

"Sure," Brodie told her, taking out his card and giving it to the girl. "Whatever makes you more comfortable."

A very interested light came into the fast-food server's pale brown eyes. "You know, I wasn't looking to get comfortable."

At this point, Kori decided that maybe she needed to come to her partner's rescue before Cyndy made an even more aggressive move on Brodie. Hooking her arm through his, she pretended to draw him over toward their vehicle. "Well, we've got other leads to follow."

"Oh wait!" the server called just before they were able to get away. "There's one more thing."

Kori sighed and turned around. Doing her best to look patient, she asked, "Yes?"

"I found this on the ground. The old lady might have dropped it in her hurry to get away from there," the server said, holding up something she had dug out of her pocket.

"But I'm not sure. It might have already been there when she went by."

"This" turned out to be an ankle bracelet, the kind that hospitals put on infants to start buzzing if they were being taken out of the hospital illegally.

Kori stared at her. "Why didn't you go to the police with this?"

"I didn't think it was anything important. I just picked it up off the ground and I forgot about it, I guess," the girl said with a shrug. "Like I said, it might have already been there before she went by."

"We're going to hang on to this," Brodie told her.

The young woman shrugged. "Sure. Whatever."

That was one clueless young woman, Kori thought. She waited until they were out of hearing range before she cryptically said to Brodie, "Maybe she needs a date for the prom."

Brodie laughed at her assessment, relieved to leave the young server behind. "Not my type," he told Kori as they got into the car.

"So, out of curiosity, what is your type?" she asked Brodie, buckling up.

He spared her a look before answering. "Older and wiser," he said significantly.

Kori started up the car, barely aware of doing it. She looked down at the ankle device one last time. "Speaking of wiser, this definitely belonged to our missing infant. At least we now know that whoever stole that baby had to work at the hospital." As she talked, Kori worked the situation out to her satisfaction. "How else would they know how to remove that ankle device?"

"Good point," Brodie said.

She barely heard him. "We need to re-canvass the maternity floor, see if we missed something else."

"We didn't miss that ankle device. That girl just happened to find it," he pointed out. He brought up another point. "There are five more names left to question on our part of this list." Taking out a folded paper from his pocket, he held it up. "That means there are five more potential witnesses."

"Five more people who *thought* they saw something," she said, pulling away from the taco restaurant.

"All it takes is one person," Brodie reminded her. "One potential witness felt they'd seen something and took it upon themselves to call in. You need to hold on to that," he told her.

He was right. She needed to hold on to that, to the fact that if everyone on the team kept at this long enough, they *would* find that one lead that would bring them to the right conclusion.

She nodded. "You're right," she told him. "Let's get going."

Out of the corner of her eye, she caught the look he sent her as she stepped on the gas. The smile caused every single nerve ending in her body to suddenly stand up and salute. It took her more than a second to focus on the road.

"My thoughts exactly," he told her.

None of the so-called witnesses panned out, although Kori was fairly certain that the people who had taken the trouble to come forward actually did believe they *had* seen something, be it the kidnapper or some sort of plan going down to either smuggle or steal the baby from of the hospital.

Then she thought of Cyndy Kellerman. Without realizing it, the young woman had provided them with their only single clue, such as it was.

Maybe they would get luckier, she thought, attempting

to remain optimistic. Even so, a sigh managed to escape her. "I really hope we're not just spinning our wheels," she lamented as they drove back to the precinct.

"Those wheels just need to make contact once and we'll have our answers," Brodie told her.

"When you graduated the academy, did someone give you a box of quaint sayings you could just whip out and use to spread joy around?" she asked, her voice growing sharp. "Or do these 'uplifting' words just naturally roll off your tongue?"

Rather than get annoyed, Brodie just grinned at her again. "I guess these things just come to me because there is no box full of sayings for me to reach into," he told her.

"Too bad," she quipped, turning down the street toward the back of the police station. "If there was, I would have requisitioned it so that we'd have something to burn for the next bonfire."

"Okay," he said gamely, "now I have a question for you."

She supposed that she had this coming to her, whatever it was. She needed so stop saying what popped into her mind. "All right. Ask."

"Your mood," he said, watching her expression for any telltale signs of her next eruption. "It does get better, right?"

Yup, she thought. She'd had that coming. But she stopped short of an apology. This was her. If he didn't like it, then Cavanaugh could request another department transfer.

"When there's something there to improve it," she answered.

His eyes met hers—and then he nodded. "I'll hold you to that."

Hold you.

For a moment, completely out of the blue, the image of Brodie holding her just flashed through her mind, wrapping her with an all-encompassing warmth she couldn't immediately shake off.

And then, just as quickly, it was gone.

How the hell could she be thinking of something like that at a time like this? Kori silently upbraided herself. They had a kidnapped infant to find. She had absolutely no business letting her mind go elsewhere.

"Hey, where are you?"

Brodie's voice broke into her thoughts, pulling her out of her mental reverie and back into the front seat of her vehicle.

Blinking, she spared a glance at him. "What?"

"That expression on your face...you weren't here," he told her. "But you were definitely thinking of something. What was it?"

Floored and at a loss for an answer, she grabbed the first thing that occurred to her.

"Dinner," Kori answered. "I was thinking about dinner," she said, recalling one of the things he had said that first day. She built on that. "And how I haven't had it. Or lunch. I guess not eating is finally catching up to me."

"I knew it would," he told her. "Why don't I take you to get something to eat after we sign out at the precinct?"

"That wasn't a hint," she told him almost indignantly.

"No," he replied mildly, "that was a suggestion on my part. You've got to eat. I've got to eat. So why don't we just do it together?" Brodie could see that his partner was about to turn him down. He cut her off before she could. "Partners do grab something to eat together—and they even talk while they're doing it. It's called getting to know each other." He looked at her, his mouth curving in amusement. "Unless you're afraid to spend time with me."

Her eyebrows drew together. Was he that full of himself? He was handsome, but not *that* handsome. "That's ridiculous. Of course I'm not afraid."

"Great. Because I know this really great place where we can grab a meal and talk for as long as you'd like."

As long as *she'd* like? He was lobbing the ball into *her* court? Just what did he think he was doing? She'd set him straight. "So it's a dine-and-dash place."

Brodie just shrugged. "It's anything you want it to be."

"I'm not sure I follow you," Kori said, her voice getting an edge to it again.

As if to tease her, Brodie went literally with the words and not the gist behind them. "Why, Kennedy, you're not a follower. You're a leader. We both know that."

"Right now, I'm just a tired detective. I just want to pick up the next list of people to interview so I can be ready to go tomorrow—and call it a night," she concluded.

When they got back to the conference area that had been set aside in the squad room, Kori found that the list of possible witnesses had shrunk—by a great deal.

"Where are all the other names?" she asked Baxter, holding up the short sheet of names that was left.

Baxter nodded at Brodie. "Why don't you ask him," he suggested.

"Cavanaugh?" Kori questioned incredulously. "He was going around in circles, same as I was. Why would I ask him?"

"Because the chief of D's—otherwise known as Cavanaugh's uncle—thought we could use some more people to conduct those interviews. Enough detectives were requisitioned for us to do the work properly," he told Kori.

There was only one thing she wanted to know. "Have we made any progress?"

"Well, we've had a few more leads," Simon told her,

"but it's going to be a while before we know if any of those leads pan out."

"So no," Kori concluded from what the other detective said.

"For now," Valente allowed, catching the tail end of the conversation. "But that doesn't mean that one of these leads won't be able to finally bring us to the actual kidnapper."

"You know, there's even talk that this might be the beginning of a new baby abduction ring forming," Spenser told her. Joining the group, he seemed even more exhausted than she felt.

Tired as she was, Kori exchanged looks with Brodie. They had the same thought and both shook their heads.

"I don't know," Kori replied. "I don't really think so. It just doesn't feel like that's the case here. Think about it," she said to the men in the room who comprised her initial task force and were now preparing to leave. "Unless this baby was the first, why haven't we heard about any other recent abductions taking place?"

Spenser shrugged. "Because maybe this baby *is* the first."

"You know that old saying?" Brodie said to the others.

It was Kori who sighed. "Another old saying, Cavanaugh? Okay, what sage piece of advice are you imparting this time?"

"When you hear hoofbeats, think horses not zebras," Brodie said with a straight face.

Simon looked at his partner and shrugged in confusion, then asked, "And that means?"

Brodie explained patiently. "That maybe this is just a single abduction. Maybe whoever made off with the baby just wanted *that* baby, or *a* baby. They didn't want to begin their own nursery." He didn't wait for anyone to agree with him—or argue, either. Instead, he went another route. "Anyway, I think we're all pretty much too wiped out to hash this out now. Let's all just go and get something to eat, then go home and get a good night's sleep. We'll take another look at this in the morning when we can think more clearly."

Baxter glanced at Kori. It was clear that he agreed, but wanted to see if she was on board. "That okay with you, Kori?"

"Right now, that's just great with me," she said without a trace of sarcasm. "But then, I'm so tired that I'd probably agree to anything—within reason," she specified when she saw the light entering Brodie's eyes.

Brodie grinned broadly at her. "Define *reason*."

"Off the top of my head, I'd say anything that doesn't cross your mind," she answered.

"Well, that's fair—I think," Simon pronounced.

"Nobody asked you," Brodie pointed out.

"Also true," Simon said, inclining his head. "Well, I'm going home. Good night, cellmates. See you in the morning," Simon told no one in particular as he walked out.

Chapter 13

Leaving the building, Kori paused on the top step before descending the rest of the stairs and out into the parking lot.

Brodie looked at her. "Something wrong?"

"You know, about going together to grab some dinner…" she began, searching for a way to word what was probably going to come off as a rejection in his eyes. "I think I'll take a rain check."

"Oh?"

Kori continued walking to where her vehicle was parked. "Yes. I'm just way too tired to chew," she told her partner. "Besides, if I know my father, he probably has something warming on the stove for me. No sense in letting that go to waste—again."

"You know," Brodie told her, "I'm getting the impression that you don't want to be seen out in public with me."

She couldn't read his expression. She didn't think that

he looked annoyed, but his comment made her wonder if maybe he felt insulted. She couldn't really tell.

"What are you talking about? I've been seen out in public with you everywhere for the last few days," she pointed out. "Every time we leave the precinct, we've practically been joined at the hip."

"Work doesn't count," Brodie answered. When he saw her begin to protest, he added, "It's not voluntary."

"I beg to differ," she told him. "If you recall, I split the task force into three groups. I could have picked anyone else, but I told you that you were with me." The moment the words were out, she realized she'd set herself up.

Amusement curved Brodie's mouth. A mouth she noticed seemed to be getting progressively more sensuous. "Why did you do that?"

"Because I needed my head examined," she answered tersely, then sighed. "And because you're my partner." She closed her eyes for a moment, regretting this path she'd just taken. But now that she had, she might as well get the rest of this out. "And as far as partners go, you're all right," she told him grudgingly.

Brodie clutched his chest. "Wow, that's a really heady compliment."

Kori frowned. Okay, time to wrap this up and go home. "Speaking of heads, don't let that go to yours."

Brodie laughed. He looked as if he knew the sound of that laugh was burrowing into her consciousness, unsettling her.

"Don't worry, I won't," he promised. Kori had already started to walk to her car. Brodie called out to her. "Hey Kennedy, you sure you don't want to stop somewhere and get a beer and some pretzels?"

She was a sucker for pretzels, although the thought of beer didn't move her. "I'm sure—and when we do go out, Cavanaugh, I'm not going be that cheap a date. Count on that."

He grinned at her. "Then I guess I'd better start saving up so I can do this right."

"I guess so," she agreed.

As she turned to her car, she felt her mouth curving in an amused smile. *Okay, so maybe he isn't so bad after all*, she thought.

Bill Kennedy looked at his daughter in genuine surprise when she opened the front door and walked in. "I wasn't expecting you home before midnight," he told her.

"Yeah, Cinderella called. She said she wanted her slippers back," Kori quipped.

It was an inside joke between them. When she had been a little girl, Cinderella had been her very favorite fairy tale. She had made her father read it to her so many times, she could actually recite the story by heart. She had even gone so far as to sew herself a makeshift ball gown. She'd worn it three years in a row for Halloween until she'd finally outgrown it.

Remembering, her father smiled. "Did you tell her she couldn't have them?"

"No," Kori answered, keeping a serious expression on her face. "I felt sorry for her. Besides, keeping those slippers would be stealing and you taught me to always be honest."

"I didn't need to teach you to be honest," Bill told his daughter with pride. "You were born that way." Then, changing the subject, he asked, "You haven't eaten, have you?"

There was no point in denying it or making up excuses. Her father would see right through that. He always had.

"You know me too well, Dad. As a matter of fact, for

the last half hour, I've been fantasizing about your fantastic roast beef sandwiches. Any chance you can whip me up one of those?"

"Every chance in the world, honey. You want it in the kitchen, or should I bring it to you out here?" he asked, thinking that every step she took at this point was an effort. If he knew his daughter—and he did—she had pushed herself too hard again.

"I'll have it in the kitchen, Dad—as long as you agree to join me and have one as well," Kori told him.

When Bill smiled, people told him that he looked just like his daughter. He smiled now. "I thought you'd never ask."

Bill Kennedy led the way into their kitchen, attempting to gauge his daughter's mood by what she was saying. Over the years, he had found that the direct route was always the simplest—and the most satisfying.

"So, how's the investigation going?" he asked as he opened up the refrigerator and rummaged around on the shelves. Because Kori was such a fan of roast beef, Bill always made sure that he had at least half a pound of the meat, thinly sliced and rare, on hand, as well as tomatoes and lettuce.

"Still stuck in first gear," Kori lamented. For now, she decided not to mention the tracking device that had been tossed away and found on the ground. It might not lead them anywhere, either.

"After that great appeal you made to the public this morning?" Bill asked his daughter in amazement. "I would have thought that you would have gotten a great many calls in response."

"Oh, we did. Trust me, we did," she told her father, a sense of weariness slipping into her voice. Kori paused for a moment to sink her teeth into her first bite of the thick roast beef sandwich, savoring the familiar, wonderful taste.

"But?" her father asked, waiting to hear the downside of the story. The way she had phrased it, he knew there had to be a downside.

"*But*," she echoed, "none of those so-called tips that were called in led us to anything remotely productive. That's not to say that they won't," she quickly corrected, "but to get to that point involves having the team wade through all those calls that had come in and *keep* coming in."

"You need help?" Bill asked, about to volunteer his services.

"Thanks, Dad, but luckily, Chief Cavanaugh gave us a boatload of officers to help man the phones." She paused again to take another bite. "He also recruited a bunch of detectives to conduct the face-to-face interviews with all the callers whose stories seemed to be at least partially credible."

"Brian Cavanaugh's a good man," her father said as he sat down opposite her at the table. "But then, you and I already knew that," he concluded with a smile.

"Yes, we did," Kori agreed absently.

"But?" Bill prodded. He could see that something else was bothering his daughter.

Kori put down her sandwich in order to share what was eating away at her. "The longer this takes, the harder it's going to be to find that little girl, Dad. I'm afraid that we might wind up missing our window of opportunity and being too late."

Bill closed his hand over hers and squeezed it for a moment, trying to will his strength to her. "You'll do it, Kori. I've got faith in you, remember?"

She laughed dryly. It was going to take more than just

her father's faith in her to get the job done. "You forget one little thing. I'm not a miracle worker."

"Don't sell yourself short, honey," he told her. And then his tone changed to a more uplifting one. "By the way, how's your new partner doing now that he's gotten used to what the job requires?"

Kori thought back to earlier that day. "Well, we went to interview the first eyewitness who called into the precinct and she wound up flirting with him. Does that give you any idea how things went?"

Her father nodded, taking the information in stride. "You never know. That sort of thing might turn out to be useful, Kori."

"How?" she asked. "How is that going to turn out to be useful?"

He thought for a second. "Well, someone calling in with a 'tip' might see Brodie and want to impress him with what she's seen."

That was what happened today and, as far as she was concerned, that sank like a lead balloon. "Dad, if what the 'witness' tells us turns out to be a lie, then what good is it?"

"Might not be a lie," her father pointed out. "It might actually be the truth, just drawn out to keep you enticed and on a string."

Kori read between the lines. "And by 'you,' you mean Cavanaugh."

"Yes," he told her, adding, "Whatever brings that little girl home."

Well, she certainly couldn't argue with that, Kori thought. She'd be willing to use whatever method she could. What was important here was to bring that infant home to the girl's mother.

Kori looked down at her empty plate. "Great sandwich,

Dad—and great talk," she added. "As always." She smiled at the man she considered to be her anchor. "You always make me see things more clearly."

"Glad to help, honey. That's what I'm here for." He picked up her plate and put it on top of his. "And glad to hear that you and Brodie are working well together."

"Well, I wouldn't go so far as to say that," she cautioned.

"But you will," Bill assured her with confidence. When he saw the skeptical look on her face, he told Kori, "Don't forget, I met your partner at a few of Andrew's family gatherings." He liked the fact that he and his daughter had been assimilated into the family. It did bother him that in the last couple of years, Kori always seemed to find excuses not to attend. "You should attend those things, you know."

She shrugged a little too carelessly to be convincing, Bill thought. "Maybe someday."

"And maybe the next time you're invited," Bill stressed.

Kori shrugged again. She didn't want to be pinned down and wind up having to lie. "We'll see."

But for once, her father wouldn't let this go. "As a favor to your old dad, Kori."

"Maybe," Kori allowed. And then she smiled. "As soon as I find this 'old dad' you speak of."

Bill laughed, pushing himself to his feet. Bending over his daughter, who was still seated, he kissed the top of her head.

"Get some sleep, Kori. Morning will be here before you know it."

She nodded, rising to her own feet. "I'm much too tired to argue with you, Dad."

"Thank heaven for the little things," he acknowledged.

Picking up the plates to take them to the sink, Bill watched his daughter as she walked to the stairs.

Kori didn't bother to turn around. She could *feel* her father's eyes on her, watching her make her way to her room.

"I can get to my room on my own, Dad. You don't need to watch me walk up the stairs," she deadpanned.

"It's one of my few pleasures, baby—and so is calling you that," he told her, anticipating the next words out of her mouth would be to protest his referring to her in that way.

Kori merely laughed and shook her head. "Good night, Dad. See you in the morning."

It occurred to her as she went the rest of the way to the stairs that she never grew tired of saying that and never took saying it to her father for granted. She still occasionally dreamed about that awful night in front of the convenience store when she'd tried to stop her father from bleeding to death with her hands. The memory was never far from her thoughts.

She was really lucky, she thought. *Really* lucky. And the only way to show her gratitude was to pay it forward.

"So, is everyone all well rested?" Kori asked the next morning. Walking into the squad room, she had called her task force into the conference area.

Simon snorted, dismissing her question. "You ask me, Rip Van Winkle had the right idea with that twenty-year nap he took."

"Well, if you take that kind of a nap, when you woke up, you wouldn't be the stud you fancy yourself to be now," Kori told him.

The men sitting around the table exchanged surprised looks. "Hey, looks like our fearless leader is back among us," Baxter said to the others.

"I was never gone," Kori informed Baxter. "But this case involves a really grim situation and, I don't know about you guys, but I'm not about to 'whistle a happy tune' until we locate that baby and I'm holding her in my arms—or at least one of us is."

More of Brian Cavanaugh's handpicked recruits kept walking in. She recognized several of them from the day before. They all appeared to be ready and willing to help field all the phone calls that were coming in again, hot and heavy.

Kori looked around the room. "Okay, so where are we?"

Officer Alexandra Harper spoke for the volunteers. "We're still talking to the 'good Samaritans' who are calling in, claiming they saw someone taking the baby off the premises. At this point, there seems to be no end to them."

"I'll say," Drew Montgomery agreed, adding his voice to Alexandra's. "We've got reports describing everyone but Santa Claus abducting the baby from the hospital."

Another officer, Kirk Conway, nodded and spoke up. "One woman swears she saw the baby being carried off in a laundry basket."

"A laundry basket?" Brodie repeated. "Why didn't she call someone immediately?"

"Well, according to our so-called eyewitness, she *thought* she saw something wiggling like a baby in the laundry basket, but when she went to try to investigate, the woman making the rounds and gathering the laundry together shooed her away."

"'Shooed her away'?" Kori questioned as she paused to take a long sip of her extremely bracing, eye-opening black coffee.

"The witness's words, not mine," Conway explained to Kori.

"And what did this woman say when she was 'shooed'?" Kori asked.

"According to our so-called eyewitness, the older woman collecting laundry was territorial. She claimed that she would get into trouble and maybe even lose her job if she let everyone touch the hospital laundry. I dunno, I guess there's a lot of call to touch hospital laundry. Anyway," Conway continued, "she asked our 'eyewitness' to move away from her and the basket."

"Doesn't that strike you as rather odd? This woman being so protective of the hospital's laundry," Brodie commented.

"Yeah, but hey, it takes all kinds," Baxter said with a shrug.

Kori thought of the taco server's story about an older nurse holding a baby. "What did this protective hospital worker look like?"

Conway thought for a moment. "All the eyewitness said was that it was some older woman who looked as if she should have been retired long ago instead of doing laundry like some kind of old-fashioned washer woman."

"'Washer woman,'" Brodie repeated. "Now there's a term I haven't heard used in decades. Maybe longer," he commented.

Simon looked at this newest member of their team. "Just how old are you?"

"We can discuss Cavanaugh's youthful appearance later," Kori told the others, then turned toward the policeman. "Tell me more about the woman who called in and this laundry basket that attracted her attention. Was she sure she saw the laundry moving?"

"That's just it, she wasn't sure. She just *thought* it might have been moving, but she didn't get a chance to check that out one way or another. For all we know, it was just wishful thinking—in hindsight."

"Hindsight?" Kori questioned.

Conway nodded. "You know, when someone is trying to be a part of the solution that led to finding the little girl."

"In other words, this so-called eyewitness might have had some sort of a desire to play hero by association," Brodie suggested.

"Or maybe just good intentions that were being pushed too hard in order to register. We'll find out today," Kori told the others. "Okay, people, we've got our list of supposed witnesses to talk to. Same partners as before. Let's hit the streets."

"You got it, boss," Simon said, speaking for all of them just before the task force filed out of the office.

Chapter 14

Kori wearily closed her phone and put it away. She had just had to tell Rose Williams that there was no new news. They still hadn't been able to locate her baby or discover who had taken her. With all the working surveillance cameras on the various floors, they had not been able to record so much as a glimpse of the crime being perpetrated. The only thing that they had managed to do was rule out a simple kidnapping because there had been no calls asking for a ransom.

Kori felt that telling the new mother, who was now home, that they hadn't been able to find the baby had just about crushed Rose.

Kori was keenly aware that she, her partner, and the rest of the task force had been working the investigation almost nonstop for close to a week now. They still had nothing of substance to show for it. Every time Kori thought they were finally getting closer, whatever they were working on just seemed to fall through and the team wound up back at square one.

Faced with yet another dead end, Brodie looked at her as they walked to their vehicle. He found himself thinking that his partner was taking this last setback particularly hard, especially after hearing her end of the phone call. In his opinion, she seemed to be wilting.

When she got into the vehicle and began driving again, Brodie debated saying something, then decided that he really needed to.

"You do know that there are some kidnapping cases that are never solved," he warned Kori. He just wanted her to keep things in perspective.

Working the case, she had done a complete about-face and was now determined to cling to hope. "I don't care about other kidnapping cases. I care about *this* kidnapping case," she snapped. Then murmured, "Sorry. I didn't mean to bite your head off."

Brodie saw that she was clutching the steering wheel to the point that her knuckles were white. *Not good*, he thought. Since Kori had initially said that she liked to be the one driving, he hadn't contested the arrangement. But now he began to think that this might have been a bad idea—at least for now.

He could detect the tension gripping her body. He could especially see it in her arms and shoulders, not to mention that it showed in her face. He felt he had to do something to help Kori deal with it before she wound up driving into something and causing an accident.

"Pull over," Brodie told her.

Kori gave him a look as she continued driving, certain that she had misheard. "What?"

"Pull over," Brodie repeated, enunciating each word slowly.

"Why?" she asked sharply.

He wasn't going to get into a discussion while they were driving. Or, more to the point, while *she* was driving. "Just do it," he told her.

Kori pressed her lips together, keeping back a host of choice words that, voiced, might have made her feel temporarily better but eventually she knew she would regret saying. Annoying though he was, she knew that Cavanaugh undoubtedly meant well.

So, taking a deep breath, she did as Brodie instructed and pulled over to the side of the road. "All right, I've pulled over," she declared, spreading her hands. "Now what?"

"Now get out of the car," Brodie told her with finality.

She stared at him, stunned. Just what was he trying to accomplish?

"What?" she cried.

"You heard me, Kennedy," he said, then repeated, "Get out of the car."

"Yes, I heard you," she agreed. "And I want to know why."

"Because I want to switch places with you," he told her patiently.

She rolled her eyes. This was getting annoying, not to mention repetitive. "Again. Why?"

All right, he would spell it out for her. "Because you're tired, you're preoccupied—" he ticked off his fingers "—and you're in no condition to drive."

Okay, she was now officially angry. "In your opinion."

"In *anyone's* opinion. C'mon, Kennedy," he urged, trying to appeal to her common sense. "You're an accident waiting to happen and I, for one, still have a lot of living left to do—and I figure you do, too."

For the second time, a number of words rose to her

lips. This time it was harder keeping them back than before, but she managed.

"Maybe you're right," she allowed, "but there is a little girl out there who might not have a lot of living left to do and I want to find her before some crazy person decides that she's used her allotment up."

"We all want to find her, Kennedy, but pushing yourself way beyond human endurance isn't going to help find that little girl. And neither is getting into an accident," he stressed.

"What are you talking about?" Kori demanded heatedly.

"If you hadn't just swerved in time back there," Brodie pointed out, "we would have undoubtedly wound up being tree ornaments a couple of minutes ago."

Kori glared at him, angry because Brodie had said that. Angrier because part of her knew he was right. "But we *didn't* wind up being tree ornaments, did we?"

"No," he agreed, "but I'd rather not take another chance on that. Now switch places with me," Brodie said a little more insistently. "I don't want to have to tell your father that you won't be coming home tonight—or any night—because you were too stubborn to listen to reason. Now, are you going to get out of the car or am I going to have to get physical and carry you out?"

The next moment he saw Kori raise her chin like a boxer about to go into the ring and face an avowed enemy. Just when he thought he was going to have to make good on his threat and carry her out of the driver's seat, Brodie saw his partner drop her chin again, obviously surrendering.

"All right, have it your way," she snapped sharply, throwing open her door.

Swinging her legs out, she stood and then deliberately

rounded the vehicle's back end. She made her way to the passenger side. Getting in and buckling up, she slammed her door defiantly. The action made the car vibrate on her side.

"Happy?" she asked between gritted teeth as she glared at Brodie.

"Let's just say I'm mildly content," he told her. "The word *happy* is reserved for when we find that baby," he told her, then stressed, "*When,* not *if.*"

Kori sighed. Cavanaugh was trying, she acknowledged, and she wasn't being fair to him. But that was because she felt so drained and really disillusioned.

"I'm sorry," she told him, apologizing in a moment of weakness "I'm usually not this down."

"You're taking this too personally," Brodie pointed out, beginning to drive. It was way past the time when they should have clocked out.

Kori's eyes flashed as she turned to look at him. "I take *every* case personally," she informed him indignantly. "It's the only way I know how to work."

"Funny you should mention that," Brodie responded.

"'Funny'?" she repeated incredulously. "I can think of a lot of words to use here, but *funny* isn't one of them."

"Which was why I was going to suggest something to help you broaden your base."

She stared at him, suddenly grateful they were calling it a day and heading back to the precinct even if they hadn't made any discernable headway.

"I don't know what you're talking about, Cavanaugh, and right now, I have to admit that my brain is way too tired to make any sense of it or to attempt to untangle the words."

"All right, I will speak in short sentences that you can

understand without even trying," he told her, doing just that by speaking very slowly and carefully.

Her eyes flashed again. "Don't patronize me, Cavanaugh. If you do, I won't be responsible for my reaction."

"No patronization intended," Brodie told her in an easy, calm tone. "Anyway, there's going to be a gathering this Saturday…" he began, staring straight ahead at the road in front of him.

He wasn't able to get any further because she declared, "No."

"You're not being very fair, you know," he told her. "You're turning this down without even knowing what it's all about."

She made an annoyed noise under her breath. "You just said it was a gathering."

"Yes, but you don't know what kind of gathering it's going to be—" Brodie noted.

"Doesn't matter," she said, cutting him short. "I don't do gatherings when I'm working a case."

"That's ridiculous." Didn't she realize how absurd her statement sounded? "Only hermits don't 'do' gatherings," he informed her, telling her decisively, "And you're not a hermit."

"No," she agreed. "I'm a frustrated detective."

He refused to back off. "And this will help take the frustration away."

"Okay," she said gamely, "you have my attention. At the risk of sounding like I'm totally lost, just how is this going to take the frustration away from me? Or are you just talking?"

"I can't speak to that lost reference you just made," he conceded, "but I am *not* just talking. This gathering on Saturday is going to include, among others, a number of seasoned veteran detectives discussing some of their old cases. Their old missing-persons cases," he stressed, "some of which involved kidnapped children. Who knows, you might pick up something useful. We all might," he added so she didn't feel singled out. "You'll also have a chance to blow off some steam—*and* make your father happy."

"My father?" she asked incredulously. "What does my father have to do with it?"

"Well, for one thing, he'll be one of the people attending." Brodie eased into a stop at the red light.

All right, she thought, now she knew he was just pulling her leg. "In case this little fact escaped you, my father's not a seasoned detective."

"No, you're right," Brodie agreed, taking his foot off the brake and going again. "But Uncle Andrew likes your father—a lot. He'd never exclude him from a gathering he was throwing. He hasn't done it in all the years he's been having these get-togethers."

She sighed as she shook her head. Did Cavanaugh really think she didn't see through this? "You're just trying to get me to go to one of these things and I really—"

Brodie laughed, interrupting her. "Getting you to come is just a side benefit. But it really is a gathering to discuss old cases." She was still looking at him as if she didn't believe him, so he added, "I should know. I'm the one who suggested it to Uncle Andrew when I saw how much not finding this little girl was really getting to you, Kennedy."

Kori raised an eyebrow. "And I suppose it doesn't bother you?" she challenged.

"I didn't say that," he pointed out. "Yes, it bothers me, but I'm not pushing myself so hard that I'm going to get sick over it, because if I did that, then I wouldn't be any good to the investigation." He paused for a moment before saying, "And there's nothing good to be gotten out of that scenario."

Kori glared at him. He had her cornered and they were going around in circles. "Got an answer for everything, don't you?"

"Not everything," Brodie told her. "But I do try my best." He glanced in her direction as he took a corner. "So, how about it, Kennedy? Can I tell my uncle that you'll be coming to this thing he's pulling together in order to help you out?"

Guilt, she thought. Now he was using guilt to get her to go. "To help me out?" she repeated, stalling for time to come up with a way out.

"That's what I said," he answered.

Kori sighed and then became silent for a good ten minutes. When her silence threatened to draw out even longer, Brodie decided to press the matter. "Well? Are you going to come?"

She blew out a long, annoyed breath. "You're not going to give up until I say yes, are you?"

His smile all but lit up the interior of the vehicle. She had her answer. "Now you get the idea."

"Why is my coming to this gathering so important to you?" she demanded.

There was no point in beating around the bush. Brodie was honest with her. "Because it's important to Uncle Andrew and to your father. And I'm thinking, in a way, to you."

"Why would you even say that? That it's important to me?" she stipulated. "Don't you think that if it actually was, I would have gone a long time ago?"

"No, you wouldn't have. You wouldn't go because you're afraid."

She stared at him, stunned and annoyed. "And what

makes you think that?" Kori asked. She was just about coming to the end of her patience—and she was getting there really fast.

"You're afraid to go because you might be reminded of everything you don't have—meaning a full family life," he explained. "Even when we, meaning my family, feel that we're alone, we're not. There are cousins, uncles, aunts—hell, there're so many relatives, it's a challenge just keeping track of them. In comparison, taken at face value, your life might feel stark to you—but it doesn't have to be."

"It's not," she insisted heatedly. Who did he think he was, analyzing her life like this? "I have my father. That's enough for me."

"All right, then come tomorrow because it's important to him. Having you there is important to him," he said with emphasis.

Kori closed her eyes, searching for strength. This man wasn't going to give up, she thought, annoyed. "And you're not going to stop badgering me until I go, are you?"

Brodie smiled at her. "Nothing slow about you. Except maybe when you drag your feet," he allowed.

She'd had enough. "All right, all right, all right!" Kori cried. "I'll go. Just stop badgering me, okay?"

"Absolutely," he said with an obliging smile.

"Yeah, right," she responded with a mirthless laugh.

"No, really."

She decided to push. "And if I ultimately don't come?"

"Well, then that's called reneging and, if you do, I'll be free to do the same," he warned with a mischievous smile.

"You're saying that all bets will be off then?"

"No, what I'm saying is that if you don't show up, I'll be free to come get you and bring you to the gathering. So you see, there really is no way out and you might as well just go with it, because one way or another, you *will* be there." He glanced at her again. "It's a lot easier that way."

"Why is this so important to you?" she demanded again, still not really understanding why it mattered to him.

"Because," he told her, "ultimately, it'll be important to you."

She sighed. "You do realize that you talk in riddles."

"All right, if it helps, think of this as a riddle. A riddle that'll be unscrambled somewhere in the middle of tomorrow—right about the time you wind up attending the gathering."

"And just so I'm clear on this, if I don't go, you'll come and get me."

"Yes."

"How? Are you going to tie me to the roof of your car?" Because, Kori decided, making up her mind, there was no way Cavanaugh was going to get her to attend on her own power. She absolutely refused to be manipulated into going.

Brodie looked completely unfazed by her sarcasm. "If I have to."

She looked at him uncertainly. "You wouldn't."

But her partner didn't back off. Instead, he gave her this look she couldn't really read no matter how hard she tried.

"I wouldn't push it if I were you," he warned. "You don't know me that well and some of us Cavanaughs can be very unpredictable. You going along with this is a lot easier than digging in your heels. Trust me on this."

"Trust you?" she echoed incredulously. "And why would I do that?"

"Because I've never lied to you."

"Yet," she pointed out.

His smile was indulgent. "For now, all we have is the

present," he told her. "So, how about it? Do we have a deal?"

"Sure," she answered, thinking it was the only way to get him to back off. She didn't have to mean it.

"Good. I'll be there tomorrow to pick you and your father up," he told her just as he pulled the car into the police parking lot.

She could feel herself literally being backed into a corner.

Chapter 15

Over the course of the next twelve hours, in the privacy of her own mind, Kori came up with one excuse after another. All the excuses were centered around why she wouldn't be able to attend this latest gathering at the former police chief's house.

But, in the end, she decided that her partner was ultimately right. It was simpler just to go along with this whole thing than to fight it and have Brodie keep bringing it up infinitum, asking her about it and teasing her about being too afraid to attend.

Even though she dawdled, Kori still wound up dressed and ready way too early. Being early was a lifelong habit she couldn't shake.

Taking in a deep breath, she came down the stairs.

Her father had just slipped on a blue-and-white pullover sweater with his gray slacks. He looked over as she came to the bottom step and smiled.

"You look very nice, Kori," he said with approval. "I'm glad you finally decided to socialize with the Cavanaughs. Don't know why you stopped. I never bought that excuse of yours about not wanting to mix business with pleasure. You're not going to regret this."

"I'm already regretting it," Kori murmured. When her father looked at her, an expression of dubious surprise on his face, she was quick to set him straight about *why* she had just said what she'd said. "This is time I could be using to work on the case, maybe even get somewhere."

"Baby, I know better than anyone what a dedicated workaholic you are," her father told her, "but maybe listening to the voices of experience might just help you actually think of something to help you solve this investigation."

Kori laughed dryly. "That's the same thing that Cav— Brodie said," she responded, deciding at the last moment to use her partner's first name rather than the surname she'd been using when referring to him. This situation, she was sure her father would point out, called for friendliness, which called for first names. "According to him, that was actually the chief's idea."

Bill nodded, agreeing with what his daughter had just said. "Just because someone retires doesn't mean his brain automatically goes into sleep mode and stops working. As a matter of fact," he continued with a genial smile, "the opposite is usually true."

Just then, the doorbell rang. Bill's smile widened. "And, unless I miss my guess, there's our ride now," her father said brightly, striding toward the door.

Out of the corner of his eye, he caught his daughter's frown. He was starting to wonder if perhaps there was another reason why Kori was fighting attending this gathering as hard as she was. Was there something going on between her and Brodie?

Or was she afraid that there would be something going on if she came to this party?

Bill smiled to himself as he opened the door, feeling a surge of hope suddenly dancing through him.

"Hello, Brodie," Bill said, greeting the young man standing in his doorway. "We were just talking about you."

Brodie laughed. "Let me guess. My new partner was enumerating all the reasons she has just decided she can't possibly attend my uncle Andrew's gathering with us."

"No," Bill replied, pleased as he took a step back to physically invite the younger man in. "As a matter of fact, she just said she could see the merit in finally doing this—or words to that effect," the older man wound up saying. For the moment, Bill avoided eye contact with either one of the younger people.

Even so, Brodie gave Kori's father a very skeptical look as he crossed the threshold into the Kennedy living room.

Still, having learned, long ago, the benefit of quitting while he was ahead, Brodie chose not to pursue the matter any further. He felt that if he did, Kori might use that to change her mind and withdraw from the gathering.

So instead, Kori's partner gestured behind him toward the opened door.

"Your chariot awaits," Brodie announced to the two people he had come to bring to his uncle's party.

Kori's attendance meant different things to different people, but the bottom line was that it was important—to his uncle, to her father and, if he were being honest, to him.

"By the way," he told Kori, his green eyes washing over her and lingering at the way her dress's soft, blue material seemed to cling to her body, "in case I didn't mention it, you clean up really nicely."

Kori told herself that she was just imagining her stomach suddenly tightening. And her mouth growing dry was just a coincidence, too.

"I could say the same to you," she finally responded. A beat later, she realized what she had just said, but it was too late to take it back.

Brodie was surprised by her comment. He didn't know if she was being serious or not, but again, he chose not to prod her for any sort of a deeper meaning. Instead, he merely smiled at her and said, "Glad you approve."

"Isn't anyone going to say anything about me?" Bill asked, extending his arms and pretending to be hurt that he had been left out.

"You are *always* lovely, Dad," Kori replied.

Bill pretended to fluff his still full, albeit gray-streaked hair.

"I know," her father answered, tongue-in-cheek. "It's just nice to hear once in a while, that's all." And then he said in a far more normal voice, "Well, shall we go?"

"Right this way," Brodie said, leading the way to the front curb and his car.

Seeing the vehicle for the first time, Kori stopped dead in her tracks. Her mouth nearly dropped open.

"That's a Cadillac," Kori said in surprise as she looked at the very large vintage vehicle. She had to admit that she had *never* envisioned him driving anything like that.

"So *that's* what it is," Brodie cried, pretending to be enlightened by her reaction.

Kori had to steel herself not to glare at him in front of her father.

"Very funny," she responded. "I just didn't see you driving something so elegant."

"What did you see me driving?" he asked, curious. "A truck?"

She shrugged, slowly walking up to the Cadillac. "I guess I thought you'd be driving something fast," she admitted.

Brodie smiled at the image. "There's a lot about me that you don't know," he told her. And then he mysteriously added, "Maybe tonight will turn into a night of more than one discovery."

Unlocking the car, Brodie held the passenger door open.

"I'll take the back seat," Bill volunteered. He sat in the rear of the vehicle before Kori had a chance to contest the matter, closing the door behind him. "More room for my legs," he explained when Kori gave him a look that told him she thought he was being way too obvious.

"Right, because you're so very large." Kori pointedly looked at his five-foot-eight frame.

"I like to stretch," her father told her, nonplussed.

"Today is about you relaxing and unwinding," Brodie reminded her as he rounded the vehicle and got in on the driver's side. "So you might as well go with the flow. You won't regret it."

"For that to happen," Kori informed her partner, making eye contact and looking at him pointedly, "I would need a time machine."

"So in other words, you're regretting this already?" Brodie asked.

Kori made no answer, but she did smile at his assumption.

Bill wasn't the type to butt into his daughter's business, but this one time, he decided to speak up.

"I guess it's up to us to prove her wrong, boy," Bill said.

Brodie glanced over his shoulder at the older man—and grinned. "Apparently."

Kori pressed her lips together. For the moment, she

decided that it was better not to say anything at all. She knew when she was outnumbered.

When they entered Andrew Cavanaugh's development twenty minutes later and drove toward his house, Kori couldn't help staring at all the cars parked up and down the residential streets.

"Wow," she finally said, "there are an awful lot of vehicles parked here." More than the usual amount, in her opinion. She looked at Brodie. "Is today some kind of holiday?" she asked as she began to unconsciously search for a space where Brodie could park his overly large vehicle.

"Yeah," Brodie answered, his mouth curving in amusement. "One of Uncle Andrew's parties."

"You're kidding," she cried. "There are *this* many people attending one of your uncle's gatherings?" she asked in disbelief. The number had certainly increased from the last time she had attended.

"I told you they were big gatherings," her father reminded her. He had been invited—and attended—more than his share over the years. Once the so-called "lost branch" had been found, the numbers had really increased.

"I know," she replied, "but there's 'big' and then there's *big*," she emphasized. "I thought you were exaggerating."

"Exaggeration was never my thing, honey," her father told her. About to say something else, he suddenly called out, "Wait!" As Brodie came to a sudden stop, Bill pointed ahead of them. "I think there's a space right up there. Right at the end of the street," he specified. "If you angle your Caddie, you might be able to get into it," he told the younger man.

"Might be worth a shot," Brodie said, studying the space.

Two attempts and some fancy angling later, he finally managed to park his vehicle.

Getting out, Brodie surprised her by helping her father out first. She didn't say anything, but she gave her partner points because he hadn't immediately jumped out on his side to help her out.

"It's a bit of a walk," Brodie said to Bill apologetically.

"Walking is good exercise for me." Kori's father smiled. "I never take that for granted," he told the younger man.

Kori still made no comment as she fell into step next to her father. Brodie was on her father's other side. That, too, surprised her and, once again, she mentally gave him points for being so thoughtful.

Brodie just glanced in Kori's direction to make sure she was there a moment before he rang his uncle Andrew's doorbell.

The door opened almost immediately and a distinguished, genial-looking man measuring at least six feet tall in Kori's estimation stood in the doorway. Deep green eyes swept over the two men on his doorstep, but they came to rest on the young woman with them.

"You've finally decided to come back," Andrew declared with a satisfied smile. He put out his hand, strong fingers taking hold of Kori's and shaking it.

Kori found that his handshake was still very strong, yet surprisingly gentle as well.

"Welcome back, Kori," he told her, still holding her hand.

His hair had gotten grayer, but it was just as thick as ever. She would have recognized him immediately. What did one say to a legend? she wondered, struggling to say something intelligent that didn't sound as if she was about to become tongue-tied.

At a loss, Kori fell back on a standard response. "Thank you for having me, sir."

Andrew laughed at that, glancing back at both her father and Brodie.

"And we only had to resort to bribery to get you to come back," Andrew told her with an amused chuckle. "But whatever it took," he concluded philosophically, "I—we—" he corrected "—are glad you're finally here. Come in, come in." He opened the door further. Once they were inside, he closed his door, leaving it unlocked. "I'll let Brodie show you around. Some things have changed. He can answer any questions you might have."

She didn't want to lose sight of what had actually brought her here. "Um, Brodie said something about veteran detectives…" Her voice trailed off, but there was no missing the hopeful note within it.

"Oh, there's no shortage of those here," Andrew assured her. "And, as promised, they'll be discussing some of their more interesting kidnapping cases. As a matter of fact, we probably won't be able to get them to stop. We are hoping that those stories might trigger something for you and Brodie to use in your investigation," Andrew told her. And then his expression sobered visibly. "Nothing more reprehensible than someone kidnapping a defenseless child, be it an infant or an older one." Andrew turned to look at Brodie. "Brodie, do the honors, please." And then he turned toward Kori's father.

To her surprise, the chief put an arm around her father's shoulder, drawing him into the kitchen. "Glad you could make it, Bill. I've got something new for you to try," the chief told him. "Based on what you told me the last time, I think you're really going to like this."

Satisfied that her father was in good hands, Kori turned to her partner. "Your uncle's really nice," she told him, watching the two men.

"He doesn't breathe fire on the weekends," Brodie wisecracked. "That's just during the week."

She frowned. "Maybe you had the wrong idea," she suggested. "I didn't *not* come to these gatherings because I thought the chief had become some kind of fire-breathing monster."

Brodie waved away her words. "Hey, what matters is that you're here," he insisted. "C'mon, let me introduce you around to some of the people you *don't* know and then maybe they can get down to swapping a few interesting old war stories before dinner is served."

"Dinner?" she echoed, looking at her watch. It was just past ten in the morning. "Isn't it just a little early for that?"

"Officially," he told her as he began to guide her toward the living room and the spacious patio just beyond that, "Uncle Andrew likes to serve Sunday dinner at around two. But you might recall that, unofficially, he begins feeding people the moment they cross his threshold." Brodie gestured to the serving tables that were scattered around the area. "Be ready to weigh approximately five pounds more when you leave than when you first walked in."

Her father had said something about the food served at these parties, but she had thought that he was just exaggerating. "You are kidding, right?"

The amusement in his eyes threw her off. She didn't know whether to believe him or not.

"Ask around. You probably know most of these people. By sight if not by name," he added, then amended, "At least the ones who work at the precinct. This is a chance to meet their 'other halves,'" he pointed out. "It'll round out who they are as people, not just as officers and detectives." Brodie watched her expression to see if he had gotten through to her.

Kori was about to protest that she didn't need to have the people she worked with "rounded out" in order to do her job, but something inside her protested her taking that stand, just as it made clear to her why she was resisting this closer association.

The idea of loss—of her losing people she'd gotten close to—had always been there, on the perimeter of her mind. If she didn't get to really know these people, then it wouldn't really be a loss if they were no longer part of her world.

That was the moment Kori realized that the night she had almost lost her father had left her indelibly marked. It made her fearful of making any other attachments because she really was subconsciously afraid of losing people. After all, her mother had died a couple of years before the incident with her father.

So she didn't make any attachments, reasoning that if there were none, then there was no danger of losing anyone. She supposed that was why her cases meant so much to her. The cases were substitutes for any real, lasting attachments.

She had grown silent, Brodie noted. He turned to look at her and saw the odd expression on her face as if she were experiencing some sort of an epiphany.

"Kori? Kori?" He repeated her name three times before he got her attention. When she looked at him quizzically, he asked, "What's going on?"

Denial was her immediate go-to place. "Nothing."

"That wasn't a 'nothing' expression on your face," he insisted. "Now," he asked again, "what's going on with you?"

Kori sighed. She had a feeling they were going to continue working together so she might as well be honest with him. "You were right," she said grudgingly.

"I'm going to need more," he told her. "I'm right about a lot of things."

"You're right about my resisting coming here—about *why* I resisted," she clarified.

Kori fully expected her partner to gloat.

Instead, Brodie said, "Well, now that you've admitted that to yourself, we can build on it and move on." He took hold of her elbow, gently guiding her to an area toward the left. "Come with me. There are some veteran detectives you might find interesting to talk to."

She certainly hoped so, Kori thought as she went with her partner.

Chapter 16

Kori didn't realize it at the start, but as the day wore on, it became clear that it was destined to be one of those days that she would always remember. For two reasons.

The major reason was, as Brodie had predicted when he'd talked her into coming to the gathering, the stories she listened to over the course of the day as well as the evening triggered something in her own mind. Something that she and Brodie might be able to use when attempting to resolve the kidnapping investigation—maybe even to actually find the infant. For the first time since the investigation began, Kori found herself able to really nurse some real hope.

The second thing that made this a day for her to remember was that she could view Brodie in an even better light. She was able to see him for the person he actually was. Rather that just a cocky, confident, glib-tongued detective who was a member of a revered law enforcement family, Brodie had transformed into a kindly, thoughtful person right before her eyes. A person who had put her father's needs ahead of his own, certainly ahead of any need he might have to attempt to impress her by displaying his vast array of knowledge when it came to law enforcement.

What she found that she liked about Brodie most was that he didn't just pretend to be a man who cared about his family—Brodie actually *did* care about his family. Not just some of the members, but apparently *all* of them.

It wasn't something he'd said to her. Kori could see it in his actions, in the way he treated the various members they came in contact with during the course of the evening.

She caught herself thinking that that was an awful lot of members for him to be concerned about. Watching Brodie in action definitely contributed to her growing regard for the man.

"So," Brodie said, turning to her as the evening was winding down and approximately a third of the guests, those with young children they needed to put to bed, had gone home or were in the process of going home. "Am I forgiven for making you come?" The glint in his eye said he already knew the answer to that. His asking the question was just a mere formality.

"Yes," Kori answered in a monotone voice, "you're forgiven for making me come."

"And can I take that to mean that you're having a good time?" Brodie asked, giving her his undivided attention and studying every nuance that passed over her face, a face he fancied himself studying for a very long time and still finding something there to fascinate him.

"Yes, I'm having a good time," she replied through gritted teeth because she felt as if she was giving him a card to play against her sometime down the line. "Do you want me to write it for you in blood?"

"No, I'll accept a verbal confirmation—for now," Brodie qualified, and then his mouth curved in a smile that showed his amusement.

Kori shook her head. "Has anyone ever told you that despite your attributes, you can have a very annoying way about you?"

Rather than take the bait, he picked up on something else. "My attributes, huh? Tell me more about what you see as my 'attributes,'" he coaxed.

"And make your head even larger than it is?" she asked with a laugh. "No, thank you. If I mislead you by using the word *attributes*, I apologize. I was wrong to say that."

Brodie pretended to be dumbstruck as he stared at her, wide-eyed. "Stop the presses," he declared, one hand flying to his chest as if to keep his heart from popping out. "Kori Kennedy claims to have been wrong about something. Unbelievable."

She shook her head. "You're an idiot, you do know that, right?" she asked, but she couldn't quite make her voice sound as if she were actually annoyed.

"Sometimes," Brodie admitted. "But then, I've never been perfect like you." There was no animosity in his tone, which was why Kori found that she couldn't take any offense at what her new partner was saying.

Still she couldn't just keep silent, which was why she told him, "I never claimed to be perfect."

"No," Brodie agreed. "Not in so many words anyway. But you have to admit that you did give off that kind of vibe."

"Fine," she conceded. "I'll be sure to work on my 'vibe.'"

"Oh please, don't change a single hair, Korinna Kennedy," Brodie told her, punctuating his words with a warm smile that insisted on dancing up and down her spine no matter how hard she struggled to block that reaction to him. "You're unique just the way you are."

He actually sounded as if he meant it. Kori had never been comfortable talking about herself, even if Brodie was just saying what he had just to pull her leg. But right now something more important had caught her attention. She deliberately shifted his attention to it.

Nodding over to a section on the extreme left, Kori indicated a pretty, animated, older woman. Every time that Kori would look in that direction, for the last hour or so—maybe even longer—the older woman seemed to have been talking to her father. In essence, the woman had been monopolizing him.

Observing the two people, Kori had noticed that the pair seemed to exclude everyone else from their small circle of two.

Unable to contain herself any longer, she asked Brodie, "Would you happen to know who that is?"

He looked toward where Kori was indicating. Recognition instantly set in as he nodded. "Oh sure. That's Maeve."

"Maeve," Kori repeated, as if saying the woman's name would answer the host of questions that had suddenly just popped up in her head. It didn't.

"Uh-huh. She's initially from Murdoch's side of the family chart. She's one of his children," he explained, referring to Seamus's late younger brother. "In a nutshell, Aunt Maeve is one hell of a dynamo. She owns an ambulance company. I hear that the lady still drives a rig on occasion."

He could see that she wanted more, so he elaborated. "Aunt Maeve also raised five kids on her own after her husband died in an accident." Brodie saved what he felt was the best for last, knowing it would set Kori's mind at ease about his aunt. "She wouldn't accept a dime from her three brothers. She had—and still has—too much pride. Sound familiar?"

She didn't rise to the bait. Instead, Kori focused on what she felt was the important thing. "So your aunt is a widow?"

Brodie nodded. "She said she never found anyone who came close to taking her husband's place. Of course, working as many hours as she did, I can't see how anyone would have been able to have a shot at measuring up to the man. Aunt Maeve was always just much too busy to even attempt to have a social life. Why do you ask?"

Kori shrugged, avoiding his eyes as she continued to watch her father and Maeve. He was laughing, like he was really enjoying himself, she thought. He almost seemed boyish.

"No reason."

Brodie laughed, drawing her attention back to him. "You know, you're going to have to brush up on your technique when it comes to lying because, as it stands right now, you really do stink at it."

Kori shrugged again, doing her best to seem indifferent. "In my defense, I never aspired to be 'good' at lying."

"Sometimes," Brodie told her, "in this line of work, you have to be."

When it came to her father, she had always been very protective, even before she had almost lost him so long ago. "It's just that my mother died when I was really young and my father never got over it," she told him. "To my recollections, the man never had so much as a single date in all those years. He swore that loving my mother had spoiled him for anyone else."

"Maybe it's time that he got back in the game," Brodie suggested.

She knew that, technically, her partner was right, but that still didn't evoke any agreement from her. "I just don't want to see my father get hurt."

"Number one, it's not up to you," Brodie pointed out kindly. "Your dad's a big boy. Number two, Aunt Maeve is not a femme fatale who gets her kicks stringing men along. She's a decent, really hardworking woman. When you think about it, this might actually be the start of something for both of them," he told her. "My advice to you is just be happy for them."

Her eyes flashed. Where did he get off, telling her what to think and feel? "I didn't ask for your advice."

"That's okay. There's no charge. The advice is free," he told her with a grin.

He was surprised to see her face cloud over and even more surprised to see her suddenly turn on her heel and walk away. When she kept on walking toward the door, he decided it was time to stop her and find out just what was going on in her head.

Mindful that she wouldn't tolerate being embarrassed in front of his family, Brodie didn't call out to stop her but he did pick up his pace. He managed to catch up with her just beyond the front door.

Grabbing her arm, Brodie turned Kori around to face him.

"You know, you *can* walk home from here, but it'll take you a very long time," he warned. "I wouldn't suggest you try it."

She attempted to pull her arm away, but she couldn't get him to loosen his grip. That just incensed her. "Let go of me," she ordered.

But Brodie just went on holding her arm. "Not until you calm down."

That just earned him an intense glare. "You can't tell me what to do," she warned.

"I'm not telling you what to do," Brodie informed her. "I'm just making suggestions until you come to your senses and act on them."

"So now I'm being irrational?" Kori snapped angrily.

Brodie continued being maddeningly calm and answered her mildly. "Your word, not mine. Now what are you *really* so angry about?"

About to protest that she wasn't angry, she realized she couldn't say that because she was.

"I don't know," she cried. She saw that he was actually waiting for an answer, so she tossed out the first thing that came into her head. "Not being able to protect my father if this blows up in his face." She remembered Brodie's comment about her father being able to make his own choices. He was right, she thought darkly. It was just hard for her to keep out of it. "Not being able to hate you."

Brodie felt somewhat confused by her response. "Not sure I can make any sense of that, but I do know I like where this is going." He smiled at her. "Especially the 'not hating me' part."

Frustrated, Kori doubled up her fists and tried to beat on him. But he caught her hands in his, keeping them still.

And then, in a move completely dictated solely by gut reaction rather than any sort of rational thought process, Brodie found himself responding to the hellcat who was his partner as if he had no free will. He brought down his mouth to hers.

The moment that his lips touched hers, rather than defuse the situation, that simple action ignited it—and very effectively managed to set both of them on fire.

The kiss took on length and breadth as well as a tremendous power that he found he wasn't able to safely measure.

That explosion morphed into something else, something gentler and, consequently, a great deal more powerful than anything in its origin had been.

An eternity later, as he drew his head away, Brodie could see that she was as dazed and confused by what had just transpired as he was.

The next moment, unable to resist, Brodie framed her face with his hands and brought his mouth down to hers again, this time in a far gentler action that still managed to burrow its way down into his soul.

As the kiss went on to build in depth and scope, it left Brodie completely shaken for the very first time in his life. Drawing his head away, he looked at Kori, totally stunned, wondering what in heaven's name was going on here.

"Are you all right?" he finally managed to ask her.

"I'm not sure," she admitted breathless with the soul-deep effects of his passionate embrace. The next second, feeling extremely vulnerable, she said, "Let's go back inside."

"Sure." It was safer that way, he thought.

Quickening his pace, he opened the front door and held it for her, then followed her back into the house.

"There you are," Bill said the moment they came in. "I thought we got our signals crossed and you had left."

Wow, this woman has really managed to rattle his brain, Kori thought.

"No, Dad, we wouldn't have left you behind. That would have been irresponsible. We were just outside— getting some fresh air," she said, avoiding Brodie's eyes, although she had to admit that she felt her face growing warmer because of the lie anyway. "Are you ready to go?"

"As a matter of fact," Bill told his daughter, "I am."

"Okay. Then we'll all say our goodbyes and we can get going," she told her father and Brodie.

"Well, that's just it…" Bill began. "I'm not going to be leaving. That is, I won't be leaving with you."

"You're planning on staying here?" Kori asked uncertainly.

People were slowly trickling out of the house, but if her father wanted to stay longer, she was certain Brodie could be talked into hanging around for a while longer. After all, it had been his idea to come to this gathering in the first place.

Kori turned toward him to suggest just that when her father's answer stopped her.

"Not exactly," Bill said. He turned to the petite woman standing next to him. "Maeve has offered to show me around her place."

Kori thought of the station where the ambulances were undoubtedly being housed. It was getting late and taking a tour through there didn't make any sense to her.

"Now?" she questioned in surprise, looking at her father uncertainly.

"What's wrong with now?" Bill asked.

"Well," Kori pointed out, "it's getting late, not to mention dark. Wouldn't you be able to see more if you did this in the light of day?"

"Every part of the day has its good points," her father answered.

He just wasn't making any sense, Kori thought. "But the ambulances…" she began to protest.

It was his turn not to understand what she was driving at. "Who said anything about the ambulances?" he asked his daughter.

"You just did," Kori pointed out.

"No, I didn't." And then it dawned on him as Brodie laughed at the error. "Maeve isn't going to show me around where the ambulances are kept. She's going to show me around *her* place. Where she lives, not where she works."

"Oh. That's great," Kori said, knowing she didn't exactly sound convincing. All this time, she had been hoping her father would get out there and find someone. He was a good man and he deserved to be happy. Now that it was happening, she told herself that she should feel happy. So why did she feel like an eight-year-old who had just been abandoned by her only parent?

"Take good care of him," she instructed the older woman.

"Oh, I intend to," Maeve said, exchanging glances with Bill.

"And don't drive too fast," Kori cautioned.

Maeve smiled knowingly. "I never do."

"Okay, I think it's time for us to hit the road," Brodie announced, putting an end to the awkward conversation. "Let's say our goodbyes," he told Kori. "Have a good time you two," he said to his aunt and Kori's father as he ushered Kori toward where the former police chief was standing.

Chapter 17

Brodie could sense his partner's uneasiness as he pulled his car up in her driveway. He was aware of the fact that Kori's mind had been elsewhere throughout the entire drive to her house.

Turning off his engine, he remained where he was as he looked at her, "Are you going to be all right?" he asked, concerned.

Her answer was automatic. "Yeah, sure. I'm fine," she replied almost too cheerfully. And then, as she began to open the passenger door, she stopped. She could sense that Brodie could see right through her. Maybe she could stand to talk to someone for a while.

"Would you like to come in for a drink or some coffee or anything?" she asked.

Kori was aware of how awkward that had to sound, but the words were already out of her mouth and she couldn't exactly take them back.

It wasn't hard for Brodie to read between the lines. Kori didn't want to be alone right now, at least not yet.

"Sure," he replied. "The 'or something' sounds interesting." With that, he opened the door on his side and got out of the car.

Kori waited until she had unlocked her front door and then walked in before suddenly turning toward her partner and asking, "What you said before…about your aunt," she clarified.

"Yes?" he prodded, closing the door behind him and flipping the lock for her.

Kori took a breath. Because he was related to the woman, this was *not* as easy as she would have thought. But this was about her father, so she pushed ahead. "She is a nice person, right?"

Brodie smiled. Temporarily, he made himself comfortable on the sofa.

Appearing to think her question over seriously, he told Kori, "Well, there's been talk about nominating her for sainthood."

Annoyance flashed in Kori's eyes. "I'm serious, Cavanaugh," she insisted.

"I'm doing my best to set your mind at ease. And to make you understand that, much as I'd like to, I can't give you a hundred percent guarantee that no one will be hurt here—this does go two ways," he reminded her. "But if your question is whether or not Aunt Maeve is a fair-minded, decent person, then my answer is an unequivocal 'yes, she is.'" He could see by the expression on Kori's face that what he had just said still didn't put her mind at ease. "Don't worry, Kori. It'll be all right."

Brodie's reassurances notwithstanding, Kori was still worried, and she couldn't help it. She didn't want her father being hurt. She should have spent more time with him, she thought, feeling guilty. Then maybe he wouldn't have gone looking for companionship.

Kori absently poured pitch-black coffee into a cup and brought it over to her partner, handing the cup to him. "Can I have that in writing?" she asked as she sat down next to him on the sofa.

"I can cross my heart," he told her loftily, then saw the error in saying that to her. "But then, if anything goes wrong, you'll probably want to cut it out."

He could create quite an image, Kori thought with a laugh. "So, in other words, you're saying I don't get to have any fun?"

Brodie placed the cup she had handed him on the coffee table, his eyes never leaving her face; a face that seemed to fascinate him more each time he looked at it.

"Maybe we can find some other kind of fun for you to have," he suggested in a light tone.

There it was again, Kori thought. That electricity, those sparks that insisted on shooting all through her, making her vividly aware of the attraction that had been steadily growing between them. Growing significantly larger and more intense every time they shared a kiss.

Her breath had caught in her throat, trapped there by the look in his eyes. "What did you have in mind?" she heard herself asking.

Every fiber in her being was screaming for her to "run for the hills" and yet, for some unknown reason, she stayed exactly where she was.

She didn't move.

It was as if she was just frozen in place, suspended in time and waiting for something—although part of her didn't have a clue what that "something" was.

Kori was only vaguely aware that she was holding on to her own half-filled cup of coffee as if it were some sort of a life preserver. But when he gently removed it from her hand, she just let it go without so much as a single protest or any effort to continue holding the cup. Brodie seemed to want it gone, so it was gone.

He set her coffee aside, placing it next to his own cup on the coffee table. He never took his eyes away from her face.

With the coffee cups safely out of the way, Brodie was free to focus his attention entirely on her.

"This," he whispered, answering her question from a thousand years ago.

And before she could ask what "this" referred to, Kori knew. Knew in her soul because Brodie had brought his lips down to hers and, just like that, had effectively managed to erase her questions even while causing an entire slew of brand-new ones to spring up in their wake.

Kori knew this was dangerous, kissing Brodie here like this in her home without a single thing she could possibly use to distract him from taking things to another higher, much hotter, level.

A level where she would wind up doing the exact same thing she worried that her father was doing.

And even so, as Brodie's delicious mouth found hers, creating havoc, Kori could just *feel* that this was something her soul had been waiting for.

For *more* than an eternity.

As Brodie continued kissing her, the kiss built in intensity, drawing her further and further into a heated area from which there was no retreat.

She felt herself surrendering before she was even remotely conscious of the process.

His hands were everywhere, worshipfully caressing her, stoking her inner fire. But even so, his fingers didn't delve beneath her clothing. Instead, his hands only made her desire for him utterly insatiable.

She wanted him.

Desperately.

It made Kori want to rip her clothes off just to feel his touch on her bare skin.

Ever mindful of the fact that her father could just come in at any moment and effectively extinguish this growing blaze with his very presence, Kori suddenly rose to her feet.

Never drawing her mouth from his, with small, measured steps, she began to guide Brodie toward the stairs.

Bracketing her shoulders with his hands, Brodie dragged his lips from hers and looked at her quizzically. "Not that this shadow dancing isn't really turning me on, but am I missing the bigger picture here?"

She hadn't a clue what he was talking about. "Bigger picture?"

"Yes." The smile on his lips encompassed his eyes as well. "Are you trying not to hurt my feelings, but are really attempting to get away?" he questioned. "Because I have to admit, this technique? This is all new to me."

Kori caught herself laughing at the bemused expression on his face.

"You know," she whispered, "for a detective, you can be awfully dense. I'm trying to get you to come to my room before my father gets home and we have to stop before he turns the hose on us."

"Can't have that," he agreed. "Where is your room?"

She didn't answer. Instead, she pointed upward just before she returned to her first method of getting her point across. She laced her arms enticingly around his neck.

Brodie paused at the base of the stairs to kiss her again, putting his entire heart and soul into it before pulling his head back and saying, "In the interest of safety, as romantic as the notion might be, kissing while making our way up the stairs is really taking unnecessary chances. Besides, we can get there much faster if our lips aren't sealed together."

With that, he grabbed her hand and raced up the stairs.

Delighted, Kori could only laugh as she raced the rest of the way just ahead of him, pulling on his hand as if that would urge him on even faster. They reached the top of the stairs in a blink of an eye, and then she was drawing him into her bedroom.

She pushed her door closed and Brodie took his cue. There was no more hesitation, no more waiting, no more delays. Clothes were tugged free, meeting the floor one after the other until there was no longer anything in the way, no longer anything to form any sort of a barrier between them.

His hands felt hot on her body, all but leaving a sizzling imprint as he glided them over every inch of her, caressing, possessing and slowly setting the groundwork of what was to come.

Somewhere along the line, although she wasn't quite clear exactly when, they wound up tumbling onto her bed. Body parts wound up around one another in a very warm, palpitating tangle of yearning flesh that forged an eagerness for fulfillment.

His body created a hot imprint against hers, which in turn excited her even more. The feel of it sent her to heights she hadn't even dreamed were possible.

Growing anticipation continued to throb demandingly through every part of her, making her suddenly want him with an intensity that shook her down to her very core. More than that, it frightened her because, outside of the night she had fervently prayed for her father to live, she had never experienced something of this magnitude and intensity before.

Kori felt as if she were literally on fire.

Brodie could feel the change in her immediately. Could feel her reaction to him, her desire to take this to a level that previously hadn't been there.

A level he could honestly say he had never experienced before.

"Oh baby," he breathed, his words blending into her hair. "Slow down before we both burn up."

But Kori didn't slow down.

If anything, she sped up and all he could do was try his very best to keep up with her, thinking that, any second now, they would both wind up being burned to a crisp.

But that was all right, he couldn't help thinking, because if that happened, it would be one hell of a way to go. Men went their whole lives without coming close to experiencing anything even remotely as soul-jarring as what he was feeling with Kori right at this moment.

Each intense kiss, every worshipful caress, had just brought him closer to the final moment of exquisite passion just before the all-encompassing explosion and release undulated through his body.

Brodie held back as long as he could, then, after having feasted on her exquisite body and at the same time, having experienced as much ecstasy as a human being possibly could without imploding, Brodie laced his fingers through hers. He held her hands above her head and then, his eyes on hers, making her feel like the center of his universe, Brodie united their bodies and slipped himself into hers.

He heard Kori's sharp intake of breath. The very sound just excited him even more. He saw her eyes widen and then fill with an emotion he wasn't altogether sure he recognized, but even so, it spoke to him.

Responding to a melody he felt rather certain only he heard, Brodie began to move, at first slowly then faster and faster still. When she began to respond in kind, he realized the same melody must have taken possession of her as well.

From then on, they moved as one being with one purpose: to climb the summit before them together until they could finally get to the very top of it.

Hearts pounding in unison, they kept moving higher and higher until they could achieve that final exhilarating thrill.

And then it happened.

The explosion came, ricocheting and vibrating through them at the exact same moment, raining an exquisite shower of mind-blowing ecstasy over them as they clung to one another, lips and souls sealed for what felt like all eternity.

Or, at the very least, for that moment.

Kori held on to him tightly, not wanting to let go because, if she did, she was certain the feeling would end.

But even now it was receding, swirling off into the mist.

She tightened her arms even more, refusing to surrender to the theft that was threatening this incredible new place she had just found.

She loathed giving it up.

"Who *are* you?" she heard Brodie whisper against her ear.

Kori shifted her head just a little, just enough to look at him.

"I was just going to ask you the same thing," she told Brodie, her voice coming out so softly, it was practically nonexistent. And then she smiled at him. "Maybe we're hallucinating," she said. "Because I've never felt anything quite like this before," she confessed. "So it must be a hallucination."

"Must be," he echoed, nodding his head. "Unless it's real."

The smile that encompassed his face drew her in, making her want him all over again.

"Well," Brodie murmured, slipping his fingers through her hair, "there's one way to find out."

She could feel the smile building within her. "And what's that?"

"We could test it out," he proposed, kissing her with each word he uttered.

She turned into Brodie, the close proximity of her nude body teasing his. "It does sound like a plan," she agreed. Her smile grew. "Well, I'm game."

"Oh, you definitely are that," he agreed, his body beginning to heat again, making demands on him. Slipping his arm beneath her shoulders, his lips marked a brand-new trail along her face, her lips and her throat.

Kori could feel that wild, whirlwind ride starting all over again.

But this time, even though the demands on their bodies were pronounced, they took it slower, savoring every step, enjoying one another now that they both knew what to expect.

And because there was more patience involved, the rewards were even more gratifying than they had been the first time around.

The explosion more intense.

When they finished, falling back against the pillows and taking refuge in each other's arms, they listened to their hearts beating in harmony.

Who would have even thought that that sound could turn out to be so very reassuring? Kori thought. For the next few moments or so, she allowed herself to revel in this and to allow herself to be vulnerable without trying to put up any barriers to protect herself.

Chapter 18

The warm glow created with last night's lovemaking, and that had wound up enveloping her, all but receded in the light of day. It left Kori suddenly bracing herself for what she felt might come in its wake—something a great deal less than the heart-stopping happiness she had experienced in Brodie's arms.

Reality might very well be a cold splash of water.

Would he think, now that they had made love, that he could tell her what to do? Or worse, would he suddenly behave like someone who had made a mistake and was worried he would have to face the consequences of that behavior, consequences he had no intentions of dealing with?

Would he think that their night together entitled him to be the one who was in charge now?

She had no answers, only questions.

Concerns whirled through her head.

Nowhere in *any* of those scenarios was there room for a live-and-let-live attitude. So when Brodie continued to act as if they were on the same footing as before, and that they were becoming friends, respectful of each other's experience and opinions, not only was she stunned, she thought it was a trick on his part.

But all that would come later. First, she had to deal with the "morning after."

Kori hadn't meant to fall asleep. The plan—all along—was for her to hustle Brodie out of the house before her father came home. Unfortunately, the rosy contentment that had taken hold after they'd made love for a second time brought with it a peacefulness that had her contentedly falling asleep in Brodie's arms—and remaining that way until after dawn.

Kori's eyes flew open nearly six hours after they had both fallen asleep. This time when her heart began pounding madly in her chest, it was because of all the consequences and resulting problems that having Brodie here in her bedroom like this created should her father walk in on them. Never mind that she was a grown woman who could do as she chose. What she didn't choose was to flaunt that in her father's face.

The only way out, as far as Kori could see, was for *both* of them to get dressed and slip out of the house as soon as possible, leaving under the guise of getting back to working the case. If they could dress quickly and make their way downstairs, they might be able to leave without waking up her father.

Kori couldn't shake the feeling that they were on borrowed time.

"Wake up," she hissed at Brodie, bending over so that her mouth was close to his ear. At the same time, she covered *his* mouth with her hand in case Brodie yelped at being summarily woken this way.

Instantly awake, Brodie stared at her in utter confusion when he opened his eyes.

Forcibly removing her hand from his face, he asked her, "What's going on?"

Unless there was a burglar in the house, there was no reason for her to attempt to keep him silent this way. On the slim, outside chance that he had actually guessed the reason for this dramatic enactment, Brodie obligingly kept his voice very low.

"I want to leave without waking my father," Kori told Brodie in what amounted to a whisper that was barely audible.

"Okay," Brodie replied gamely in the same sort of whisper.

"Now," she stated emphatically.

Throwing off the covers, she hurried into jeans and a sweatshirt. When she glanced over her shoulder, she saw that Brodie hadn't moved a muscle. Instead, he was watching her dress and was obviously enjoying what he saw.

"*Now*, Cavanaugh," she ordered in a low growl.

So they were back to Cavanaugh again, were they? He was going to have to make her see that they were way past that at this point, he thought with a smile as he complied with her order and started to get dressed.

"Ready," he announced, spreading his hands to facilitate her view.

Kori stopped getting her things together, looked in his direction and frowned slightly, although it wasn't because of anything she saw. Her thoughts were at odds with one another. She would love to crawl back into bed with Brodie, but that wasn't possible. For all the reasons that had just gone through her brain. In lieu, Kori wanted to put this scenario behind her and slip out of the house, even though she felt cheated because she would have much rather stayed in bed and relived some of last night's highlights with the man who had helped her create them.

Slowly.

"Okay, let's go," she said once he was dressed. "When we pass my father's room downstairs, please be extra quiet."

"I guess bursting into song is out of the question," he quipped.

The fact that he didn't know which was her father's room was a point Brodie decided not to raise. He figured that would occur to her soon enough.

They quietly made their way down the stairs, then cautiously moved in the direction of the front door.

Kori's sharp intake of breath as she came to a stop before an open door alerted Brodie that something was most definitely wrong. Kori was staring into a bedroom. A masculine bedroom, from the looks of the decor.

Kori's next words, mumbled under her breath and strictly to herself, confirmed his suspicions. She appeared genuinely worried, not to mention upset.

"He never came home."

The *he*, Brodie assumed, referred to her father. "What makes you think your father didn't come home?" he asked.

"Because his bed's made," she answered sharply, walking into the room.

"Maybe he made his bed after he got up," Brodie suggested.

Kori glared at her partner, uttering a dismissive noise. "My father's a wonderful man, but he has *never* made a bed in his whole life," she told Brodie. Distressed, she could only come to one conclusion. "He didn't come home last night."

Brodie gave her a look that had "calm down" written all over it, although he did refrain from using the phrase.

"Kori, your father's a big boy. He deserves a night out once in a while and, from the way you're reacting, I take it that the man never goes out. Ever."

Her face clouded over. "That's not the point," Kori insisted.

"Then what is the point?" he asked her patiently, waiting to see what she would come up with.

"I didn't want him thinking less of me for casually sleeping with someone and it obviously doesn't bother him if I think that about him." She quietly closed and locked the front door behind her.

He didn't see why anyone had to think less of anyone for going with their feelings, but he knew that raising that point was just asking for trouble. It would undoubtedly sink him further into this pool of quicksand that was forming, so he decided the best thing was to gloss over it.

"Chalk it up to a life lesson and just move on," he advised. "We've got bigger things to focus on. Or have you decided to give up on our current case?"

Kori glared at him. "I hate it when you're right."

"I'll try to be wrong once in a while," Brodie told her, then couldn't resist adding with a grin, "But it won't be easy."

Kori made a guttural sound and just continued walking toward his car.

They wound up driving to the precinct in Kori's car because as Brodie went to open up his vehicle, Kori put her foot down.

"I am not going to the precinct in a tank. If you want to drive over there together, it's going to have to be in my car," she informed him.

Brodie spread his hands genially. "Fine by me."

They drove in silence for exactly two minutes before, unable to keep her concern to herself, she glanced in Brodie's direction and asked, "Do you think he's okay?"

Brodie congratulated himself on not laughing at her question. He sensed that, to her, her concern about her father was very real.

"I'm sure he is, Kori. Unlike a black widow spider, Aunt Maeve does not eat whoever she, um…spends the night with," Brodie said tactfully. Keeping a straight face as he said this was definitely *not* easy since he was biting the inside of his cheek to keep from laughing out loud.

"I'm not worried about that," she informed her partner, annoyed. "I'm worried about my father being hurt."

Brodie looked at her profile for a long moment. He decided to answer her seriously and stop teasing. "Well, we all risk that if we let our guard down and get close to someone."

Was he warning her about himself? Kori wondered. No, she couldn't let herself go there, she insisted. She already had enough going on without worrying about Brodie's feelings about her—or lack thereof.

"Why don't we stop for breakfast before we go in?" Brodie suddenly suggested out of the blue.

Food was just about the last thing on her mind. "You could eat?" she queried, her voice filled with marvel.

Brodie laughed in response. She had to be kidding. "I could always eat, Kori."

She had already gotten too personal last night. It was time to retreat, to rebuild barriers before something went very wrong and she wound up paying for dropping her guard.

"I liked it better when you called me Kennedy," she told him tersely.

"And I liked it better when you called me Brodie," he

countered. His eyes washed over her. "Guess we can't always get what we like."

Suddenly, Kori found herself wanting to put him in his place, to raise her voice and yell at Brodie, or maybe just punch him. But as she tried to summon the proper amount of indignant anger, all she could manage was to relive last night as images flashed through her mind, warming her all over again.

Annoyed with herself, Kori deliberately shut her mind to any extraneous thoughts and instead just focused on Brodie's last request. Breakfast. At least that was safe.

"Do you want to go anywhere in particular?" she asked him.

The moment the words were out of her mouth, Kori realized her mistake. She had wanted to look like the one in charge.

"Never mind, I'll pick," she announced, negating any selection Brodie might have been about to suggest.

"Fine with me," he told her with a broad smile.

She got the feeling that he could see right through her.

Kori sighed. She had to stop looking at him, stop letting that smile of his get to her. She was a decorated detective for heaven's sake and she had a case that needed her entire attention, not just a piece of it.

If nothing else, she was being totally unprofessional.

"Mind if we get that breakfast to go?" she asked.

She was extending a courtesy to him by asking. The fact was she had already made up her mind that whatever order they got would be "to go." She had no intentions of sitting across from him at any fast-food restaurant, giving him another chance to totally wear her down with those liquid green eyes of his that were already wreaking havoc on her entire being.

"I was just going to suggest that," Brodie told her cheerfully, managing to catch her off guard again.

So Kori could only nod her agreement. "I guess great minds do think alike," she told him with a touch of sarcasm.

But Brodie seemed to be entirely serious as he answered, "I guess they do at that."

It wasn't until breakfast had been ordered and secured and they were driving to the precinct that Kori finally dug deep and apologized. It was, she told herself, the right thing to do.

"I'm sorry, Cavanaugh, I didn't mean to bite your head off back there."

"No harm done. My head's still where it's supposed to be, firmly attached," he told her, amused as he let her off the hook.

Stubbornly, Kori ignored his absolution. Instead she forged on with her apology. If she didn't do it now, she never would—and then she would feel guilty about it.

"It's just that I've never been in this situation before, going to work with the man I slept with the day after I slept with him." She avoided his eyes and stared straight at the road.

"No explanations necessary," Brodie told her, doing his best to make her see that he didn't need her to make any apologies. His skin was tougher than that. Much tougher.

She lost her patience. "Damn it, Cavanaugh, it *is* necessary. I don't know what I'm doing here. It's all new for me," she said, referring to the situation she found herself in.

He nodded, but it was a noncommittal nod and she didn't know what to make of it. And then he said, "Even God had to have a first day. It's okay, Kori, really," he stressed. "If it helps, I've never been in this kind of situation before, either. And for the record," he added softly, "I'd really like to see where this goes."

Kori smiled at the man in her passenger seat, oddly comforted by what he had just said even though there was a part of her that upbraided her for being a fool and baring her soul this way to him.

"And," Brodie continued, "I'm going to call my aunt sometime later today to see if she had a nice time at Uncle Andrew's gathering—and afterward," he added significantly after a pause.

She saw the smile in his eyes and tried not to be drawn in by it. "Won't she get angry at you? You know, for prying?"

"Maybe," Brodie allowed. There was no defensiveness in his voice. "But we're Cavanaughs. It's what we do. We pry into each other's lives because we care about one another," he explained. "It might not be spoken, but it is still understood."

She stared at him in disbelief. "And your aunt really won't get angry with you for prying?" Kori asked in surprise.

"Perhaps," Brodie replied, not certain about Maeve's initial reaction, "but ultimately, one way or the other, I'll get to the bottom of this and find out what happened—and then you'll have your answer."

From where she stood, that sounded like a pretty big favor. The man was going out on a limb. "You'd do that for me?"

"Yes, but having you affected is a by-product of this whole exchange. I'm doing it for Aunt Maeve because I do care about her and want her to be happy. I also want to know if she's not happy for some reason. I owe the woman a lot."

"You're a good man, Brodie Cavanaugh," Kori told him with feeling.

"That's what I've been trying to tell you," he dead-panned. And then he said, "Drive faster, partner."

She didn't understand. "Why?"

"Because the smell of breakfast is really tempting me and I can feel my stomach growling—big-time."

"Are you sure that's your stomach?" she asked, slanting a glance in his direction.

"We could pull over somewhere, act like a couple of teenagers in one of their parents' cars and find out," Brodie suggested.

Kori shook her head as she kept driving. "You are totally incorrigible."

"That all depends on what the situation is," he answered. "But right now, if you don't drive any faster, I can't be responsible for what I do."

"To—?"

"That breakfast you're packing back there," he said, indicating the back seat.

"Driving faster," she announced, stepping on the gas in order to arrive at their destination a little quicker than she intended.

His laughter was ringing in her ears.

Chapter 19

Brodie was on his way with Kori to talk to one of the hospital employees they hadn't interviewed yet when his phone rang. He stepped to the side and turned away to answer his phone.

Kori watched Brodie's body language and sensed that this call wasn't about the case, but she couldn't begin to guess what it actually was about. She knew she was going to have to wait until he got off his cell phone.

Waiting patiently had never been her strong suit.

She held her breath as he ended the call and tucked his phone back into his pocket. "Well, you'll be happy to know Aunt Maeve just called back," he told her. He'd placed at call to her earlier and had been forced to leave a message on her voice mail.

"And?" Kori prodded, wanting to jump in and squeeze the words right out of his throat. He was drawing this out and taking much too long.

"And," Brodie told her with a smile, "she thinks that your father is an extremely nice man."

Kori wanted to scream. This wasn't telling her what she asked.

"I could have told her that," Kori said, and then looked at him as questions insisted on popping up in her head. "'Extremely nice man' as in 'I wouldn't mind having Bill Kennedy sit next to me in a movie theater' or as in 'where has he been all my life' nice?" Kori questioned.

"I got the impression it was the latter," Brodie answered.

Kori's smile worked its way up to her eyes with lightning speed. "Really?" she asked, making no effort to hide how pleased that made her.

"Really," Brodie confirmed. "Which brings me to my own question. Just how nice is your father?" he asked, doing a theme and variation of the question she had asked him yesterday at the gathering.

"The kind of nice they rarely make anymore," Kori told her partner.

"Good, because Aunt Maeve could use a little personal happiness in her life. It's always been about her kids, or her job, or the family. It's never about her."

Kori heard what he wasn't saying, "And you think it's about time that it was."

"Absolutely," Brodie said with enthusiasm. "Isn't that how you feel about your father?" he asked.

"Yes," she answered. Then a thought hit her. "Well, what do you know. We seem to be in agreement here."

"Twice in two days," he joked with a laugh as they got to the car. "Who would have thought?"

"And by twice, you mean…" She let her voice trail off because she wasn't about to take *anything* for granted.

There was a sparkle in his eyes when they met hers.

"I do," he confirmed. The way he said it left no doubt in her mind as to his meaning. He wanted to make sure that both her father and his aunt enjoyed one another.

A lightness filled Kori, making her feel happy, much the way she had last night when Brodie had made her feel like she was walking on air and collecting rainbows for the very first time in her life.

It was way past time to get back to the case and focus her attention on it. Maybe, given her fresh frame of mind, something new would jump out at her, something that they had missed earlier.

"Did Valri make any headway with the tapes we had her look at?" she asked Brodie after they had gone to see yet another hospital employee. Valri had called him right after that.

Brodie shook his head. The news wasn't good. "She didn't and the tech she had looking over her shoulder didn't find anything new, either," he told her.

"Think it might be worth another go-round?" she asked him. "Maybe if we took another look at the tapes…"

"Honestly, no," he answered flatly. "If Valri couldn't find anything, and her assistant couldn't find anything, then there's just nothing to be found in those tapes."

Kori reexamined his reply and her face brightened slightly. "Which in turn does tell us something."

He looked at her, trying to understand where she was going with this. "How do you figure?"

"Don't you see? Whoever took that baby had to know where all the surveillance cameras' blind spots were located. Which, in turn, just confirms what we already suspected because of the removed tracking device—that this had to be an inside job." Her voice grew in excitement. "That means that the baby was taken not by some random visitor coming to see someone in the hospital. That little girl was taken by someone who works at the hospital," she concluded, barely containing herself.

Brodie rolled over what she had just said in his mind, nodding. "You're right. And it just reinforces what we already thought when that so-called eyewitness we talked to told us she had found that ankle bracelet the hospital uses as a tracking device. I mean, it was cut off. Someone had to know how to do that without setting it off."

Kori leaned back in her chair for a moment, closing her eyes and centering herself. She knew what they needed to do.

Brodie saw the expression on her face. "You all right?" he asked, concerned.

She opened her eyes again and nodded. "I'm fine," she answered wearily. "But I think, focusing on this idea that it was an inside job, we're going to have to re-interrogate all the hospital employees who were on the maternity floor any time before the baby went missing that day." It was a daunting idea, but there was no way around it. "It's the only way we can effectively follow up on all this."

Brodie nodded, looking none too happy about the matter. "I know."

They went back to the beginning.

Since this was the second time around for a lot of the people—in some cases, this actually made three times—those whom Kori, Brodie and the rest of the task force spoke to were not exactly ecstatic to retrace old ground that was now painfully familiar. Not to mention, for the most part, fruitless.

One of the nurses, Jenny Wong, one of the first people they had originally questioned, seemed almost hostile to be going over all this with the police again.

"Look, it's not that I don't sympathize with that mother—although I hear she was going to give that baby up for adoption anyway," the less-than-patient nurse told Brodie. Rather than sit for the interview, she'd insisted on continuing to work while he asked her questions. "But I've already told you everything that I know," she pointed out. It was obvious that the woman was barely containing her irritation. This was a stain on the hospital's reputation and she just wanted to move past it and have it buried.

"If you wouldn't mind, could you tell me again?" Brodie prodded the sharp-featured woman with an encouraging smile.

The nurse rolled her eyes and made an impatient noise, then began to answer in an almost robot-like tone of voice.

"I came in that morning, checked Rose Williams's vitals, then did the same with the baby after first reading the baby's name on her small wrist bracelet to make sure that the right baby was with the right mother." When Brodie looked at her with an unspoken question in his eyes, the nurse said, "Yes, I know it *does* happen. But I did my part. End of story, end of contact," she concluded. "I didn't see either one of them until the alarm went out that a baby—that baby—had been stolen. Nothing has changed since the last time I went over this with one of your other people. Now, if you don't mind, I have a lot of work to get back to," she said. With that, she turned away from Brodie.

"One more question." Brodie spoke up. The nurse reluctantly turned back to face him, waiting. "Would you know how to remove the tracking device from the baby's ankle?" Brodie asked.

"I would—but I wouldn't," she insisted. "Removing those tracking devices is not part of my job description. Why are you asking me that?" she challenged.

"Because whoever took the baby had to know how to remove the ankle bracelet without setting it off," he told the woman.

"Well, all I can tell you was that it wasn't me," the nurse replied flatly. "Now, can I go?"

Kori, who had listened to the entire exchange—feeling that she needed to back Brodie up with this hostile nurse—nodded and gestured toward the doorway, silently indicating that she was free to leave...for now.

"Thank you," the woman said icily, her words directed at both of them just before she left the area.

Kori sighed. "You know, this is starting to feel like we're stuck in a rerun of *Groundhog Day*," Kori complained. "We're just going around and around the same territory, leaving tread marks and getting absolutely nowhere."

"Until it winds up all falling into place for us and makes sense," Brodie insisted.

"You're right. We're missing something. Something that's staring us in the face," Kori said. "I just don't know what it is." Frustration all but vibrated in her voice.

"It's a process," Brodie told her, then promised, "Don't worry about it, Kori. We're going to get there—as long as we don't give up."

"Will we?" She found herself battling a hopelessness that threatened to swallow her whole. "In time?" she questioned. "I'm not as sure as you are."

"One foot in front of the other, Kori," Brodie counseled. "We still have a lot of people left to re-interview."

Kori looked at the list she had complied earlier. There were still a great many names on it. "Back to *Groundhog Day*," she said with a sigh.

The re-interviews continued through the day. Most of the people they wanted to talk to weren't at the hospital

and weren't very happy about having to talk to police detectives on their day off and on their home territory. But,
to a person, because there was an infant's life at stake,
they did all cooperate.

Some, however, were a bit less willing than others.

By the end of the day, Kori, Brodie and their teams
were still no wiser about the abducted child's whereabouts
than they had been to begin with.

"Second verse, same as the first." Kori mocked herself,
feeling like they were just spinning their wheels, going
nowhere. "What are we missing, people? What am I not
seeing?" she asked of no one in particular.

"Maybe it'll be clearer in the morning," Spenser suggested hopefully.

"And maybe it'll be that much further away," Kori
said, crushed. "Sorry," she apologized. "You're right.
We should go home. Shower. Change our clothes. Maybe
that'll help."

"Hug our kids," Valente, the only team member with
children, said, adding his two cents to Kori's plan for the
evening. "We get this guy—or woman—" he added "—and
I get dibs on stringing him up from the nearest flagpole."

The man was only putting into words what they were
all secretly thinking, Brodie thought. "I'll help, but first
let's find this baby," he said to the rest of the force, getting his things together in order to leave the squad room
for the night.

Concurring murmurs greeted his statement as the other
members of the task force filed out of the room.

Brodie found an excuse to hang back until only Kori
and he were left in the room. "Want to get something to
eat?"

She laughed, shaking her head. "I keep forgetting that

you're a growing boy," she told him. "No. But I'll watch you eat."

"What fun is that?" he asked.

"I wasn't thinking about fun." She sighed, deciding to level with Brodie. "I was thinking that I don't want to be alone just yet. My dad took your aunt out dancing." Even as she said it, she laughed, shaking her head. "Dancing. The man I was so terrified would never walk again is out dancing tonight." A smile took over her features. "You were right, Brodie. Your aunt *is* very good for my father."

Brodie was very pleased at the conclusion she had reached. "I told you. She's got a big heart even if, at times, she comes on a little gruff."

Kori slipped a couple of files into her purse. She thought she heard something in his voice. "You sound as if you have a special connection with her."

Brodie smiled and nodded. "I do."

When he didn't say anything to follow that up, she asked, "Are you going to tell me about it, or am I going to have to use my detective skills?"

"Save your skills," he told her. "It's no big secret. I'll tell you." The truth of it was, he didn't like revisiting that period of his life even though it was years ago. "My mother died when I was still pretty young. Despite everything she was involved with and that put so many demands on her time, Aunt Maeve stepped in to help my father cope with his loss. Moreover, she made sure she was there for every one of us—my brothers and sisters and me," he specified.

"She did what she could so that none of us would feel as if we'd been abandoned by the woman we all loved and needed. But that's just the way that Aunt Maeve is," he told Kori simply. "I'd go to hell and back on my knees for that woman."

"Wow," she said, impressed. "That is some endorsement."

"I don't know about an endorsement, but I wouldn't say it if I didn't mean it. Now, about that dinner…" Brodie's voice trailed off as he looked at her for any input.

Kori shrugged. She had no preferences. "It can be whatever you want. My only request is that we get it to go."

Brodie smiled. "You read my mind. And since we're on the subject, can it 'go' to my place?"

Her eyes met his. For a moment, she thought it was just wishful thinking on her part, that she was just reading into what he was saying, but a second later, she realized that he *was* inviting her over to his place.

Much as she wanted to go, she didn't want to push it. "Are you sure about this?" she asked Brodie.

"Very sure," he replied. "But if you'd rather not, I understand completely."

"You might," she laughed dryly, "but I wouldn't."

His eyebrows drew together. "I'm not sure that I follow," he admitted.

"That's okay. I promise I'll walk slow so that you don't lose me." And then she smiled. It was a weak smile, but it was definitely there.

They wound up getting Chinese food—several entrées when she had trouble making up her mind which one she wanted.

"Makes for a good breakfast the following day," he told her, paying the tab and then carrying the oversize large bag out of the restaurant and to her car.

"I've never had leftover Chinese food for breakfast," Kori admitted.

"Then you are definitely in for a treat," Brodie promised, getting into the car on the passenger side. The bag filled with their order was put on the floor.

"There's just one problem," she told him as she turned her key in the ignition.

Brodie braced himself. "And that is?" he asked.

She looked at him. "If we're going to your place, I have no idea where you live."

He laughed then, as relief slid through his body. He'd been prepared for almost anything, including her changing her mind, or even doing a complete about-face. Having her confess to this minuscule lack of knowledge was exceedingly gratifying.

"Fortunately, that's a very easy problem to solve," he told her, and then proceeded to give Kori directions to his home.

Chapter 20

As she followed the directions Brodie gave her, Kori wasn't really sure just what to expect. She had to admit that she'd thought Brodie probably lived in some sort of an apartment complex. Since no building in Aurora was over fifty years old, she'd just assumed that Brodie lived in one of the newer residential complexes.

She hadn't thought that he actually owned his own home.

So when the address he gave her turned out to belong to a single-story, newly painted structure, it was a surprise. There was even more of a surprise, she discovered, when Brodie unlocked the door.

Leading the way, he walked into the kitchen and put the bag of Chinese food on the counter. Since Kori hadn't said a word from the time he had opened the door, Brodie turned around to look at her.

"You're not saying anything. Is there something wrong?" he asked.

"No, nothing's wrong," she replied, the words coming out slowly as she continued taking everything in. "I was just admiring the place." She looked back at her partner. Everything looked absolutely immaculate. "I guess your maid must have just been here today."

"My 'maid'?" he echoed, bewildered as he unpacked the bag he had brought in. Where had she ever gotten the idea that he had a maid? "I don't mean to correct you, but I don't have a maid."

"Sure you do," she argued, looking around again. The place looked so clean, Kori thought, she could have eaten right off the floor. "Everything looks so incredibly neat and clean. You *have* to have a maid."

So that was it, he thought with a smile.

Brodie finished emptying the bag, then absently folded it before lining up the containers next to one another. "Well, contrary to popular belief, not all men are slobs," he told her. "My mother, bless her, always insisted that we clean up after ourselves. After she got sick, we kids just kept on doing it. We were trying to please her." Brodie smiled more to himself than at Kori. "Skylar and I thought that if we were very, very good, then our mother would eventually get well and stay with us.

"When she didn't," he continued, "we were pretty devastated, certain that we had somehow failed in some way."

Kori ached for him then, ached for the wounded boy he had been all those years ago.

"Oh, Brodie, I'm so sorry," she whispered.

"Don't be. At least I got into the habit of being neat. See, there's something positive to be gleaned out of every bad situation." He prudently changed the subject. "Now, I know you said you weren't hungry…" he told her as he opened the last of the containers. The alluring aromas all melded together, wafting up so that they could both smell them. "But you have to admit that this does smell tempting."

She smiled. He was right. And now that she thought about it, maybe she *was* hungry. "All right, you win. I'll have a little bit," she relented.

"Atta girl." He took two plates out of the overhead cabinet and brought them over to the containers. "I knew I could get you to change your mind and eat something."

"Well, don't get your hopes up. Hitting dead end after dead end has just about killed any appetite that I might have had budding up inside me. I keep thinking about what I'm going to say to that poor young mother if it turns out that we can't find her baby. It's tying my stomach up in knots," she admitted, helping herself to a serving of Beef Lo Mein.

"The chief of D's gave me some really good advice when I originally started working in the homicide department."

He held up a fork as well as the chopsticks that had been packed with the containers, giving her a choice.

Since she wasn't all that handy using chopsticks, Kori reached for the fork.

"I was afraid of falling flat on my face," he continued, "you know, not living up to the Cavanaugh name and all that. Let's face it, there's a lot to live up to—not that anyone would rub my nose in it but, well, I didn't want to be remembered as the guy who failed. Anyway, the chief saw that I was struggling with some issues," Brodie said, taking a serving of Moo Goo Gai Pan. "He took me aside and said, 'Don't think about failing. Just focus on succeeding. The rest will take care of itself.'"

"Nice sentiment," she said as she took an egg roll out and put it on her plate. "But—"

"No. No 'buts,'" Brodie told her, then underscored the

one word that he wanted her to take away from all this.
"Succeeding."

"Succeeding," she echoed, indulging him.

Brodie flashed her a smile. Somehow it managed to
hearten her even though she felt as if she were initially
just going through the motions and playing along with
what he said.

Kori didn't go home that night, but then she knew that
she wouldn't.

Things between them progressed naturally and although she had promised herself that there wouldn't be a
repeat performance of the night before, she neither needed
it nor wanted it. But deep down inside, she knew that was
a lie, created just to protect herself from being hurt if Brodie pulled away from her.

But he didn't pull away.

The complete opposite was true.

Brodie acted as if this was a very natural part of the
evening. That after a full day of working together and
then spending the evening together, they would wind up
retreating to their own personal haven, have a little dinner and then find solace in each other's arms—not out of
habit but out of a strong, mutual need to enjoy one another.

And, to Kori's delight, this time was even better than
the night before.

When the lovemaking was over and Brodie fell back,
stunned, pleased and completely spent, he drew Kori to
him and cradled her against him in his arms.

"You know," he said once his breathing began to level
off and return to normal, "we're going to have to come
up with a safe word."

"'A safe word'?" she repeated, unaware that her breath

was tickling his bare skin as she spoke. "Why would we need a safe word?"

He smiled at her. "Because you get my blood rushing so much and so hard, I just might wind up expiring while I'm making love with you."

She slanted a dubious look at Brodie. "Okay, now you're just making fun of me by exaggerating."

Brodie tightened his arms around her. "I would never make fun of you," he told her. He took one of her hands and placed it on his chest, putting his own hand over it to emphasize his point. "And does that feel as if I'm exaggerating?"

She could feel his heart all but pounding against her palm. He might be teasing her, but oh lord, she wanted him again. Those walls that she had kept around herself had been up for so long, she had just assumed that they were a fixture.

A permanent one. Which was why she was so stunned by the feelings madly racing through her like a herd of wild horses that had been set free.

Kori took a deep breath and then said, "Elephant."

Brodie blinked. He raised his head slightly and looked at her, somewhat bewildered.

"What's that now?" he asked, thinking he had to have heard wrong.

"I've decided that's my safe word," Kori explained and then said it again. "Elephant."

"Elephant," he repeated and then he laughed, delighted. "You know, you really are a very unique woman, Kori Kennedy," he told her as he leaned in and pressed his lips against hers.

A quick, fleeting kiss bloomed into something more, something longer and far more stirring, within a matter of seconds.

Before either one of them knew what was happening, they were making love with one another again and soaring above the clouds, creating an indescribable rapture that wrapped itself tightly around them. Within moments, they had managed to seal themselves away from the rest of the world as they slipped into paradise.

The insistent buzzing of the cell phone she had placed on his nightstand muscled its way into the dream she was having. The very nice dream that had brought indescribable contentment with it and managed to evaporate without leaving any sort of form or even a hint as to its content once it receded from her brain.

Brodie had trained himself to be a light sleeper years ago and was already awake.

"Your phone's ringing," he told her, rubbing his face and erasing the last trace of sleep from his system.

Kori sat up. "It must be the precinct," she noted, reaching for her phone.

"I don't think so," he told her. "My phone's not ringing." And he was fairly certain that if it was something that had to do with their current case, both of their phones would be ringing.

Kori pulled the phone to her as she leaned against the headboard. Blinking, she focused on the screen. If it wasn't the station, she was fairly certain that it was probably her father, wondering if she was at the station, pulling an all-nighter again.

But it wasn't her father, either. The number on her screen was one she didn't recognize.

Well, she was up now. She might as well answer.

"This is Detective Kennedy," she said. "Who am I speaking to?"

There was a small sob on the other end in response and

then she heard a very shaky, timid voice begin to speak. "Detective Kennedy? This is Rose."

Kori braced herself. The young woman was going to ask her if there had been any progress made in locating her baby. She didn't know how to give Rose a negative response and still find a way to keep her hopes up. This was the part of her job she really hated.

Unconsciously, she leaned into Brodie, as if that would somehow help her through this.

Her voice sounded almost hollow to her own ears as she said, "Hello, Rose."

She could feel Brodie become instantly alert.

He took her hand, wrapping his fingers around it and silently giving her his support as he listened to her end of the conversation.

"I wish I had something positive to tell you, Rose, but right now—"

Rose cut in, breaking into what Kori was about to say. She sounded almost breathless as she told the detective, "I got a letter."

Kori quickly assimilated the information, straightening. "From the kidnapper?"

"I think so," she answered uncertainly, then followed that with a slightly more positive, "Yes."

Kori was kicking off the covers and looking for her clothes. "You still have the letter?" she questioned. She wasn't about to take anything for granted.

"Yes, it's right here. Someone slipped an envelope under my door. I found it this morning and put it on the table. I called you as soon as I read it." Rose was talking faster and faster.

"Good," Kori told her. "Don't do anything with it. Leave it exactly where you put it."

"Okay," she answered. "Are you going to want to see it?"

"Oh yes," she said with emphasis. This could be the break they'd been waiting for. "Are you calling from home?"

"Yes." For good measure, Rose rattled off her address, stumbling at first, as if she was having trouble remembering the exact order the numbers came in.

Kori nodded out of habit, committing the address to memory. "Don't go anywhere," she told Rose. "We'll be right there."

Getting all the way out of bed, Kori terminated the call.

Brodie had put two and two together, but now that Kori was off the phone, he wanted to be sure, so he asked, "Was that what it sounded like?" as he began to throw on his clothes.

Kori was gathering up her own clothing. All the items were scattered all over the floor. In the middle of all this, Kori found it ironic that she had been so amazed at how neat Brodie kept everything while she was the one whose clothes were tossed all over the place as if they had weathered a really severe blizzard of disarray.

"Rose just called that someone had pushed an envelope under her door. She didn't go into any detail, but I'm assuming that there was a message inside about the baby," Kori said as she pulled on her sweater.

"Asking for a ransom?" Brodie prompted as he put on his shoes.

The call had been scarce on details. Kori hadn't pressed because she'd wanted to read the note herself.

"Rose didn't say anything one way or another," she admitted. "Although probably. Why else would the kidnapper drop off a note? "She just sounded very confused when I talked to her. But she seemed pretty certain that whatever that note said, it was written by the kidnapper."

Brodie nodded, taking everything in. "We'll need to notify Crime Scene Investigation. They're going to have to bag the letter and put it into evidence so they can dust it for prints."

They were both thinking the same thing, Kori thought as she heard Brodie say, "With any luck, our kidnapper just made his or her first mistake and we'll find some telltale fingerprints on the envelope or note to trace. Maybe we can finally put a face to this monster who made off with Rose's baby."

Kori slowed down and swung by the kitchen. She knew that Brodie had set the timer on his coffee maker to go off first thing in the morning—which was now.

The scent of brewing coffee greeted her even before she walked in. Breathing it in, Kori turned to look at Brodie, who was right behind her. "You know, you are definitely going to make someone a very thoughtful, wonderful wife," she teased as she poured coffee into two vacuum mugs, then put on the lids, tightening them so that there wouldn't be any mishaps when they took the mugs with them.

Brodie, meanwhile, was packing two containers of the leftover Chinese food to serve as their breakfast on the run.

"Don't go getting ahead of yourself," Kori warned him.

"I'm going to need more before I can take you up on that," Brodie told her, not sure just what she was referring to. He'd learned very quickly that he needed to reserve any sort of judgment until Kori clarified things for him.

"About this note that the kidnapper probably left. It might not have any fingerprints on it, or anything else we can use. This person has been clever so far, avoiding the surveillance cameras, getting rid of the baby's tracking device. Most likely the note was handled when the kidnapper was wearing gloves."

"You know, your optimism can really be overwhelming at times," Brodie quipped.

She gave him a long-suffering look. "It's called being a realist."

"Whatever you say." The expression on his face told her that he wasn't buying the excuse she was giving him. "You know," he suggested, "why don't we reserve judgment like you said and deal with things as we come up against them?"

Kori nodded. There was no point in arguing about it. Besides, part of her was really hoping that Brodie was right.

"Works for me," she told him. "Did you happen to bring the rest of the egg rolls?" she asked him as they left his house.

"As a matter of fact, I did. I figured they would be easy enough to eat without needing to use a fork."

"You've thought of everything," she said, smiling and nodding her approval.

"I usually do," he answered. "Now let's go and find out if that so-called clever kidnapper slipped up and made his or her first mistake."

The fact that he was holding up crossed fingers didn't escape Kori. She figured that Brodie wasn't quite as certain about things as he pretended to be.

Chapter 21

"According to this address," Kori said as she drove herself and Brodie to Rose Williams's apartment, "if I'm reading this right, I think Rose lives on the ground floor of one of the oldest apartment complexes in Aurora. These days real-estate agents like to refer to them as 'apartment homes.' I guess that's to make them sound more appealing to the renter."

"Apartment homes, huh?" Brodie scoffed. "Whatever happened to truth in advertising?"

She pulled up in what she mused served as a guest parking area. "There is no such thing," Kori said, turning off her engine.

Stepping out, she looked around the grounds. "Not homey, but definitely better than some of the places I've seen." Getting her bearings, she pointed to her immediate left. "I think her 'apartment home' is right over there."

Taking a breath, Kori knocked on the ground-floor

apartment door. Less than a second later, they heard a timid voice ask, "Who is it?"

Kori looked at the man at her elbow. "That has to be Rose," she said just before she announced, "Detectives Cavanaugh and Kennedy, Rose. You called me to say you received a note under your door."

She was barely finished saying that before the door flew open. "Please, come in," Rose cried, beckoning them into what was a very small studio apartment.

Kori was surprised at how crammed it appeared.

Given the limited space, the first thing that struck Kori as she walked in was that there was a crib set up next to what had to be a fold-out sofa. For the moment, it took her attention away from how very pale Rose looked.

Kori stared at the crib. A crib meant that the new mother had been expecting to come home with an infant, not give it up for adoption. Had she somehow gotten her facts mixed up?

She looked quizzically toward Brodie. The discrepancy had apparently struck him as well, because Brodie was the one who brought the crib up to Rose.

He turned to face her as he closed the front door. "Maybe I got things mixed up, but I thought you said that when you went into the hospital, you were going to put the baby up for adoption."

The reminder brought a wave of fresh tears to a person who had obviously been crying off and on since the baby had vanished.

Rose struggled to collect herself. "I was," she answered Brodie, a labored sigh escaping her lips as she wiped her eyes.

Wadding her handkerchief up, she looked from one detective to the other, searching for words that she could use to make these two people understand what she was going through. And then she blurted out what had been haunting her since the moment she'd realized that the baby had been taken.

As she spoke, a fresh wave of tears began to choke her. "I didn't deserve this little being and now I'm being punished for it."

"Explain something to me," Kori requested, trying to get the distraught mother back on track.

"Anything," Rose breathed, looking at the two detectives as if they performed miracles on a regular basis.

"If you were going to give the baby up for adoption, then why did you buy a crib?" Kori asked. She could see by Brodie's expression that the same question had crossed his mind.

"I didn't," Rose protested.

"Then how did this crib get here?" Brodie asked.

She stared at the piece of furniture as if she hadn't noticed it until just now. "Oh, that. My grandmother bought it." Guilt colored her cheeks. "She didn't know I was going to give the baby up," Rose confessed. "She's a very religious person and I couldn't bring myself to tell her until just before I was being wheeled into the delivery room. She was really upset when I told her. I guess none of that matters now."

Brodie could see that Rose was slipping away from them. They needed her to be as clear-headed as they could get her so that she was able to answer their questions.

"When you called earlier, Detective Kennedy said you mentioned that you thought the kidnapper had slipped an envelope under your door," he prodded, trying to get her talking about the incident.

Rose seemed to come to then, as if she had one last purpose to see to before she totally withdrew from reality. Nodding, the young woman pointed toward the small table where she took her meals.

"The letter is over there. I opened it," she said, as if they couldn't already guess as much. "But I put it back in the envelope and away as soon as you told me to."

"We're going to need your fingerprints," Kori told her as she pulled on a pair of rubber gloves before picking up the letter.

"Why?" Rose asked, confusion and fear in her voice.

"So we can rule you out when we look for other fingerprints on the envelope or letter," Brodie explained to the quivering young woman.

It struck Kori that her partner sounded as if he was speaking to a frightened child rather than to a grown woman. The man had patience, she'd give him that.

The next moment, she turned her attention to the envelope and, more importantly, to what was inside it. Gingerly opening the flap, she very carefully withdrew the folded paper. Even before she unfolded the paper, she could see that they weren't going to need someone to analyze the writing.

Because there *was* no writing to analyze.

"Brodie, come look at this," she called to him.

Brodie excused himself from the frail young woman who, despite the words of encouragement he was giving her, seemed to be slowly falling to pieces.

"What's up?"

The words were no sooner out of his mouth than he saw why Kori had called him over. He emitted a low whistle, careful to keep the sound under his breath.

"Looks like our kidnapper is a fan of grade B murder mysteries," he commented.

Kori frowned. "Maybe, but the person is being clever, not to mention extremely patient," she commented, staring at the note. The sheet of paper contained a missive completely comprised of letters of all sizes, shapes and colors that had been cut out of at least half a dozen different publications so that none could be used for even the slightest identification purposes.

The resulting note read:

Do not worry about your baby. She is safe and being well cared for.

"This must have taken *hours* to cut out and paste," Brodie commented, reading the message over Kori's shoulder.

Kori glanced back at her partner. "You sound as if you almost admire the kidnapper's patience."

Instead of answering, Brodie raised his eyes and looked in the baby's mother's direction. Speaking up, he asked her, "Do you have any idea why the kidnapper would send this to you?"

Rose appeared just as bewildered by the note. "I don't know. I think I might have told someone that I just wanted to be sure that my daughter wasn't being harmed. That I wouldn't worry so much about her if I just knew that she was okay."

"Who, Rose?" Kori pressed. "Who did you say this to? Think, honey."

"I don't know," Rose cried, covering her face with her hands as she began to sob. "I don't know. Maybe it was the orderly who was there. Maybe it was someone else. Everything is all jumbled up." Totally distraught, she looked from one detective to the other. "I don't remember."

Letting out a long breath that sounded suspiciously like a shudder, Rose made another halfhearted attempt to try to collect herself. "Maybe this is a sign," she said to the two people in the room.

"A sign?" Kori questioned.

Rose nodded again, her head bobbing up and down like a cork being tossed around in a flood. "Maybe I shouldn't be trying to find her to get her back. She's probably better off without me. Whoever has her says that they're taking care of her. They could probably do a better job of it than I can," she told them, her lower lip quivering again.

Kori stared at the young woman. This was something she hadn't expected. She decided that the only way to snap Rose out of her mental quagmire was to get tough with her. "And maybe the kidnapper is going to lose his or her patience with your baby the first big crying jag she has and sell her to the first couple who comes along—after knocking her around a little.

"No, Rose, he or she had absolutely no right to steal your baby. This person needs to be brought in and made accountable for what they've done, and your baby needs to be in the care of a law-abiding person or persons. If you feel you can't give her the kind of care that she needs, then you're free to make that sort of decision. But you don't just give those rights away to someone who stole the baby in the first place."

Kori was struggling to hold on to her anger and keep it from erupting. This case was hard enough to deal with without having to try to make the baby's mother not just mentally abandon the baby in a fit of so-called selflessness.

She saw Brodie looking at her. Taking a deep breath, Kori regained control over herself.

Brodie called the CSI team so they could dust for any and all prints that might have been on the envelope as well as the paper with all the cut-out letters.

The team arrived in what felt like record time. When

they came, the head of the investigative unit, Sean Cavanaugh, was with them.

Nodding at his nephew and Kori, the tall, rugged man who looked like a younger version of Brian Cavanaugh, his older brother, modestly explained his presence to Kori. "When I heard it was that kidnapping case you two caught, I thought that maybe I could help."

Kori was grateful for the man's interest as well as his offer. "We'll take anything that you might be able to give," she told him in all sincerity.

Sean looked over to the area where his two assistants were dusting for prints. "Caleb, why don't you dust around the bottom half of the outside door?" he suggested. When Kori gave him a quizzical look, he explained his thinking. "You said that someone slipped that envelope under the door."

"They did," Brodie confirmed.

"Maybe they braced themselves against the door when they knelt down. You never know. The knees are the first to go," he commented. "At least it's worth a shot," Sean said.

"I would have never thought of that," Kori admitted. She had been completely focused on the actual note to the exclusion of every other possibility. "I guess that's why you're the head of the crime scene investigations," she told Sean with a grateful smile.

Sean laughed. "I'm already on your side, Kori. There's no need to try to flatter me," he assured her. He glanced in his nephew's direction. "Tell her, Brodie."

"I think she's already picked up on that, Uncle Sean," Brodie said. He winked at Kori. "She's quick that way."

"I just wanted you to know that I'm really grateful for any and all help," Kori explained. "And I know you're busy," she added.

Sean inclined his head. "Message received," he told Kori. "I'll get back to doing my job. The sooner we dust everything for prints, the sooner we can get out of that poor girl's hair," he concluded, nodding toward the baby's mother.

Since the apartment was so small, there was hardly any place for Rose to go in order to be out of everyone's way, but she still tried. Sitting down by the window, she seemed to almost completely draw into herself as the CSI team did their work, dusting for prints and being as thorough about it as they could.

Kori's attention was drawn over to Rose. She seemed so sad and forlorn, Kori could almost feel her heart breaking for what she knew Rose had to be going through. Not only had the child she had just given birth to been taken from her in less than two days after the momentous event, now her very belief that she had a right to keep that child had somehow been stolen from her as well.

She and Brodie needed to get going, but there was no way she was going to leave Rose when the young mother was all but drowning in self-doubt and who knew what else.

Kori made up her mind and crossed to the young mother. Squatting down in front of Rose, she took the young mother's hands in hers.

The look in Rose's eyes was almost excruciatingly sad. "It's going to be all right, Rose. We're going to find your baby."

Rose's lower lip trembled. "You haven't yet."

There was no blame, no recrimination, in her voice. It was just a sad, simple statement of fact, one totally devoid of any hope.

"No, we haven't," Brodie agreed, coming up behind Kori and adding his voice to hers. "But that note from the kidnapper just might have given us the ammunition that we need."

Rose turned her body toward Brodie. "How?" she asked.

"Well, first of all, the kidnapper just assured you that your baby is not just still alive, but is also being cared for. And second, this kidnapper went out of his way to put your fears to rest. He took a chance on being caught just to get that note to you. That has to mean something to you."

Following Brodie's example, Kori picked up where her partner had left off.

"It means that he doesn't want to cause you any undue anguish about your baby's welfare. The kidnapper undoubtedly took the baby because he or she must have found out that you were going to give the baby up for adoption—"

"But I changed my mind," Rose pointed out.

"Yes, you did," Brodie continued patiently, "but maybe the kidnapper didn't know that and hadn't heard that you'd changed your mind at the time when he took your daughter."

"But you said he put together that note for me to put my mind at ease," she cried.

"We don't have all the answers yet," Brodie told her, feeling it safer to back off for now. "This is still a work in progress. There might very well be an explanation for all of this that'll come out in the end," he said, doing what he could to keep her hopes up about the matter without getting too involved in any sort of further explanation.

Still sitting beneath the window, Rose wrapped her arms around her knees and hugging them to her, she began rocking in her seat. It was obvious that she was trying to generate some sort of self-comfort from the action.

Kori rose to her feet. She lightly placed one hand on

Rose's shoulder, briefly making contact. "We're going to go now," she told Rose. "If you think of anything else—or if you just want someone to talk to—you do have my card."

Rose nodded. "Thank you." She sniffed. "I usually just talk to my grandmother, but she hasn't been around for the last few days."

"Oh?" Brodie said, pausing before they left the apartment. "Is that unusual for your grandmother?"

"Yeah, even though things have been strange between us, she's come to see me when she had time off. But these days, work does keep her pretty busy. I guess she just got busier this last week. It doesn't seem fair because I could really use her now."

She couldn't quite put her finger on it, but alarms went off in Kori's head. She exchanged looks with Brodie. "What does your grandmother do?" Brodie asked Rose. She had a gut feeling they were on the brink of something.

"She's a nurse," the young mother replied. As an afterthought, Rose told the two detectives in her apartment, "My grandmother works at Aurora General Hospital."

Chapter 22

Kori could feel her breath suddenly standing still in her chest and her eyes darted toward Brodie's. This was just *way* too much of a coincidence. She could see that the same thing was obviously going through his mind as well.

Still, she knew that neither one of them wanted to get ahead of themselves. "Would you happen to have a picture of your grandmother anywhere?" Kori asked in as calm a voice as she could manage.

"Yes," Rose answered. Standing, the young woman crossed to the tiny, pseudo fireplace that was up against the opposite wall. The fireplace with its small mantel was decorative rather than functional. "The picture's right…" Her words disappeared, much the way the photograph she wanted to show them had. Rose looked bewildered. "Well, I thought it was right here," she told Kori and her partner. She looked at the empty mantel, then sheepishly back to the detectives. "I guess I must have put that picture someplace else."

The only problem was, Brodie thought, there was hardly any place else where she could have misplaced the photograph.

"Will this do?" Rose asked, taking her wallet out of her purse. Searching through several credit cards, she found a faded photograph of herself when she was around ten or eleven years old. She was standing next to a stern older woman. "That's my grandmother," she told them.

Kori looked at the photograph. It wasn't all that clear, but at least it was something.

"How about a name?" Brodie asked their victim. "Can you tell us your grandmother's name?" Armed with that information, he felt it would be simple enough to obtain everything else they needed. That would include a better, updated, picture that they could circulate and finally get somewhere, provided Rose's grandmother had been the one who'd kidnapped her own granddaughter's baby.

It sounded unbelievable, but he was also aware that stranger things had happened.

"Sure," Rose answered him. "But why would you want that? I mean, she's my grandmother."

Kori quickly came to the rescue. "She might be able to shed some light on all of this, see it from a different perspective," she explained. "Right now, we're still pretty much groping around in the dark. Your grandmother might have seen something we missed."

"It's usually the smallest clue that winds up breaking a case," Brodie told her, adding his voice to the explanation.

Rose appeared almost solemn as she nodded her head. "Her name is Peggy McGuire, although she might be going by Peggy Larabee. Grandma was married a couple of times," Rose explained, "and I don't know which name she likes to use better."

That sounded like a very strange explanation, Kori thought, but then this was turning into a very strange case. The woman they were looking to interrogate might have a number of aliases. This whole thing wasn't as simple as it had initially seemed.

"What's your grandmother's maiden name, Rose?" Kori asked, thinking that might be as good a place as any to start.

"Her maiden name?" Rose repeated, looking somewhat confused.

Brodie rephrased the question. It occurred to Kori that he was showing a great deal more patience with their victim than she was feeling. "What was her name before she was married to her first husband?"

"That happened before I was born," Rose replied in all innocence.

"We understand that," Brodie continued. "But a bright young woman like yourself could still know that piece of information," he told her, his voice still sounding very calm and soothing.

Kori could only marvel at how controlled he was. Either Rose was so stressed by what had happened that she was incapable of thinking clearly, or she had never been able to do so in the first place.

Meanwhile, Rose had paused, thinking. And then her face lit up as the answer to Brodie's question came to her. "It was Williams," she announced proudly. "Same as mine."

Brodie nodded, appearing pleased. "Good. Very good, Rose. We're going to go now, but we'll let you know the minute we find anything out."

Rose nodded her head, taking what he said to heart

and appearing to clutch it to her chest with both hands. "Okay," she replied. And then, looking over her shoulder at the CSI team still in her studio apartment, she asked Brodie, "What about them? Are they going to go with you, too?"

"They'll be going as soon as they finish up. It shouldn't be much longer," he told her.

Rather than look happy to be gaining back her tiny apartment, Rose just grew sadder. "Oh," she cried. "Then I'll be alone."

Kori glanced at the young mother. Rose's words felt like a sharp arrow going right into her heart. Though they needed to get back to doing their job, she couldn't bear just to leave her like this.

"Rose, is there anyone we can call for you?" Kori asked and then came up with several possibilities. "A friend, a relative, someone you worked with?"

But the young woman shook her head in response to every suggestion.

"I don't have any friends," Rose told her. "And except for my grandmother, there is nobody else. My mother doesn't want to have anything to do with me after I got pregnant. And that goes for my cousin, too."

"How about the baby's father?" Brodie asked, knowing that was probably a very long shot.

His last question was met with a negative response as well. Rose shook her head and said, "He took off the minute I told him about the baby and said I wasn't getting rid of it—not in the way he wanted, anyway," Rose clarified. She flushed. "I guess part of me always knew I was going to keep it. Except now I can't because I don't know where she is."

"Hang in there," Kori urged.

She turned toward Brodie to have him back her up, but

her partner was talking to someone on his phone. Anticipation surged through Kori. She hadn't heard the cell ring, but there was noise in the tiny studio apartment. Maybe they had finally gotten a lead.

"Skylar," she heard Brodie say into his phone, "you mentioned you were taking a few days off."

He was talking to his sister. Why? What did his sister have to do with anything? It didn't make sense in the middle of all this. And then, as Kori listened, it all began to fall into place.

"Listen," Brodie was saying, "I need a big favor. Yes, I know I already owe you big-time, but this is important," he stressed, apparently cutting into what his sister was saying. "I need you to come and spend a couple of hours with that young mother I was telling you about. Right, the one whose baby was stolen from the hospital," he confirmed. "You will?" As Kori watched, that smile she had become so partial to took over his features. "Knew I could count on you, Sky. Let me give you the address. It's a ground-floor apartment. Oh, and Uncle Sean's here with his team, collecting evidence."

As she listened, Kori could tell from Brodie's body language that his sister was asking him more questions.

"Right, I'll let him tell you all about that when you get here," he said, winding the discussion up. "You're one in a million, Sky. Okay, one in two million," he amended with a laugh. "See you in a few minutes."

With that, he ended the call. Crossing back toward Rose, Brodie told the young woman, "You won't have to be alone when we leave, Rose. My sister said that she can come by and keep you company. She's a police officer, too," he added.

Rose watched him, wide-eyed. "There certainly are a lot of cops in your family." She sighed, somewhat awed.

There was a trace of wistfulness in the young woman's voice that was impossible to miss. "It must be nice to have a big family."

Kori caught herself thinking the exact same thing.

"Yes, it is," Brodie readily agreed with a wide smile as he made eye contact with his uncle who had come in a couple of minutes ago. The latter had apparently overheard at least part of what was going on and he nodded his approval.

Making his way over to Sean, Brodie told the man, "Skylar is coming over to keep Rose company. She's already on her way and should be here pretty soon. Would you mind staying until then?" he asked. He nodded toward the distraught victim in the center of all this, his meaning clear.

Attuned to the situation, Sean didn't need convincing. He readily agreed. "Sure. It should take us a while to pack up all this evidence anyway. We'll just pack slower," he told Brodie with a wink.

Brodie's smile deepened. "Knew I could count on you," he told his uncle.

Sean spread his hands wide. "Hey, as your father would have said, 'what's family for?'"

"'Would have' said?" Kori repeated. It was obviously a question, aimed at her partner.

But it was Sean who answered her, looking to spare his nephew. "His father, Donal, passed eighteen months ago."

Open mouth, insert foot. She hadn't known, she thought, distressed that she'd asked so clumsily.

She looked at Brodie. It was the first time she had seen a totally impassive expression on his face.

"I'm so sorry," she said. Since she had broached it so awkwardly, she might as well know the rest of it. "In the line of duty?" she asked, assuming that, given the nature of the Cavanaughs, it probably had to be.

"In bed," Brodie corrected.

Kori's face turned crimson as she thought she had made another awkward blunder.

Seeing her color change, Brodie was quick to set her straight. "From the flu that turned into pneumonia. My father's biggest failing was that he took care of everyone but himself," he told Kori.

Kori debated how to rescue this situation when she heard the doorbell. *Saved by the bell*, she couldn't help thinking.

Brodie was instantly alert. "That should be Skylar," he said, anticipating his sister's arrival.

Going to the door and opening it, he smiled. "You're a life saver," he told his sister.

The tall, slender, pretty blonde dressed in jeans and a comfortable work shirt walked in, instantly owning the space she crossed.

"Remember that when I need your kidney," Skylar told her older brother. Bright green eyes swept over the small room. She nodded a greeting at her uncle's assistants and smiled at Sean. "Hi. Brodie told me that you were working the crime scene."

"That I am. Hopefully," he told Brodie and Kori, "I'll have something you can use soon." He closed the case he had been packing up with a decisive movement of his hands. "All right, see you at the old homestead," he said, addressing his niece and nephew. And then he nodded at Kori. "Detective Kennedy, nice to be working with you."

Sean glanced toward the large-eyed young woman whose home they had just dusted for prints. With all the evidence that had been collected ready to go, he crossed over to Rose. He couldn't help thinking that she looked like a lost waif.

"Don't worry, Ms. Williams. If anyone can find your baby, it's these two," he promised her, nodding at Kori and Brodie.

Rose raised her eyes toward him, gratitude shining there. To her, Sean Cavanaugh was a father figure— something she hadn't had in her life—and he was kind enough to take the time to reassure her. Rose was more than happy to believe what he'd said to her. She hung on to it like a lifeline.

Brodie was quick to take care of the introductions. "Rose, this is the sister I told you about, Officer Skylar Cavanaugh."

Skylar smiled at the petite woman. "You can just call me Skylar," she told Rose, putting out her hand to shake it. She readily dispensed with formalities since she could see how very vulnerable the young woman obviously was.

It didn't take much to envision her being afraid of her own shadow.

"Rose," the stolen baby's mother said, grasping Skylar's hand like a lifeline and shaking it.

Brodie made eye contact with his sister and mouthed, *Thank you*, before taking the lead and telling Rose that they were leaving now.

"But if you need anything at all, just tell Skylar," he advised. "She knows how to reach me."

The relieved smile he saw on Rose's face told him he had made the right call, asking his sister to come and keep Rose company for the next few hours.

Saying goodbye to his uncle and the rest of the CSI team, Brodie left with Kori.

* * *

"You realize that this doesn't solve the problem," Kori told him as they walked to where she had parked their vehicle. "It just puts a temporary Band-Aid on it."

"Maybe by the time the Band-Aid has to be ripped off, between all of us, we will have located that stolen infant," Brodie replied.

Kori looked at him. Just when she thought she knew what he was capable of, he surprised her by rising to an even higher level. "That was really nice of your sister to agree to stay with Rose—and really nice of you to think of calling her."

"What can I say?" Brodie quipped. "We're terrific people."

Kori got into the car. She wasn't about to let him shrug it off this time.

"Yes, you are," she agreed. "I'm really beginning to see that."

"Just beginning?" he asked with a laugh.

Opening up like this wasn't a joke to her. "Hey, this is hard for me."

Brodie turned his head in her direction and his eyes were smiling at her. He could tell she was being sincere. "And you're doing very well. Although I have to say that there is room for improvement," he deadpanned. "But don't worry, I'll go slow."

She thought of their night together as well as the night before. The very memory made her skin tingle even though they were in the middle of a very serious case. "Oh lord, I hope not," she murmured under her breath.

The very wide smile on his face told Kori that he had overheard her.

Kori forced herself to focus her attention on what was

important at the moment, not in the way Brodie made her feel.

"C'mon, let's find out if we can put a face to Nurse Peggy-McGuire-Larabee-Williams-or-Something-or-Other," she urged.

Kori hadn't thought it was going to be easy and she was right. When they went to the head of the hospital's HR department, they found the director had taken some time off. But his assistant was there. They asked the woman to help them with their search. The older woman listened to them, then shook her head.

"We don't have a nurse named Peggy here," she informed them.

For a moment, that seemed to take the wind out of their sails. Had this supposed grandmother lied to Rose about what she did for a living? Had Rose gotten confused about where the woman worked for some reason? The young woman was definitely not the brightest bulb in the array, but they both doubted that Rose would knowingly mislead them.

"Wait a minute," Kori said suddenly. "Isn't Peggy short for something?" she asked. She looked at Brodie for his input.

"Don't look at me," he told her. "Nicknames aren't exactly my field of expertise."

His response had Kori turning toward the assistant personnel director. Her own mind had temporarily gone blank. "Help us out here, Mrs. Fielding. Isn't 'Peggy' short for something?"

The woman thought for a moment, then brightened. "Yes, it's short for Margaret."

"Okay, do you currently have a nurse named Margaret or Maggie working here?" she asked. "This nurse would be at least sixty—probably older," Kori amended. "And she could have any one of three last names. Williams, McGuire, Larabee or maybe even something else." Kori looked at the assistant director hopefully.

The woman laughed, shaking her head. "You don't make this easy, do you?"

"Trust us, this is a lot easier than it was an hour ago," Brodie assured the older woman.

The woman merely rolled her eyes. Moving her chair in, she began surveying current personnel files on the computer records.

Chapter 23

"Ah, here we are," Angela Fielding declared, seeming very pleased with herself. She had finally managed to locate the person whose file she had been trying to find for the last half hour. "Margaret McGuire," she proudly announced. Scanning a few of the lines in the file, she looked up at Brodie. "We don't have this woman working on the maternity floor. Margaret McGuire is one of our pediatric nurses." The assistant personnel director kept reading. "But she's been with the hospital for over ten years. Before that, she worked over at Madison General. She did work on the maternity floor there. Anything else?" she asked brightly, looking from one detective to the other.

"Yes," Kori interrupted. "Do you have her picture on file?"

"Of course we have her picture on file," the woman replied shortly. And then she apparently heard her own tone of voice and attempted to temper it, sounding more amicable. "These days, everyone's got a picture every-where," she added with a weary sigh. "This is probably the most photo-obsessed generation in history."

"May we see it?" Brodie gently prodded.

The small, dowdy woman seemed to come around. "Sure. Help yourself," Mrs. Fielding said, turning her monitor around so they could both get a better view of the photo of Margaret McGuire that was on file.

It wasn't a very flattering photograph and if Kori were to make a guess, she would have said that it had probably been taken on the day the nurse had been hired, which meant that the photograph was dated. But there definitely enough of a resemblance to a nurse they had seen on one of the surveillance cameras on the day the infant had been kidnapped.

Kori studied the photograph. Maybe it was her imagi-nation, but the woman in the photograph definitely looked a lot like an older version of Rose. That *couldn't* have been a coincidence, Kori thought.

"And that's Margaret McGuire?" Brodie asked the as-sistant personnel director just to be completely sure.

"That's what her employee record shows," Mrs. Field-ing answered.

"Could we speak to her?" Kori requested. She couldn't help feeling that they were on to something. Or maybe it was just wishful thinking on her part. But either way, they needed to speak to the woman.

"Let me see," the assistant personnel director said, holding up her index finger as she pulled up the latest in-formation that had been entered into the file and scanned it slowly. Coming to the bottom of the page, she looked up and shook her freshly colored ginger head. "I'm afraid that's not possible right now," Mrs. Fielding told them.

"Why not? She's not in today?" Brodie prompted, thinking they would just seek the nurse out in her home.

"According to her file, she's not going to be in any day, at least not for the next month." Her eyes met Brodie's. "Nurse McGuire put in for a leave of absence from the hospital."

Kori had a bad feeling about this. "When?" she asked.

"As a matter of fact—" the assistant director went back to scanning the file for the answer "—she took it three days ago." The look on the woman's face was clearly sympathetic. "The poor thing, I think the turmoil at the hospital because of the kidnapping was just too much for her. According to her file…" Mrs. Fielding paused to read further in the file. "She's always been a very dependable, slow and steady worker. She didn't like her routine deviating from its normal path." She looked at the two people sitting before her. "I guess you could say she's a perfectionist. But her patients' parents loved her."

"Good to know," Kori mumbled. She really wasn't interested in how much her patients' parents loved her, she was only interested in her interaction with one patent in particular. "Do you have her current address and phone number on file?"

The woman looked as if she took that question as a personal insult. "Of course we have her current address and phone number on file. What sort of a hospital would we be if we didn't keep up on things like that?" she asked.

One that apparently could be easily fooled, Kori thought, but she kept that to herself. She also avoided Brodie's eyes, sensing that he might disapprove of the way she was handling this woman.

"Thank you for your help," she told the assistant personnel director as the woman handed them a printout of what she had just asked for. Kori was anxious to leave to see if they could find the woman in her home. "We'll get back to you if we need to," Kori promised.

She and Brodie left within a couple of moments.

Kori was all but pulsating with eagerness to see this nurse. "So, what do you think?" she asked Brodie the second they were out of Mrs. Fielding's office and had closed the door behind them.

"I think that we need to pay Nurse McGuire a visit," he told her. "Because unless Rose's grandmother has a twin or a doppelganger somewhere, that is most definitely Rose's grandmother in that file. The one she doesn't seem to be able to reach," he added significantly.

"This doesn't make any sense to me," Kori admitted as they got back to the car. "Why would the woman steal her own grandchild?"

"I'll be sure to ask her that once we find her," Brodie said. "But the important thing right now is that we do find her—*and* the baby."

They drove to the address that was listed in the nurse's personnel file. Though Aurora had the very unique distinction that none of its neighborhoods, no matter how old, were run-down, this was definitely one of the oldest residential areas in the city. It had been built before Aurora had even been incorporated.

Margaret McGuire's house was an older, single-story home. It appeared somewhat dated, but it still seemed far from falling apart. It looked as if it had been painted in the last decade and, while fading, had not yet begun to peel or flake.

"What do you think the odds are of finding Rose's grandmother here?" Kori asked.

Rather than parking right in front of Margaret McGuire's house and possibly alerting the woman that anyone was coming, Kori parked her vehicle in front of a house several doors down.

"Honestly?" Brodie asked as he got out of the car on his side. "Slim to none, but you never know. My guess is that for whatever reason, the woman is obviously not thinking clearly."

"I'm not so sure about that," Kori said, slowly scanning the immediate area around the grandmother's house. There was no sign of the woman's car, but it could very well be parked inside the garage. "To her way of thinking, this woman is probably sacrificing everything in order to save an innocent child."

"From what?" Brodie challenged. "From being adopted?"

Kori shrugged, trying to put herself in the older woman's place. "From being passed to someone else like an unwanted stray cat or dog."

That sounded rather extreme to him. "Well, here's hoping that she's not too far gone and we can still reason with her," Brodie said as they walked up to the house in question.

Approaching the door, Kori knocked on it. "Mrs. McGuire? This is the Aurora Police Department. Please open the door. We need to speak to you about your granddaughter."

Only silence met her request. After a couple of beats had passed, Brodie knocked on the door. His deep voice asked that she come to the door and open it.

Still nothing.

"Mrs. McGuire, please open up. We don't want to have to break down your door," Kori said, raising her voice as she tried again. "But we will if we have to."

"She's not home," a reedy, high-pitched voice behind them said.

Surprised, Kori and Brodie both turned around to see

a woman in her late sixties, possibly early seventies, with wispy, blond-colored hair framing her round face like a fluffy halo. She was standing on the sidewalk several feet away from the house in question.

Brodie addressed the neighbor first. "Do you know where Mrs. McGuire is?"

The woman, who obviously enjoyed knowing everything that was going on in the neighborhood, shook her head. "No. I saw her drive away on Thursday and, as far as I know, she hasn't been back since. I just thought she went on vacation, which is odd," the woman confided, "because Peggy *never* goes on vacation. I've lived here for fifteen years and in all that time, I've never seen Peggy do anything except go to work and come back. She's very dedicated that way," the woman told them as if she was imparting a major confidence. "I'm Edna Barrett, by the way," she said, introducing herself to them. Her sharp eyes shifted from Kori to Brodie. "Why are you looking for Peggy?"

So, the woman apparently did go by Peggy, Kori thought.

"We have some questions for her," Brodie answered the neighbor.

"Is it about the kidnapping?" the woman asked, clearly thinking that it most likely had to be.

"How do you know about the kidnapping?" Kori asked.

Had Rose's grandmother let something slip while she was talking to this woman? Or maybe she had even confided something to her. Kori felt her hope rising.

But that hope quickly evaporated when Edna looked at her as if her intelligence had been insulted. "Huh. Everybody with a TV knows there was a kidnapping. That poor little girl who was stolen from Aurora General," the woman said, shaking her head like a lamenting member of a Greek chorus. And then she sniffed. "Well, if you ask me, Peggy doesn't know anything about it. If she did, she would have definitely told me."

"So I take it that you two are close?" Brodie asked, leaving the end of his statement up in the air.

Edna sniffed again. "I live next door to her," the woman replied, as if her proximity was the answer to the question he had asked.

"So, what do you think?" Brodie asked after they had left the curious neighbor holding one of their cards in her hand and promising that she would call them the moment that she saw "Peggy" return home.

Kori laughed softly under her breath. "I think that if Nurse Peggy was close to this woman, that would have been the very first thing out of Neighbor Edna's mouth," she told her partner.

Brodie tended to agree as he nodded in response. "Yeah, I think you're right. She's not the type to keep that—or anything—to herself."

Kori got in behind the wheel, but she didn't start the car right away. Instead, she took out her phone and tapped in the phone number the personnel director had given them for the nurse.

She let the phone ring, counting each ring. When she had reached ten rings, she was about to terminate the call, but she abruptly stopped when she heard what she took to be the nurse's voice.

"Hi," a rather bright, cheerful voice said. "You've reached Peggy McGuire. I can't pick up right now, but leave your name and number and I promise I'll call the minute I'm free."

Kori saw her partner looking at her as she terminated the call, an obvious question in his eyes. "That was the nurse's voice mail. At least we know her phone is on," she said philosophically.

Brodie knew exactly what she had to be thinking. "That means that Valri can trace it for us and tell us where she is." They were all the way on the other side of Aurora, far from the police station. "How fast can you drive?"

He didn't really ask her that, Kori thought. "Just fasten your seat belt, Cavanaugh, and do your best to hold on."

Brodie grinned as he saluted her. "Yes, ma'am," he said.

Taking a breath, Kori put the siren on and stepped on the gas.

The twenty-five-minute trip took less than ten minutes.

"You weren't kidding when you said to hold on," Brodie told her as Kori brought their vehicle to a stop in the precinct parking lot. Pretending to look over his shoulder, he commented, "I think my breath is still trying to catch up." He unbuckled his seat belt. Part of him still felt as if they were driving. "Who taught you how to drive like that?"

"Sorry, I promised never to tell anyone his name," Kori deadpanned, pretending that someone had actually taught her how to make hairpin turns like that and drive like a racecar driver.

"Yeah, I can understand why," Brodie replied, opening the passenger door and getting out of the vehicle. Damn, his legs felt wobbly, he thought, taking a cautious step. "If I'd taught you how to drive like that, I wouldn't want it getting around, either." He looked down at his sides. "I think it's going to take a few minutes for my hands to unclench."

"I didn't know you had such a penchant for overstatement," she said as they made their way to the back stairs that led to the police station entrance.

"There's a lot of things about one another we still need to get to know," he replied.

Kori looked at him just as they entered the building. If she didn't know better, that sounded like a plan for their future.

The next second she told herself she was letting her imagination run away with her. There was no time for this. All that mattered was solving this case and, if the anticipation coursing through her veins was any indication, they were right on the brink of that. This feeling she was experiencing was coloring everything else right now, distributing hope where it had no absolute business being.

She could feel her heart pounding with every step she took as her hope kept multiplied. "Do you think that Valri can ping this phone for us and actually locate where Rose's grandmother took her baby?"

"Are you kidding?" Brodie asked her. "Hell, this is the kind of thing that Valri lives for. She can do it in her sleep while juggling building blocks with her free hand."

"While I admire and envy family loyalty, I really hope that your faith in your cousin isn't misplaced," she said to Brodie.

Brodie looked at her. It occurred to him that Kori had obviously not availed herself of his cousin's services on any sort of actual level, otherwise she would have already had her answer.

A smile played along his lips as they went to the elevator. "I won't tell Val you said that. As a rule, she's too sweet to carry grudges, but there is always a first time and I wouldn't want your kidnapping case be the first place it starts," he told her. "That doesn't mean that she won't do what she needs to do to help, but after the dust settles, you will have been relegated to the bottom on her list."

Kori hardly heard him as they rode down to the basement. She was trying her best not to get excited, but it was really hard not to. If all this went right, then they were just hours, possibly even less than that, away from recovering a baby that everyone believed had been stolen and whose fate could have wound up being a great deal worse than it now promised to be.

As she stood there next to Brodie in the elevator, she was hardly able to breathe.

"Hey, are you all right, Kori?" her partner asked, concerned, as he suddenly realized that the woman standing next to him wasn't breathing, or at least she wasn't breathing in any sort of normally accepted way.

"Just praying," she murmured as the doors closed and the elevator began to descend.

Brodie thought over her answer. "It couldn't hurt," he replied. And then Brodie took her hand and wrapped his fingers around it, giving it a squeeze. "But don't worry, it's going to be all right," he promised Kori. "I can just *feel* it," he added as the elevator doors opened and they got out.

They quickly made their way to the computer lab and Valri.

"I really hope you're right," she whispered. And then she thought of Rose. "It's time for this awful nightmare to finally be over for that poor girl." Kori raised her eyes to Brodie's. "Over in a *good* way," she emphasized with feeling.

She wasn't about to get an argument out of him, Brodie thought.

Chapter 24

Valri looked far from happy to see her cousin and his partner approaching her again. Anyone could see that they obviously were going to make yet another request. Drowning in work, she felt her patience slipping away at an incredible rate.

She frowned at the duo before either one of them could say a single word.

"You do realize that there's a system here, right?" she asked her cousin. "I'm sure you're familiar with it, Brodie. Every fast-food place in the state uses it. It's called 'waiting in line.' And all these people—some of whom, amazingly, you are related to," she said, waving her hand at the piles of paper on her desk, "are in line ahead of you."

"Valri, please…" Kori began.

But Brodie cut in, saying what he felt needed to be said to win Valri over. "This is the same case we were working earlier, Val. We think that the baby's great-grandmother stole her from the hospital," he told her, getting down to the crux of the matter. "The woman's a nurse and could have easily moved in and out of the rooms without raising any suspicions. Moreover, when we went to her house, she appears to have taken off. Nobody's seen her since she took a leave of absence from the hospital right *after* the baby was taken," he said, his voice growing progressively more intense.

Talking, Brodie drew closer and closer to his cousin. "We've got Margaret McGuire's cell phone number. We've tried calling, but all we get is her voice mail," he said, answering the question he sensed his cousin was about to ask. "That means that, for now, her cell is on, but that can change at any second. She could just shut it off at any time and then we won't be able to locate her. We've got a limited time frame here," he emphasized.

His eyes pinned Valri down, silently appealing to her humanity.

Valri sighed and put her hand out for the cell phone number. "You're lucky your partner's got puppy dog eyes," she told Brodie, nodding at Kori.

Amused by the description, Brodie laughed and glanced over toward Kori. "You're right," he agreed, his smile deepening. "Maybe I should start calling you Sparky."

"You do and I'll rip your tongue out," Kori told him with a complacent smile that was nowhere as easygoing as it appeared at first.

"Okay," he nodded. "Looks like 'Sparky' is out for the time being."

"Try forever," Kori replied.

Meanwhile, Valri's fingers were flying across the keyboard, typing the cell phone number Brodie had given her into the website that she had pulled up.

"All right," the lab tech declared as her fingers continued typing at an almost breathtaking speed. "I've managed to triangulate the phone's signal." She drew her words out as more screens came up. Valri hit a few more keys, which brought out a triumphant, "There!" from her lips.

"There?" Brodie questioned, waiting for more of an explanation from his cousin than just that single word.

"I've managed to narrow it down," she told them. "The signal's coming from the Airport Inn across the street from the Aurora County Airport on—"

"That's all right, Valri," Kori said, cutting Brodie's cousin off. "There's no need for us to take up any more of your time. I've lived in Aurora for a good part of my life," she told the lab tech. "I know where the airport is located, and so, I'm sure, does Brodie. MacArthur and Main," she said to prove her point, referring to the major cross streets right at that area. "Okay, let's go, Cavanaugh," Kori said, not bothering to hide her eagerness as she looked at Brodie.

Her partner grinned as he pretended to salute her. "Yes, ma'am."

Swamped though she was, Valri paused to grin at the departing detective next to her cousin. "I *knew* I liked you the first time I met you," she said just before she reimmersed herself in the files that were spread out all over her desk, still waiting for her attention. "Good luck," Valri called out, never raising her eyes from the file she pulled over and had initially been working on when her cousin and Kori walked in.

The airport and the motel that catered to the passengers who availed themselves of its facilities were located only a few miles from the police station.

Without impeding traffic to get in their way, they managed to reach their destination rather quickly. For once, the numerous traffic lights along the way cooperated, allowing them to experience practically an unencumbered trip to the motel.

"Not bad," Kori commented as she parked the car in a lot that was only partially filled.

He caught the surprised note in his partner's voice. "Did we catch you in a lie, Detective Kennedy? I thought you said you were familiar with the place," he reminded her.

"I'm familiar with the airport, not the motel," she told Brodie.

He smiled, his eyes all but shining. "I guess that makes us the perfect pair because I'm familiar with the motel."

Kori picked up on what he *wasn't* saying. "Have you been here before?"

Brodie's shrug was noncommittal. "A time or two."

"Oh?" The single word was probing, asking for more information.

Though he could have continued with this for a while longer, he decided to just tell her the truth. "I was undercover—and alone," he emphasized. "Nothing 'oh' about it."

She believed him. Heaven help her, but she believed him, Kori thought. He wasn't the player that she had initially thought he was. That was a role other, less secure people had assigned to him, most likely out of jealousy.

Kori gestured toward the front of the motel entrance. "I bow to your superior knowledge. Lead the way, Cavanaugh."

He grinned and winked at her as he proceeded in front of her. "I could get used to this."

Kori only had one word for him. "Don't."

Brodie opened the door to the motel registration office and held it for her.

When they walked in, the man behind the desk didn't notice them at first. He appeared to be completely engrossed in the game show he was watching on the small set tucked to the side of the reception desk.

Clearing his throat, Brodie rapped on the desk and spoke up to get the man's attention. "Hey, fella, we're going to need your help here."

Embarrassed at being caught, the man pulled back his shoulders and straightened his shirt. The latter was having some trouble fitting adequately over his expanded girth.

"Sorry. I guess I didn't hear you. Welcome to the Airport Inn," he said, greeting people who he took to be potential customers. "And how long will be you staying with us?" he asked as he flipped the motel's registration book around to face them.

Kori ignored the book. "That all depends on your answer, Mr....Clovis," she said, reading his name on the nameplate on the desk. "Have you seen this woman?" she asked him, holding up the photograph she had taken of Margaret—or Peggy—off the employment file with her phone.

"Why, yes. She checked into the motel three days ago. She had only one request—that I give her the room that was located the farthest from the motel entrance. She paid cash, which was a first for me," the reception clerk confided.

"What room is she in?" Brodie asked.

The clerk didn't have to look to know. "She checked into room twelve, but if you want to catch her, I'd hurry if I were you. She just paid her bill and is checking out of the room right now."

The man ended up saying the words to their backs as

Brodie and Kori turned on their heels and hurried out of the small office.

"Come again," he called after them, retreating to the game show he had been watching.

The words *so near and yet so far* echoed in Kori's head as she all but sprinted toward the room number the desk clerk had given them.

What if they had just missed the baby-snatching grandmother? If the woman wound up boarding a plane and flying to another location, they might never be able to find Rose's baby.

She *really* needed to catch up to the woman, Kori thought, moving fast.

Brodie found he had to really pour it on to keep pace with his partner. That caused him to be both surprised and really impressed. There had been nothing about Kori Kennedy to alert him to the fact that she was a runner.

The woman, he thought, was just full of surprises.

At the very far end of the parking lot, Kori saw an older-looking woman carrying what looked like a small, wrapped-up loaf of bread, at first. But as she came closer to the woman, Kori could have sworn that she heard a mewling noise coming from the bundle in her arm.

It was most definitely *not* a loaf of bread.

"That's her!" Kori cried to Brodie. "That's Rose's grandmother. With Rose's baby!" Raising her voice, she shouted, "Stop!" To the woman. Kori was holding her credentials up in the air for the woman to see. There was no way their escaping fugitive would be able to read those credentials from where she was, but Kori knew the woman would be able to surmise what they were.

"Mrs. McGuire," Brodie called out to the woman, "This is the Aurora Police Department. Stop where you are immediately!" he ordered.

A haunted look descended over her features as the woman they were trying to detain looked around, desperately searching for an escape route. She looked like a hunted animal that had been trapped—and knew it.

"Mrs. McGuire, it's over. You can only help yourself if you cooperate," Brodie gently advised. "The baby belongs with her mother," he told her, talking in a slow cadence so as not to fire the woman up. He was fairly certain she wouldn't hurt the baby, but he wasn't about to risk everything on that.

Rose's grandmother looked incensed. "She belongs with someone who doesn't want to give her away like she's some sort of inconvenience."

Kori cut in, thinking that if she and Brodie chipped away at the nurse on two fronts, they could get her to give up.

"Mrs. McGuire, Rose has been crying ever since you abducted her daughter from her room. Your granddaughter doesn't want to give her daughter away. She wants to keep her. To raise her," Kori emphasized.

"She wants to keep her now," the nurse stressed, her arm unconsciously tightening around the bundle she was holding. "But what about tomorrow?" she challenged. "What if she decides to give the baby away tomorrow?"

"You'll be there for her," Kori told the nurse. "You can help her over the rough spots, just like you can help her savor the good moments as well. Raising a baby is hard work," Kori said, her voice low and gentle, as if she were trying to approach a skittish pet. "You know that." All the while, she took small steps toward the nurse, her body language coaxing the woman to eventually give her great-granddaughter to her. "But if she has someone who can be there for her, someone she knows can help her, then she'll be able to get through anything."

Peggy made a small, helpless noise as she looked down at the infant she was holding. "I won't be able to help Rose," she said, raising her chin as if to keep her tears from falling. "I'll be in jail," she told them, looking first at Kori then at Brodie. "I know the consequences of what I did."

"Then why did you do it?" Kori asked her gently.

"Because I wanted this baby to be raised with love," Rose's grandmother insisted. "Strangers can't love her the way family can."

"I beg to differ with that," Kori said, thinking of the couples she knew who had adopted children. "But that's not the point right now. And I can understand your motivation," she said with all sincerity. She turned her attention toward Brodie. The way she saw it, if there was any way around this, then he would be the one who would know. "You've got connections, right, Cavanaugh?"

He understood where she was going with this. Kori was talking about finding a way to keep this grandmother from being arrested and made to pay for taking the baby from her mother.

Brodie wasn't sure if anyone within his family's network was capable of pulling that off.

"I've got connections," he admitted and then added guardedly, "Within reason."

She pretended not to hear the last part. "Well, see if you can reason with your group and find someone in their number who can pull a few strings and have this family reunion become a reality," she said, nodding at Rose's grandmother and then at the baby she was holding in her arms.

Brodie shook his head. "You don't ask for much do you?"

Her eyes met his. "I have faith in you, Brodie," she told him quietly.

He took a deep breath, as if to fortify himself for what he was about to do. And then he took out his phone. "Well, that makes one of us," he murmured.

She put her hand on his. Brodie looked into her eyes, an unspoken question in his own. "Don't make a liar out of me, Brodie."

"I'll give it my best shot not to, Kori," was all he could promise.

She smiled at him. "That'll do just fine." And then she turned toward the nurse who had come so close to making off with the infant she had taken from her grand-daughter's room. "It's time, Peggy. You need to hand the baby over to me," she told the nurse in an extremely calm, coaxing voice.

She and Brodie watched as the tears filled the woman's eyes. Holding the small bundle to her, Peggy raised the infant up to her face and brushed her lips against the very soft skin.

"Goodbye little one. I only wanted the very best for you. Great-grandma loves you," she whispered, her voice breaking. And then she looked up at Kori. "Take her," the nurse cried, "before I change my mind."

They both knew that was an empty threat, uttered just to underscore the inner turmoil that Peggy McGuire was going through as she contemplated surrendering the tiny infant.

Very carefully, Kori took the baby into her arms. "You obviously care about your granddaughter's state of well-being, Mrs. McGuire. Otherwise you wouldn't have gone through all the trouble of getting that letter to her, letting her know that her baby was all right. You meant well, and you have a good heart. That's all going to count in your favor," Kori told the older woman.

"The only thing the law cares about is that a crime was committed and I was the one who committed it. Reasons don't matter," Peggy said as if she was already resigned to her fate and to living out the rest of her days behind bars.

"Let's go, Mrs. McGuire," Brodie said, taking the nurse by the arm. He began to steer her toward the vehicle that Kori had driven.

The nurse looked at him in surprise. "Don't you want to handcuff me?" she asked, confused.

"Not really," Brodie answered. He looked toward Kori for confirmation and the latter nodded her head, indicating that she was willing to forego that as well.

"You're not planning on running away, are you?" Kori asked the nurse.

The nurse looked down at her legs. "My running days are long over," she confided.

"Then, no," Kori said. "No handcuffs—as long as you stay on your best behavior."

Brodie escorted the nurse into the back seat of their vehicle, then turned to Kori, prepared to take the baby from her.

But his partner didn't seem ready to relinquish the infant.

"Why don't you drive us back to Rose's apartment?" Kori suggested.

Peggy McGuire looked surprised. "You're not taking me to the precinct?"

"Not to the precinct," Kori confirmed. "I think that this little girl's been away from her mother long enough and it's time for a reunion. That takes precedence over everything else." Holding the infant to her with one hand, she dug into her pocket with the other. Producing the car keys, she held them out to Brodie. "Let's get this little girl home, Cavanaugh."

"Absolutely," he agreed as he carefully helped Kori and her precious bundle into the back seat.

Chapter 25

When he looked back at it later, it would have been hard for Brodie to say who cried more when they were reunited with the infant who was the center of the drama, Rose or her grandmother. In his opinion, it was a tie.

Wanting to afford them space, Brodie backed away from the two women, allowing them to fully unleash all the pent-up emotions that had been building inside them during this last chaotic week.

As he glanced in Kori's direction, he saw that she wasn't above shedding a few tears herself, although he could see that she was doing her best to attempt to hide them from him.

Maybe she felt that tears were unseemly, Brodie thought.

"Here," he murmured, handing his partner the hand-kerchief he always kept on him. The handkerchief was something his late mother had insisted on. He kept up the habit as a way of keeping her memory with him all these years later.

A week ago, Kori would have pushed his hand away, pretending she didn't need the handkerchief, saying it was just dust that had gotten into her eyes. But because of the intense way they had worked together, there weren't any more walls or pretenses left between them. There was only the honesty of what each of them was going through at the moment.

"We're going to have to take you in, Peggy."

"You're taking me to jail," the woman concluded. "I deserve it," she said, tears gathering in her eyes.

"We're going to take you before my cousin Callie's husband, Judge Benton Montgomery. Benton's fair and he'll be willing to listen to the extenuating circumstances. With any luck, you'll wind up paying a fine and have to do a lot of public service, but there won't be any time served in jail."

Hope instantly entered the older woman's eyes. She looked from Brodie to Kori. "Do you really think so?" she cried.

Brodie nodded. "Yes, I do. For now, stay here with your granddaughter and great-granddaughter. I'll have a police officer stay with you until this can be resolved. Meanwhile, we're going to make an appeal on your behalf with the judge."

The sobbing woman threw her arms around Brodie, thanking him profusely.

When the police officer arrived, Brodie and Kori left to see the judge. Because of the circumstances, Benton Montgomery had agreed to meet with them tonight.

"So we're not bringing her in?" Kori asked, wanting to be perfectly clear as to exactly what he was thinking.

"Not until after we talk to Judge Montgomery. It's not like Peggy McGuire was part of an active baby kidnapping ring that was stealing babies in order to sell them. This was a very specific occurrence that was slated to only happen the one time. I'm pretty sure that the judge will see it that way."

"What about all the money that this cost the city?" she asked. "People are going to want answers, not to mention a resolution."

Getting back to their vehicle, Kori paused by the car, then got in behind the steering wheel. She put her key into the ignition, but for the time being, she left it where it was.

"That's why we're going to go see Callie's husband. In this particular case, all Judge Montgomery will care about is that there was a happy resolution to what could have wound up being a really terrible situation," Brodie informed her.

That explanation sounded far too simplistic for her. "Are you sure?" she asked doubtfully.

Brodie didn't even have to spend any time reviewing the facts. "I know the man," he told Kori. "I'm sure. All we have to do is tell him that there was a family misunderstanding, that somehow things got out of hand. Lord knows the man is familiar with those. And if we can assure him that this is the end of it, I'm sure that the judge will be more than happy to accept that as the final result to an uncomfortable episode. Trust me, he would only place that grandmother in jail if there was no hope of this being resolved. Everyone just wants life to get back to normal."

"So we just tell him that mother and child have been reunited and it's all over but the shouting?" she questioned.

"It'll be a little more complicated than that, but essentially, yes," he told her.

Still leaving her key inserted in the ignition, Kori

leaned to her right, framed Brodie's face between her hands and then kissed him.

Hard.

When she drew her lips away from his, he said, "Not that I minded what just happened in the slightest, but what was that for?"

She was suddenly relieved and happy, not just that the baby had been recovered, but that Rose and her grandmother had a good shot at rebuilding their lives—for the better this time.

"For absolutely nothing at all," she told Brodie. "I'm just happy."

"Okay, I can work with that," he told her, nodding his head. "Why don't we go in to the station, give the team the good news that the baby's been recovered alive and well, and after we sign out for the day, we conduct our own private celebration?" he proposed, looking at Kori to see if she was on board.

He could read her answer in her smile. "I think I'd like that."

Brodie nodded. "I don't plan on making you regret saying those words."

"You know," Kori said nearly four hours later after meeting with the judge, presenting the case and getting the man to see things their way, "I am really glad all that is behind us."

It had gone more or less the way Brodie had predicted. The judge had ruled for a great many hours of public service, plus a small fine, but no jail time. Everyone involved was infinitely grateful.

"Considering what a disaster it could have been—at any moment," Kori said. "I'm really amazed that everything went as well as it ultimately did. And not just with the kidnapping," Kori added, turning her body into Brodie's.

Despite the fact that they had just finished making love a few minutes ago, Brodie was finding it very hard to concentrate. The closeness of Kori's nude body was creating havoc within him, making him want her all over again.

Desperately.

There was just something about this woman that made him completely insatiable and sapped his ability to even think straight. He'd never felt like this before and it did scare him a little.

"'Not just with the kidnapping.'" Brodie repeated the words she had just said, confused. "Well, what else is there?"

"Well, for one thing, there's my father and your aunt," she said, reminding Brodie that the issue of their relatives was still very much in the offing. "That whole thing could have ended in a disaster seven ways from sundown," Kori stressed. "Instead, I don't think that I've *ever* seen my dad any happier. And I gather, from the few things he's told me, the same sort of thing can be said about your aunt."

Brodie grinned at that. "Oh yeah, that. I think we're seeing the making of quite the couple," he agreed, running the tips of his fingers lightly and seductively along the outline of her face. He knew that aroused her—as it did him.

Kori could feel herself heating up all over again as her breaths grew shorter.

She wasn't all that experienced when it came to intimate relationships and she willingly admitted it. But the way her heart was hammering, she *knew* she was standing on the brink of something that was really special. Something that was incredibly wondrous.

"Wouldn't it be wonderful if they wound up getting married?" she heard herself saying. The next moment she was reeling back the question. "I know, I know, I'm getting ahead of myself," Kori granted, talking quickly before he could interrupt her, "but I think my dad is way overdue for some happiness in his life and I really believe that your aunt is the one who is more than capable of delivering it."

"No…" Brodie began, but got no further.

"No?" Kori cried. She propped herself up on her elbow, ready to launch into a lengthy explanation of why he was wrong.

Brodie put his finger against her lips, stopping the flow of words he knew were about to burst forth. "No," he repeated, "I don't think you're getting carried away. I happen to think that you're absolutely right. I've never seen two people who were more right for each other than your dad and my aunt—except maybe for you and me," he added.

Kori stared at him, her eyes wider than he'd ever seen. "You and me?" she repeated in disbelief. Was he teasing her?

"Maybe it's 'you and I,'" Brodie amended.

"I'm not correcting your grammar here, idiot!" Kori cried in frustration. "I'm trying to get to the bottom of what you're saying. What *are* you saying?" she asked him in the next breath. "Because it sounded to me as if you were saying that we belong together."

Kori waited for Brodie to correct her, her breath once again threatening to back up in her lungs.

"I was," he told her quietly. "Because I do. Maybe I'm the one getting ahead of myself," he said, repeating her initial statement, "but I've never met anyone who made me as crazy as you do."

"Thank you?" she said uncertainly, not sure if that was a compliment or a criticism.

"And I never met anyone who made me so happy to be crazy at the same time," he continued. Warming up to his subject, Brodie talked faster. "And I don't want to just be related to you by marriage because my aunt winds up marrying your father. I want to be related to you by marriage because we're the ones who are married to each other."

Her mouth fell open as she sat up so that she could stare down at Brodie. "Wait, did you just propose to me?" she cried, stunned.

He looked almost embarrassed as he nodded. "Badly, but yeah, I did. You don't have to answer right away. As a matter of fact, I'd prefer that you didn't—if the answer's no. It would be better if you think about it—for a long time, because I know that this is the sort of thing that really might need to percolate before it can finally—"

Kori attempted to cut him off. "Cavanaugh—"

Good at being able to talk above a noisy crowd of relatives, Brodie didn't even seem to hear her. "Because I don't want you saying something that I'm going to regret hearing so maybe we should revisit this in six months or so—"

"Cavanaugh—"

"Or maybe I should leave," he said, throwing back the sheet, then stopping short of putting his feet on the floor. "Oh wait, this is my house, so then I guess that maybe you—"

"*Cavanaugh!*" Kori shouted, clamping her hand over his mouth to stop what promised to be an endless stream of words.

Her eyes on his, Kori slowly drew her hand away, ready to clamp it back down again if he insisted on talking again.

But all Brodie said this time was, "Yes?"

Kori inclined her head then repeated the word he had just said. "Yes."

The uncertain look in Brodie's eyes remained as he questioned, "Yes?"

This time she smiled at him, her mouth curving and the smile rising to her eyes as she repeated, "Yes."

And then, just like that, things fell into place. "Then you'll—?"

"Yes," she answered before he could finish forming the question. "Yes," Kori said again for emphasis, then followed it up with several more yeses in case there was any lingering doubt in his mind. "Now shut up and get back to making love to me. My body's getting cold," she told him.

Brodie drew her back into his arms, glorying in the way her body felt against his. "Certainly can't have that," he whispered.

"No," she agreed, "Can't have that. And with any luck, we never will again."

"I'm a great believer in luck," Brodie told her.

"Yes," she said, humor sparkling in her eyes, "Me, too." Her smile grew wider. "Thanks to you."

Any further conversation on the subject—or any subject—was tabled for the moment.

And for a long time after that as well.

Epilogue

"You would think that a man my age who's been through as much as I have wouldn't be so incredibly nervous about taking part in having his own dream come true," Bill Kennedy said, looking at his daughter in the reflection of the mirror that was before him.

He had been trying to tie a bow tie for the last ten minutes and failing miserably.

With a smile, Kori finally stepped in. Gently pushing her father's hands away, she made quick work in creating what in his estimation was the perfect bow tie. "Just proves you're human, that's all, Dad." She stepped back to admire her work. "There," she pronounced with a smile. "Done."

"Thank you," Bill exhaled. "I'm sure Maeve isn't nervous like this. That woman would be as calm as a cucumber in the middle of an earthquake." And then Bill looked at his daughter as fresh thoughts occurred to him. "She is here, isn't she?" he asked his daughter. "You don't think that she had a sudden change of heart and decided she could do better than—"

Kori framed her father's face with her hands, attempting to center him with her gentle touch. "Dad, take a deep breath. It's going to be fine."

He did as she directed, taking in a deep breath. And then he slowly exhaled it. "Funny, you said the same thing to me that night in front of the convenience store," her father recalled.

"You heard me?" Kori asked, surprised. "You looked like you had passed out from the blood loss and were pretty much beyond hearing anything."

"I know. I was struggling to hang on. The sound of your voice was my lifeline, Korinna." He turned from the mirror to face his daughter again. "You've always been my lifeline, sweetheart."

"Well, your lifeline is telling you to get a grip, pull yourself together and go begin the rest of your life by marrying that wonderful woman who's waiting for you," Kori instructed, the smile on her lips lighting up the rest of her face.

Bill laughed, briefly giving his daughter a quick hug. "I make it a point never to disobey a beautiful woman."

"Yeah, yeah, save it for Maeve," Kori told him with a laugh. "Now let's get you to that altar before those very sturdy legs of yours buckle."

Bill nodded. "Good point."

At that moment, there was a knock on the door and Brian Cavanaugh, looking resplendent in a tuxedo, peered into the tiny room.

"Ready?" Brian asked his friend.

"He's more than ready," Kori told the chief. Gesturing toward her father, she said, "Take him."

Brian laughed. "You know, your daughter is bossy enough to be a Cavanaugh woman," he told Kori's father.

"Tell me about it." And then Bill looked at the man who had saved his life, a touch of anxiety in his voice. "Maeve is here, right?"

"I think she actually opened up the church," Brian told him.

"See, I told you so, Dad," Kori said. "Unlike you, the woman has nerves of steel. Don't make her come looking for you. Go on up there," she ordered.

Leaving her father and his best man in the small back room, Kori made her way into the front of the church. She slipped into the first row, taking a seat on the left side, the one that was reserved for the groom's family and friends.

She had just enough time to nod at several people before she heard the beginning strains of the "Wedding March" filling the air. Rising with the rest of the people in the pews, she turned around to watch Brodie, with Maeve on his arm, slowly make their way to the front of the altar. Her future stepmother was tastefully attired in a lacy, beige, street-length dress.

She looked perfect, Kori thought.

Maeve was beaming as she made her way toward the man who had won her heart.

Watching Brodie accompany his aunt and then step back after he brought the woman to her father, Kori could feel her heart swelling. Never in her wildest dreams had she ever thought that this was possible—that she would ever see her father *this* happy. It was obvious that she felt he had a totally new lease on life and something to look forward to: a life to build with a partner he loved beside him.

Kori held her breath as she listened to the chords from the "Wedding March" fade off.

Though tears had suddenly risen in her eyes, almost blinding her, Kori could still see Brodie smiling at his aunt, then squeezing her hand as he whispered something to the woman who had helped raise him and his siblings after his mother had passed away.

Maeve smiled up at him, beaming and obviously responding to what he had said just before she turned to her fiancé and husband-to-be.

Brodie stepped away and took his place right next to Kori. After a beat, he bent his head and whispered, "So, what do you think about us being the next ones to march up the aisle?"

Stunned, thrilled, Kori's heart was hammering wildly as the priest began the ceremony, addressing the congregation.

"Dearly beloved…"

"I'd like that very much," she whispered back to Brodie, the man she already envisioned as her partner in every sense of the word.

"Yeah," Brodie agreed. "Me, too."

Filled with anticipation of what was to come, Brodie and Kori grew silent so that they could hear the priest say the words that would join her father and his aunt for all eternity.

They knew that they would be standing like that before the priest as well as their family and friends soon enough.

They could hardly wait.

* * * * *

**WE HOPE YOU ENJOYED
THIS BOOK FROM**

**HARLEQUIN
ROMANTIC
SUSPENSE**

Danger. Passion. Drama.

These heart-racing page-turners will keep you guessing to the very end. Experience the thrill of unexpected plot twists and irresistible chemistry.

4 NEW BOOKS AVAILABLE EVERY MONTH!

HRSHALO2020

COMING NEXT MONTH FROM

H HARLEQUIN

ROMANTIC SUSPENSE

#2175 COLTON'S DANGEROUS REUNION
The Coltons of Colorado • by Justine Davis

When social worker Gideon Colton reports a parent for child abuse, he never thought he'd put his ex—the child's pediatrician—in harm's way. Now he and Sophie Gray-Jones are thrown back together to avoid danger...and find themselves reigniting the flame that never really went out.

#2176 FINDING THE RANCHER'S SON
by Karen Whiddon

Jackie Burkholdt's sister and nephew are missing, so she returns home to their tiny West Texas hometown. The boy's father, Eli Pitts, might be the most obvious suspect, but he and Jackie are helplessly drawn to each other. As secrets come to light, it becomes even harder to know who is responsible—let alone who it's safe to have feelings for.

#2177 BODYGUARD UNDER SIEGE
Bachelor Bodyguards • by Lisa Childs

Keeli Abbott became a bodyguard to *avoid* Detective Spencer Dubridge. Now she's been tasked with protecting him—and might be pregnant with his baby! Close quarters force them to face their feelings, but with a drug cartel determined to make sure Spencer doesn't testify, they may not have much time left...

#2178 MOUNTAIN RETREAT MURDER
Cameron Glen • by Beth Cornelison

When a mysterious death finds Cait Cameron's family's inn, she enlists guest Matt Harkney, father to a troubled teenager, to help investigate recent crimes. Love and loyalty are tested as veteran Matt risks everything to heal his family, catch a thief and save Cait's life.

YOU CAN FIND MORE INFORMATION ON UPCOMING HARLEQUIN TITLES,
FREE EXCERPTS AND MORE AT HARLEQUIN.COM.

HRSCNM0222

SPECIAL EXCERPT FROM

Ⓗ HARLEQUIN

ROMANTIC SUSPENSE

*When a mysterious death finds Cait Cameron's family's
inn, she enlists guest Matt Harkney, father to a troubled
teenager, to help investigate recent crimes. Love and
loyalty are tested as veteran Matt risks everything to
heal his family, catch a thief and save Cait's life.*

Read on for a sneak preview of
Mountain Retreat Murder,
*the first book in Beth Cornelison's
new Cameron Glen miniseries!*

He paused with the blade hovering over the crack between
boards. "Are you sure you want to keep prying up planks?
Whoever did this could have loosened any number of
boards in this floor."

The truth of his comment clearly daunted her. Her
shoulders dropped, and her expression sagged with sorrow.
"Yes. Continue. At least with this one, where I know
something was amiss earlier." She raised a hand, adding,
"But carefully."

He ducked his head in understanding, "Of course."

An apologetic grin flickered over her forlorn features,
softening the tension, and he took an extra second or two
just to stare at her. Sunlight streamed in from the window
above the kitchen sink and highlighted the auburn streaks
in her hair and the faint freckles on her upturned nose. The

bright beam reflected in her pale blue eyes, reminding him of sparkling water in the stream by his cabin. A throb of emotion grabbed at his chest.

"Matt?"

"Do you know how beautiful you are?"

She blinked. Blushed.

"What?" The word sounded strangled.

"You are." He stroked her cheek with the back of his left hand. "Beautiful."

Her throat worked as she swallowed, and she glanced down, shyly. "Um, thank you. I—"

"Anyway…" He withdrew his hand and turned his attention back to the floorboard. He eased the pocketknife blade in the small crack and gently levered the plank up.

As he moved the board out of the way, Cait shined the flashlight in the hole beneath.

She gasped at the same moment he muttered, "Holy hell."

In the dark space they exposed was a small plastic bag. Cait moved the light closer, illuminating the contents of the clear bag—a large bundle of cash, bound by a white paper band with "$7458" written on it.

When she reached for the bag of money, he caught her wrist. "No. Don't touch it."

When she frowned a query at him, he added, "Fingerprints. That's evidence."

Don't miss
Mountain Retreat Murder *by Beth Cornelison,*
available April 2022 wherever
Harlequin Romantic Suspense
books and ebooks are sold.

Harlequin.com

Copyright © 2022 by Beth Cornelison

HRSEXP0222

Get 4 FREE REWARDS!

We'll send you 2 FREE Books <u>plus</u> 2 FREE Mystery Gifts.

FREE
Value Over
$20

Both the **Harlequin Intrigue®** and **Harlequin® Romantic Suspense** series feature compelling novels filled with heart-racing action-packed romance that will keep you on the edge of your seat.

YES! Please send me 2 FREE novels from the Harlequin Intrigue or Harlequin Romantic Suspense series and my 2 FREE gifts (gifts are worth about $10 retail). After receiving them, if I don't wish to receive any more books, I can return the shipping statement marked "cancel." If I don't cancel, I will receive 6 brand-new Harlequin Intrigue Larger-Print books every month and be billed just $5.99 each in the U.S. or $6.49 each in Canada, a savings of at least 14% off the cover price or 4 brand-new Harlequin Romantic Suspense books every month and be billed just $4.99 each in the U.S. or $5.74 each in Canada, a savings of at least 13% off the cover price. It's quite a bargain! Shipping and handling is just 50¢ per book in the U.S. and $1.25 per book in Canada.* I understand that accepting the 2 free books and gifts places me under no obligation to buy anything. I can always return a shipment and cancel at any time. The free books and gifts are mine to keep no matter what I decide.

Choose one: ☐ **Harlequin Intrigue**
                      Larger-Print
                      (199/399 HDN GNXC)

☐ **Harlequin Romantic Suspense**
   (240/340 HDN GNMZ)

Name (please print)

Address   Apt. #

City   State/Province   Zip/Postal Code

Email: Please check this box ☐ if you would like to receive newsletters and promotional emails from Harlequin Enterprises ULC and its affiliates. You can unsubscribe anytime.

> **Mail to the Harlequin Reader Service:**
> **IN U.S.A.:** P.O. Box 1341, Buffalo, NY 14240-8531
> **IN CANADA:** P.O. Box 603, Fort Erie, Ontario L2A 5X3
>
> Want to try 2 free books from another series? Call 1-800-873-8635 or visit www.ReaderService.com.

---

*Terms and prices subject to change without notice. Prices do not include sales taxes, which will be charged (if applicable) based on your state or country of residence. Canadian residents will be charged applicable taxes. Offer not valid in Quebec. This offer is limited to one order per household. Books received may not be as shown. Not valid for current subscribers to the Harlequin Intrigue or Harlequin Romantic Suspense series. All orders subject to approval. Credit or debit balances in a customer's account(s) may be offset by any other outstanding balance owed by or to the customer. Please allow 4 to 6 weeks for delivery. Offer available while quantities last.

Your Privacy—Your information is being collected by Harlequin Enterprises ULC, operating as Harlequin Reader Service. For a complete summary of the information we collect, how we use this information and to whom it is disclosed, please visit our privacy notice located at corporate.harlequin.com/privacy-notice. From time to time we may also exchange your personal information with reputable third parties. If you wish to opt out of this sharing of your personal information, please visit readerservice.com/consumerschoice or call 1-800-873-8635. **Notice to California Residents**—Under California law, you have specific rights to control and access your data. For more information on these rights and how to exercise them, visit corporate.harlequin.com/california-privacy.

HIHRS22

**IF YOU ENJOYED THIS BOOK
WE THINK YOU WILL ALSO LOVE**

⊕ HARLEQUIN

INTRIGUE

Seek thrills. Solve crimes. Justice served.

Dive into action-packed stories that will keep you
on the edge of your seat. Solve the crime
and deliver justice at all costs.

6 NEW BOOKS AVAILABLE EVERY MONTH!

HIXSERIES2020

SPECIAL EXCERPT FROM

H HARLEQUIN

INTRIGUE

*Wounded army veteran Shane Adler is determined
to rebuild his life, along with the canine who came to
his rescue overseas. Turning Decoy into an expert
search-and-rescue dog gives them both purpose—even if
their trainer, Piper Lambert, is a distraction Shane hadn't
expected. And when he learns Piper's life is in danger, he
and Decoy will do whatever it takes to keep her safe...*

Keep reading for a sneak peek of
Decoy Training,
the first book in K-9s on Patrol,
by New York Times *bestselling author Caridad Piñeiro.*

He was challenging her already and they hadn't even really
started working together, but if they were going to survive
several weeks of training, honesty was going to be the best
policy.

"My husband was a marine," Piper said, but didn't make
eye contact with him. Instead, she whirled and started
walking back in the direction of the outdoor training ring.

He turned and kept pace beside her, his gaze trained on
her face. "Was?"

Challenging again. Pushing, but regardless of that, she
said, "He was killed in action in Iraq. Four years ago and
yet…"

Her throat choked up and tears welled in her eyes as she
rushed forward, almost as if she could outrun the discussion
and the pain it brought.

The gentle touch of his big, calloused hand on her forearm stopped her escape.

She glanced down at that hand and then followed his arm up to meet his gaze, so full of concern and something else. Pain?

"I'm sorry. It can't be easy," he said, the simple words filled with so much more. Pain for sure. Understanding. Compassion. Not pity, thankfully. The last nearly undid her, but she sucked in a breath, held it for the briefest second before blurting out, "We should get going. If you're going to do search and rescue with Decoy, we'll have to improve his obedience skills."

Rushing away from him, she slipped through the gaps in the split-rail fence and walked to the center of the training ring.

Shane hesitated, obviously uneasy, but then he bent to go across the fence railing and met her in the middle of the ring, Decoy at his side.

"I'm ready if you are," he said, his big body several feet away, only he still felt too close. Too big. Too masculine with that kind of posture and strength that screamed military.

She took a step back and said, "I'm ready."

She wasn't and didn't know if she ever could be with this man. He was testing her on too many levels.

Only she'd never failed a training assignment and she didn't intend to start with Shane and Decoy.

"Let's get going," she said.

Don't miss
Decoy Training *by Caridad Piñeiro,*
available April 2022 wherever
Harlequin Intrigue books and ebooks are sold.

Harlequin.com

Copyright © 2022 by Harlequin Books S.A.

HIEXP0222